continued . . .

"A charming, witty, exciting new entry in the genre, featuring the best realized and most personable fictional character on four legs. You'll love Shadow. And Sunny's fun, too."
—Parnell Hall, author of *The KenKen Killings*

"A fun amateur-sleuth tale . . . [A] whimsical spin to the light-hearted whodunit."
—*The Mystery Gazette*

"With a deft hand at plotting, an appealing small-town setting, and a determined protagonist, Donally has created a series opener that aficionados of whodunits and felines will find rubs them exactly the right way."
—*Richmond Times-Dispatch*

"[Sunny and Shadow are] a cute twosome . . . I am looking forward to the next in the series!"
—*Book Dilettante*

"Interesting and engaging . . . [An] enjoyable novel."
—*Genre Go Round Reviews*

"A lighthearted romp with plenty of suspects in a quirky little town . . . A great start to a series that shows much promise."
—*Escape with Dollycas into a Good Book*

"*The Big Kitty* falls squarely between dark, intense thrillers and comic detective romps . . . A fast, enjoyable read."
—*Fresh Fiction*

Last Licks

Claire Donally

BERKLEY PRIME CRIME, NEW YORK

THE BERKLEY PUBLISHING GROUP
Published by the Penguin Group
Penguin Group (USA) LLC
375 Hudson Street, New York, New York 10014

USA • Canada • UK • Ireland • Australia • New Zealand • India • South Africa • China

penguin.com

A Penguin Random House Company

LAST LICKS

A Berkley Prime Crime Book / published by arrangement with Tekno Books

For information, address: The Berkley Publishing Group,
a division of Penguin Group (USA) LLC,
375 Hudson Street, New York, New York 10014.

ISBN: 978-0-425-25255-0

PUBLISHING HISTORY
Berkley Prime Crime mass-market edition / May 2014

PRINTED IN THE UNITED STATES OF AMERICA

10 9 8 7 6 5 4 3 2 1

Cover illustration by Mary Ann Lasher.
Cover design by George Long.
Interior text design by Laura K. Corless.

To the youngest member of our family,
my grandnephew, sweet baby James.

And as usual,
many thanks to Larry Segriff of Tekno Books
and Shannon Jamieson Vazquez of Berkley
Prime Crime, who have so ably shepherded
this project along.

1

The midsummer sun was finally going down—not that the brilliant afternoon sunshine had given him much in the way of trouble. He'd found a good patch of shade to lounge in when the sun was still high overhead. It not only kept him comfortable, but allowed him to stay inconspicuous as he checked out the area around him.

Now it looked as if that had paid off. He kept still, only his eyes moving to follow her. She took silly, flouncy steps, her head bobbing in time with her skinny legs as she wandered along in her haphazard way.

She came right past him, not even looking in his direction. He wondered how far she could run on those ridiculous legs—and how fast.

Doesn't she know it's dangerous to come down around here, especially when it starts to get dark? His eyes narrowed and he dropped his head a little, taking a couple of slow steps after her. *Well, I guess she's going to find out she'd have been better off staying with her little ones.*

She paused to examine something on the ground, completely unaware that she was being stalked. He looked right and left. No one around to stop him, no place for her to run . . .

He made his move, uncoiling powerful muscles, leaping for her, reaching out for her back . . .

She unfurled her wings and took off, leaving his claws a bare inch short of her tail feathers.

He recovered before he sprawled on the ground and rose up to sit on his haunches, his tail flicking around in annoyance as he glared upward. The prey that had gotten away fluttered to a branch high, high out of reach, dropping for a landing onto those absurd-looking legs.

Stupid bird, he thought, sulkily licking the back of his paw and then running it along his whiskers. *Maybe she learned her lesson and won't come around here again.*

An unexpectedly cool breeze ruffled his gray fur, and he glanced at the house behind him. Where were his people? Hanging around in the yard was fun, but he'd just missed out on a picnic supper. There was a stout door between him and his bowl and dish in the kitchen. He needed a two-legged type to open that for him.

Where were they?

*

Sunny Coolidge puffed a little as she trailed her father around the cinder track. They'd made six circuits of the quarter-mile track and had as many more to go before Dad finished his daily three-mile walking quota. That was a pretty good showing for a guy who a year and a half ago had been flat on his back after a heart attack.

Mike Coolidge moved easily, his unruly white curls bobbing with each step, his face only a little pinker than usual from his exertions.

Sunny, however, found herself falling farther behind.

Too much time in front of a computer and too little time on your feet, that annoying voice in the back of her head scolded. Well, it was an unfortunate fact. Her job kept her at the keyboard most of the day. Despite an active-sounding name, the Maine Adventure X-perience, MAX for short, did most of its travel-booking business online. If Sunny wasn't receiving e-mails and organizing responses, she often wound up tinkering with the MAX website to fix problems or update software that seemed to change every time she turned around.

Even when she managed to escape from the world of virtual business, she found herself answering the phone or organizing packages of tourist information to go off via snail mail. All in all, not the most physical line of work.

Still, that wasn't any reason for letting her dad walk her into the ground.

Mike looked around, stopped, and pulled loose an ear-bud. Sunny got a brief snatch of a song from about forty years ago, sounding as if it were played by an insect rock band.

"What's the matter?" Mike asked. "Got a pebble in your shoe?" He frowned, looking at her more closely. "You're sweating off your bug repellent, Sunny. Keep that up, and the mosquitoes will fly off with you."

Claire Donally

That wasn't quite an overstatement. Maine had a lot going for it in summer: quaint villages, camping, boating, pretty scenery. But the infamous Maine mosquitoes were definitely not a drawing card for tourists—or natives, for that matter. Sunny should've pointed out that exercising at dusk put them outdoors at a peak time for the bloodthirsty critters, but Mike had had a busy morning dealing with all sorts of errands, and then had wanted to wait until the afternoon heat had died down a little.

"Maybe we should have tried taking this walk in one of the malls over in outlet-land," she suggested, trying to keep the faint croak out of her voice. "At least they're air-conditioned."

In addition to the other enticements of summer in Maine, Kittery Harbor also boasted mile after mile of outlet stores. That alone brought an impressive number of potential tourists to the MAX site.

"I'm stuck in those stores all winter," Mike complained. "This is the time of year to get some nice, fresh air."

Sunny shook her head as something went whining past her right ear. "I think maybe I could do with a refresher on the repellent—and maybe some water, too."

"We've got both in the car," her dad said. "You can catch up with me." He continued at his usual pace while Sunny headed to the parking lot. Sunny felt a little weird being here, at her old high school, now a community center. This place was supposed to have been the launching pad to her future. She'd pretty much left Kittery Harbor behind after graduation, moving on to college, journalism school, and then a job at a New York City newspaper.

But after her dad's heart attack, she'd come home to take

care of him, got laid off from the paper in absentia, and was forced to deal with her old hometown—even when it seemed to be erasing her own past. Sunny reached her Jeep Wrangler and opened the bag of supplies her dad had (rightly) insisted on carrying along, taking a long sip from the water bottle and then reslathering on the insect repellent.

She was just closing the car door when her cell phone went off. The screen identified Will Price as the caller—a nice surprise. Sunny knew his schedule as town constable meant he'd be working this Friday evening, so she hadn't expected to see him, much less hear from him.

"What's up?" she asked as she put the phone to her ear.

Will was definitely in cop mode as he replied. "Just got news of a car accident along Woodcrest Road. Ollie Barnstable is in County General."

"Yikes," Sunny said, frowning in thought. Ollie the Barnacle, as she'd nicknamed him, was her boss . . . and a very difficult man. "He hadn't been drinking, had he?" Even this early on a Friday night, that was strong possibility.

"I wasn't there, I only got this secondhand from one of the sheriff's guys," Will told her, "but according to him, it seems Ollie got struck while trying to assist an injured deer off the road."

This didn't sound like the hard-nosed employer Sunny knew, not even after a couple of cocktails. "Was the deer blocking his way?"

"Barnstable claimed he just saw the injured deer and stopped to help."

Definitely not normal Ollie behavior.

Will cleared his throat, trying to keep a chuckle from

his voice. "Evidence at the scene, however, suggests that Ollie wasn't so much the discoverer as the perpetrator. There's a suspicious dent on his Land Rover."

"Ah." That was more in character.

"Anyway, while he was trying to get rid of the evidence, another car came along. The deer shook off both accidents and took off, but Ollie went down."

"He's not really hurt, is he?" A little belated concern crept into Sunny's voice. Cantankerous as Ollie was, he *had* given her a job.

"They think he broke a leg." Will said. "At least, that's what the ambulance guys said."

"And he's at County General now?" Sunny glanced over at where her father completed another circuit on the old high school track. Mike wasn't a fan of Ollie's. He complained—probably rightly—that Ollie underpaid Sunny. But the gig at MAX was the only paying work in town that had some connection to Sunny's skills. Oh, there was a local newspaper, the *Harbor Courier*, but Ken Howell put it out almost single-handedly, right down to the printing. Sunny knew only too well that he had no budget to pay a reporting staff. Kittery Harbor was a nice little town, but it was heavily blue-collar. If Ollie hadn't taken her on, Sunny would probably be flipping burgers or running a cash register in outlet-land.

"Well, thanks for letting me know," Sunny told Will. "I'll check in on him."

"Maybe we can get some pancakes or something on Sunday," Will suggested.

Not the most romantic date, but still . . . "Sounds good,"

Sunny said. "Give me a buzz in the morning, and we'll make plans."

After a quick good-bye, she clicked the phone shut and sighed, trying to figure out how to tell Will that their dates needed more moonlight and less maple syrup. Not coming up with an answer, Sunny set off across the track to her dad. "Ollie Barnstable's in the hospital," she announced.

"I'm not surprised, the way he takes care of himself," Mike grumped. "Stroke, heart attack, or galloping gout?"

"He got hit by a car." Sunny watched her father's stern expression change to shock.

"That, I didn't expect," Mike admitted. "So, do you want to get going?"

"I suppose I'd better," Sunny said. "Do you want me to drop you off at home?"

"What?" Mike almost looked offended. "Of course not." Mike might not particularly like Ollie, but if he was in the hospital, he was supposed to be visited. That was the Kittery Harbor Way, the tradition that Sunny had grown up in, even if afterward she'd taken off for foreign parts like New York City.

Back in the Jeep, heading north along tree-lined roads, Sunny put on her headlights. In the woodsier areas, it had probably been dim even while the sun had still been higher in the sky. She could see all too easily how an accident could have happened.

Sunny kept a careful eye on the road ahead, fighting her impulse to hurry. Ollie was already in the emergency room by now. There was probably nothing they could do but offer moral support.

Elmet County General was up near the county seat in Levett. As they drove northward and inland, Sunny passed along the info Will had told her.

"Broken leg?" Mike repeated. "Could be worse. A fella can get killed, stepping out onto a road."

As a former long-distance trucker, delivering road salt all over the Northeast, Mike knew what he was talking about. He'd lost friends to accidents like that, pals who'd left the cabs of their trucks, trying to warn others about dangerous situations—an accident ahead, a flooded-out road, black ice. Some had been struck even while they were laying out safety flares. And the worst, when Sunny was in college, her mom had died in a road accident during a huge ice storm.

Neither of them brought up the topic now. Instead, Mike went out of his way to shrug off Ollie's situation as inconsequential.

"Eh, a broken bone? That used to get people laid up. But nowadays, they've got all sorts of new stuff they do— putting in pins and suchlike. He might not even get a cast."

Sunny was willing to take her dad's word for it. Certainly a lot of their older neighbors had suffered broken hips and made decent recoveries.

"Yeah, the way they do things now, he'll be back on his feet fast enough. But walking is another thing. I betcha he's going to need physical therapy. Rehab. The boss probably won't be back in the office to bother you for at least a month—maybe two." Mike grinned at her as they arrived at the hospital.

They walked over to the security guy at the emergency room entrance, who wasn't exactly helpful. "Supposed to be family members only," he told them. Sunny inflated her position at MAX to almost-partnership with Ollie, but that still only got them into the waiting room.

After a while, though, a harried-looking doctor in surgical greens and her hair pulled back in a bun came out to talk with them. "You work with Mr. Barnstable?"

"Yes." Sunny wasn't about to get all editorial and suggest *for* instead of *with*. "I'm Sunny Coolidge, and this is my father, Mike. We just heard about what happened to Ollie—Mr. Barnstable. Is he all right?"

"Physically, he's doing about the best we could hope for. We've given him something for the pain, and if he lies quietly, he shouldn't suffer." The doctor took a deep breath. "Otherwise . . . well, he's threatened three times to buy the place and have us all fired."

"Only three times?" Sunny managed a smile. "For him, that's being fairly mellow."

"Well, a lot of the other patients—and staff—would appreciate it if he were a little less loud." The doctor pulled back a wisp of hair that had gotten loose from her bun and fallen onto her forehead. "Does he have a wife? Any family?"

Sunny shook her head. "He was an only child, and his folks died years ago. He never married"—*for obvious reasons*, that snarky voice in her head chimed in—"and the only relations I know of are a couple of cousins who live several hours away."

From the look on the doctor's face, several hours was longer than they could put up with. She came to a sudden decision. "I'm going to let you in," she said. "Maybe you can calm him down."

Sunny and Mike followed the doctor into the emergency

room proper—a good-sized area with flooring, tiles, and walls in various shades of muted green. Maybe the color was supposed to be calming, or maybe the doctors hoped their surgical scrubs would blend with the walls and make them invisible. But if the colors were quiet, the ambiance wasn't. Machines gave off all sorts of blips, blurps, and beeps; doctors, nurses, and aides all seemed to be talking together; and of course, visitors and patients had questions and requests for help. And then the public-address system came on, announcing some mysterious code.

Gee, I can't imagine why Ollie couldn't calm down in the middle of all this serenity, Sunny's sarcastic side commented.

The ER patients all lay on gurneys separated by curtains with suitably soothing patterns (in green, of course). The curtains didn't do much to block out sound—like the moaning that got louder as the doctor led them to a completely curtained-in space.

Pulling the curtain open, the doctor announced, "Some visitors for you, Mr. Barnstable."

Ollie responded with a "Hanh?" He tried to see over his big belly, which mounded up the hospital sheet like a minor hill, then winced and let out a loud groan, reaching his hand down to his right thigh. "Why don't they do something? This leg is killing me."

At least, that's what Sunny thought he was saying. The words came out awfully mushy—like when he actually recognized her. "Shunny! Wa'ry'doonere?"

Sunny correctly interpreted that into, "Sunny! What are you doing here?" But then, she had the advantage of having dealt with plenty of peremptory phone calls from

Ollie the Barnacle after one of his multiple-martini lunches.

"We heard you got hurt and came to see how you were doing," she said. "You remember my dad."

"Hiya," Ollie said to Mike. "S'awful here! Tryna kill me!" He attempted to shift on the skinny mattress and let out a howl. "My leg!"

"You have to keep still," Mike advised. "Otherwise, you aggravate the broken bone."

"From the looks of things, I'd say they gave you something for the pain," Sunny said.

"Yeah." Ollie's big, round face had paled to a light pink from its regular red. "Shtuff makes m'soun' thrunk!"

Ollie assured them, however, that he'd been sober as a judge during his accident. "I shaw th'deer lyin' there, an' I wash tryna help 'im off th' road." His look of civic responsibility might have been more convincing if he hadn't been peering blearily up at them.

He blinked and suddenly sounded a little less drunk . . . and a lot more scared. "They want to cut into my leg." Again, he pointed to his thigh.

"They probably want to put in a plate to hold everything together," Mike said, his voice calm and soothing. "You know, the femur is one of the strongest bones in your body. It has to bear a lot of weight."

Sunny couldn't help glancing at Ollie's bulk on the gurney. Then she turned to her dad. "How do you know about all of that?"

Mike shrugged. "When you take friends to appointments with orthopedic surgeons, you hear a lot."

"They said if I go along with this surgery thing, I could

be out of here in a couple of days." Ollie looked hopefully at Mike. "Is that true?"

"Yes, but you won't be going home," Mike warned. "You'll probably have to put in some time at a rehab facility—not to mention a lot of work."

Ollie's face stopped looking loopy and became honestly confused. "Rehab? Where?"

"If you want my advice, I'd say you should go with Bridgewater Hall," Mike promptly replied. "They've got a good reputation, do a lot more therapy work with the patients. Also, I hear the food is decent."

"Bridgewater Hall," Ollie repeated, sagging back against the folded blanket that was serving as his pillow. Maybe the painkiller was finally kicking in. "Couldja tell 'em that for me?" He closed his eyes and was out like a light.

"Well, you managed to calm him down," Sunny told her dad. "That was pretty impressive. How did you know about Bridgewater Hall?"

"It was my first choice after I had the heart attack and didn't know if you were coming up to help out," he replied a little grimly. "Sounded great to me, except for one little thing."

"What was that?" Sunny asked.

"They told me I couldn't afford it," Mike replied. "But I figure Ollie is loaded. He should be able to swing their fees."

2

After Ollie finally settled down, Sunny got a chance to talk with some of the doctors. Surgery to implant a brace on the broken bone was tentatively scheduled for the next afternoon, and shortly afterward a social worker would be turning up to get the ball rolling on some place for rehab. Mike made sure to mention Ollie's preference for Bridgewater Hall. The discussion took a while, and by the time Sunny and her dad got out of the hospital, true dark had already established itself.

As they drove home, Mike discussed the pluses and minuses of other nursing homes in the area. "I think physical and occupational therapy, they're the big considerations," he explained. "Otherwise, you're just being warehoused, lying in bed, watching daytime television. Bridgewater Hall has two hours a day, one in the morning and then one in the afternoon. Everywhere else I looked into only had an hour. The place isn't all that big—only seventy-five beds both for the old folks who are permanent residents and the short-timers in for recuperation. But the rehab patients have a separate wing of the building with exercise space and equipment. And the therapy staff has a reputation all over the state. They get good results."

"The physical therapist who came to the house and worked with you was pretty good," Sunny pointed out. "Getting results when he could only come once a week— well, that depended a lot on my nagging."

Mike sighed. "I know I gave you a hard time about my exercises. It's easier taking orders from a stranger than from your own kid."

"Having a hard time taking me seriously because you once changed my diapers?" Sunny inquired, grinning.

"That's probably part of it," Mike said with a laugh. "Also, in a facility, it's harder to escape when they want you to do stuff. You can't get away with giving them guff about wanting a nap or not feeling up to exercising."

"Looks as though it turned out pretty well for you despite convalescing at home," Sunny told him. "Nowadays you can walk your kid right into the ground." She glanced over at her dad. "Do you really feel you missed out on the fancy-schmancy rest home?"

"I was really glad when you came home to help out." Mike's voice grew rueful. "But maybe if you'd stayed in New York, you'd still have your job."

Sunny briefly turned to give Mike a pat on the arm. "I wouldn't blame yourself for that, Dad. The *Sentinel* was bleeding jobs well before I took my leave of absence. Sooner or later, my number would have been up."

Although it kind of stings when the editor who cans you is also your ex, Sunny's uncompromising back-of-the-head voice felt compelled to add.

They continued on in silence until Sunny made the turn home onto Wild Goose Drive. "What was that?" Her voice grew sharp. For just a second, the Jeep's headlights had ignited an answering glow in a pair of animal eyes.

Mike rolled down the window and peered out into the gloom. "It's the damn cat."

"Shadow? What is he doing out?" Sunny exited the SUV and stepped forward. With his striped gray fur, Shadow was almost invisible against the dark grass.

"I think he figured out how to gimmick the screen door in the kitchen," Mike said. "Come to think of it, I didn't see him all afternoon."

Shadow came toward Sunny, but stayed just out of reach, then turned away, his legs and back stiff, his tail a flag of offended pride.

"Shadow!" Sunny called after him.

"You missed his supper," Mike said. "I guess he's peeved." Despite having turned his back on Sunny and stalking off, Shadow somehow still managed to zip between her legs and into the house as she unlocked the front door. He elaborately ignored her as Sunny headed to the kitchen and got out a can of the good cat food, and even stayed aloof as she scraped the can into his dish and added fresh water to his bowl. He waited until she was well away before he came up and began taking small, determined bites.

He's got to be starving, but he won't let himself be hurried, Sunny thought, watching him from the kitchen doorway "Hey, how come the furball gets fed first?" Mike demanded, reminding her that there were other hungry people in the house.

Sighing, Sunny went to the refrigerator and got out the deli salads she'd picked up at Judson's Market the day before. They might be leftovers, but with some bread and cold cuts, they'd make a decent cold supper.

Mike came into the kitchen to get plates and scowl at Shadow. But when he saw Mike, the cat abandoned his bowl and advanced on Sunny's father, reaching out a paw to pat at his shin.

Mike's grim expression melted to a wry grin. "Crazy cat."

Yeah, the sarcastic voice in Sunny's head commented, *but he's still getting fed first.*

*

Four days later, Sunny had fallen into a routine with the hospitalized Ollie. At the end of the day, she'd bring any business that needed his approval up to County General. Thankfully, with the weekend there hadn't been much for Ollie to deal with when he was really out of things, just a real estate deal with somebody in Portland who kept making phone calls to the MAX office.

Although Ollie had a boatload of businesses, the tour office served as headquarters and nerve center of his miniature financial empire. That's where all the files were kept, all the mail was delivered, and all the calls kept coming in from Mr. Orton in Portland.

Today was the big day when Ollie transferred out of the

hospital and into the nursing home. Sunny left the office early, carrying a fat envelope full of papers that Mr. Orton had express-mailed over for Ollie's signature ASAP. Placing the bulky package on the passenger seat of her trusty maroon Wrangler, Sunny set off for Bridgewater Hall.

The orthopedic surgeon had worked quickly to pull Ollie's broken bone together—and the hospital had worked just as quickly to get him out of there. An ambulance arrived to take Sunny's boss to Bridgewater Hall around noontime. Mike Coolidge had volunteered to help with the move and get Ollie established in his new digs.

Heading north from Kittery Harbor, Sunny stayed on the interstate until she reached the exit that would take her to Levett. Then she followed a series of country roads until she came to the stone bridge that gave Bridgewater its name. The village had a downtown about a block long—a food store, Laundromat, barbershop, gas station, and dry cleaner's. Following the instructions she'd downloaded, Sunny passed the business district, took the next left, and five minutes later pulled up in the driveway of Bridgewater Hall.

"Yikes!" she muttered, taking in the view. Except for the cyclone fence and the parking lot taking up a good piece of the front lawn, the place had a distinctly baronial feel. A three-story stone structure rose up on the left, complete with a two-story bay with battlements on top. And just to the right of those rose a heavy arch framing a pair of bronze and timber doors that would probably require a major battering ram to bust through if the local peasants ever decided to revolt.

Extending off to the right was a two-story wing set

farther back, rising at the far right end to another three-story structure, sort of a miniature of the first hall.

Must have started out as someone's stately home, or maybe a hotel, Sunny thought as she got out of her Jeep and headed up the walk. The doors, for all their imposing size, swung open easily, and Sunny immediately left medieval times for the world of twenty-first-century medicine—or at least twentieth century. The floor was institutional green terrazzo, and a guard's desk flanked the doorway. The buildup had left Sunny expecting maybe a Beefeater with a halberd; instead, she saw a guy maybe a few years younger than she was behind a chest-high wooden counter. He was burly, with sandy hair in a military buzz cut and a wide, open face that was maybe softening a little along the jawline. But he wore his short-sleeved blue shirt and dark striped tie like a uniform, and there was plenty of heavy muscle on his arms as he took up a pen and pushed a sign-in book toward her. Still, his smile was cheerful and friendly as he said, "Welcome to Bridgewater Hall. How can I help you?"

"Yes, a . . . friend of mine just arrived today." Maybe she was having a flashback to the Kittery Harbor Way, but Sunny didn't want to call Ollie just a boss or employer. "Mr. Barnstable."

"Oh, yes, he's settled in by now." As the guard ran down a list, Sunny got close enough to read the name tag over his breast pocket: R. WARNER. "Ah," Warner said, "they put him in 114 with Mr. Scatterwell. Well, you should get some entertainment. Mr. Scatterwell's the mayor of the rehab unit."

"Thanks." Sunny tried to figure out which way to go. Beyond the guard's desk was a large open area done up as a sort of parlor, with armchairs, couches, paintings, and even a huge, ancient grandfather clock. Large fish tanks took up one wall. Opposite that stood what appeared to be a pair of elevators. Beyond those was a long hallway.

One of the elevator doors opened, and a calico cat sauntered out.

Sunny blinked to make sure she wasn't seeing things. The cat padded across the corridor, then broke into a sudden run to jump onto one of the parlor chairs.

Warner followed her eyes. "Therapy animal," he explained. "We've got several cats and dogs here." He called out, "Portia, what are you doing over there?"

The cat's head briefly appeared over the arm of the chair, responding to her name. Then Portia disappeared again, no doubt arranging herself on the upholstery for a nap.

"Wouldn't it be nice if we could all do that?" Sunny asked with a smile.

"Wouldn't get much done if we followed Portia's schedule." But Warner's smile was fond as he looked over at the chair. Then he glanced back at Sunny. "Sorry, ma'am, You're probably wondering how to get to your friend's room. Just follow the corridor—it'll take you to the nurses' station. They can direct you from there."

I'm not so much older than you that you've got to call me ma'am, Sunny thought. She signed in, then extended her hand. "Sunny Coolidge."

Warner replied with a firm handshake. "Rafe Warner."

"I guess I'll be seeing a lot of you." Sunny hefted the bulging envelope she'd brought. "I work for Mr. Barnstable, and I'll be bringing papers and stuff for him."

Rafe smiled. "Well, welcome again. I hope Mr. Barnstable enjoys his stay."

Sunny thanked him and set off for the corridor. Along the way, she stopped by the armchair that Portia had claimed. "Hello, there," she said, extending the back of her hand. Portia was up before the hand got close, but she didn't skitter away. Instead, she raised her head and gave Sunny a delicate sniff, staring up at Sunny's face with greenish-gold eyes, their color heightened by the markings on her face. Black fur surrounded her right eye, ginger fur encircled her left. Against the white fur on the rest of her face, it made Portia look as if she were wearing a multicolored mask.

Barely had Portia checked out the hand than she lowered her head in a gesture Sunny had learned early in her relationship with Shadow. It was a silent command to be petted.

Maybe she's catching a whiff of Shadow on me, Sunny thought as she ran gentle fingers over velvet fur. Portia thrust her head more determinedly against Sunny's caress, wanting the space between her ears scratched.

Hearing a laugh, Sunny glanced over to the guard's station and Rafe Warner's smiling face. "Should have warned you, the critters around here are very touchy-feely. Spending time with the residents means a lot of petting."

"So I see." Portia wordlessly directed Sunny to take care of her neck and then arched her back to get a nice scratch there, too.

Rafe Warner came over. "Poor Portia isn't getting as much attention as she likes." He glanced around, then lowered his voice. "Hope you're not superstitious. She's gotten a sort of—reputation—lately."

"Reputation for what?" Sunny asked.

Rafe shrugged uncomfortably. "As a jinx. A lot of the people she's picked to hang around with—they pass away."

"Is that so?" Sunny asked the cat. "What's your weapon of choice? Is it fish breath? Or maybe a gas attack under the covers?" She'd learned from harsh experience that whenever Shadow closed his eyes and looked blissfully content, it was time to abandon the nearby premises until the noxious cloud dissipated.

"Folks seem to take it more supernaturally," Rafe explained, chuckling.

"You mean people think that once Portia the Psychic Cat puts her paws on them, they'll die?" Sunny shook her head. "Seems to me I read something about a cat doing the same thing in a hospital, and there turned out to be a simple physical reason. Really sick people are usually bundled up, making them nice and warm. That's pretty attractive for a cat."

Rafe nodded. "I've heard the same thing. But even people who pooh-pooh the idea of a cat choosing people to die get skittish if Portia takes a shine to them."

"That's silly." Sunny smiled down at the cat. "You wouldn't go around marking people for death, would you, Portia?"

The calico cat raised guileless eyes to her, purring loudly as Sunny's fingers went back to work. Rafe reached down and joined in. It was obvious he knew all the spots where Portia wanted to be petted.

Sunny glanced over at Rafe. "Well, you don't seem to be scared off."

"I found Portia and her brother Patrick abandoned as kittens outside in the parking lot," he explained. "Used to take care of them through the night shift, bottle-feeding them, keeping them warm, and petting them when they got lonesome or scared." He gave Sunny an embarrassed smile. "I guess you could say they think I'm their mother."

The phone at his post rang. "Sorry," he said, hotfooting over to answer it.

"I still think you're getting a bum rap, Portia." Sunny gently kneaded muscles while Portia purred. She knew how those things happened.

I wouldn't mind some magical abilities, though, Sunny silently told the cat. *Help get some idiots to steer clear of me if they thought that taking up my time might make them keel over.*

*

Shadow marched along the hallway at a determined lope. He'd checked all the windows in the room with the picture box, trying to find a loose screen. The one by the couch had seemed like a possibility, but even though he worked very hard, he hadn't been able to get it to move.

Stupid screen, he thought, investigating the eating room. The windows here were small and hard to reach, and besides, they were rarely open. Shadow needed the combination of an open window and a loose screen. Whenever he came to live in new places, he always made sure he had a way to leave if he had to. Shadow couldn't imagine leaving Sunny, but he still managed to find an exit. He'd learned to jump up and bang the handle on the screen door until it finally opened enough that he could squeeze out. That was fine—he'd used it to get out of the house that day he'd stalked that stupid bird. Bad enough the bird got away, but then Shadow had found himself stuck outdoors.

Now he had a new hunt—to find a way *in*. Most two-leggity types he'd lived with hadn't paid much attention to screens. They let corners get loose or left spaces where a careful cat could lever up the frame on the screen . . . In one place, if he'd hit the right place when he jumped, the whole screen fell right out of the window. Of course, the human he'd stayed with hadn't liked that. But it seemed as though Sunny and the Old One who lived here took care of things too well. Wherever windows were left open, the screens were sturdily in place.

He moved on to the kitchen, jumping onto the table. The window there was barely open at the bottom, just about the width of his paw. Shadow crouched down, poking his paw out. The screen was solid, and he couldn't catch hold of the frame. With a hiss of annoyance, he dropped down to the floor and then leaped up onto the counter and the place where Sunny washed dishes. He had to stretch to reach the window there, and he didn't have any luck anyway.

Even more maddening, as he fruitlessly poked around, a bird came fluttering by.

Shadow looked over to the door. *Maybe I'll go outside and give that flapper a surprise,* he thought. But then he realized that not only was the screen door closed, but the glass one was closed, too. He couldn't find a way in *or* out . . . at least not on this floor.

He started for the stairway. *Stupid house.*

*

Sunny finally managed to disentangle herself from Portia the cat and continued down the corridor, passing several closed doors and a connecting hallway until she came to a broad open space with a desklike island in the middle, where several white-clad figures were working. This must be the nurses' station.

"Hello," Sunny said to the nearest nurse. "I'm looking for Mr. Barnstable in Room 114—"

The woman immediately rose and pointed down the leftmost of the three corridors that radiated from in front of her desk. "That's down in the rehab wing. He's with Mr. Scatterwell." She gave Sunny a smile as she said it.

Hope that means this Scatterwell is a nice guy, not the joke of the floor, Sunny's annoying internal voice piped up. Sunny thanked the nurse and set off down the hallway, checking room numbers—although she could just as easily have followed the sound of her dad's laughter. *He's still here?*

She entered a space larger than the living room in her house, with an Impressionist-style landscape on the wall between two wardrobes. A pair of wheelchairs sat in front of a closet door, along with a pair of walkers—the kind with wheels on front, the frames all folded up. And, of course, there was the pair of hospital beds, with fancy coverlets that matched the drapes on the windows and the curtains hanging from tracks in the ceiling, everything neatly arranged to camouflage the institutional nature of the room.

Sunny's dad sat on a large, comfortable armchair under the painting, talking with the occupants of the beds. The man in the bed by the window was a stranger to Sunny, but he spoke to Mike as if they were old friends. Ollie lay on the other bed, still in pajamas, looking a lot less comfortable.

"Sunny!" Mike rose from his chair, turning to the stranger. "Gardner, this is my daughter, Sunny. Sunny, Gardner Scatterwell."

The man fumbled for a device like a TV remote, and the bed moved him to a more upright position. He wore a track suit and had a pear-shaped, jowly face with just a fringe of white hair over the ears. His eyes were so pale blue they seemed almost colorless, and his nose was a sizable beak knocked a little off center. The creases around his mouth extended down toward his chin. Between the fixed gaze of those odd eyes and the slight bobbing to his head, he gave Sunny the impression of a life-sized marionette—with a less-than-experienced operator at the strings.

But Gardner Scatterwell gave her a wide smile and clasped her hand in both of his. "So you're this old reprobate's daughter? I knew your dad when we were in high school, back in the New Stone Age."

"How do you do, Mr. Scatterwell?" Sunny said politely. She had a moment's struggle extricating her hand from his double clutch. "Excuse me, I have to deliver something to Mr. Barnstable."

Ollie wasn't looking his best—not surprising when turning in his sleep or even sitting up to eat could trigger a stab of pain if he wasn't careful. His skin looked a half-size too large on him, he had bags under his eyes, and he'd apparently collected a new crop of wrinkles. Sunny thought she'd seen her boss in a bad way those times he'd come in seriously hungover, but that Ollie had looked positively chipper compared to the way he looked now.

And the situation hadn't improved his notoriously uncertain temper. "What is it?" he snapped. "Can't a guy get any rest around here?"

Sunny held out her thick envelope. "Mr. Orton rushed this over."

Ollie pushed the package away. "You think I'm going to worry about that, the way I feel?"

"The man said it was urgent."

"Urgent for him maybe." Ollie grabbed the envelope and glared at her over the big, dark, pouchy bags beneath his eyes. "He may lose a few bucks if the deal drags on, but it's not costing *me* money. This can wait."

Ollie contemptuously tossed the overstuffed envelope into his lap—then let out a stifled howl of pain as it landed on his bad leg. Sunny quickly collected the papers and deposited them on the hospital table at the foot of his bed.

"Oliver, you need something to take your mind off things." Gardner looked at the gold watch on his wrist. "There's some music over in the other wing right now."

"I don't feel—" Ollie began.

But Gardner just kept smiling. "Think you'll feel better just lying here?" He hit a button on his souped-up remote, and a second later, a voice came out of a speaker. "Yes, Mr. Scatterwell?"

"Can we get an aide in here?" he asked. "My roomie and I want to get into our wheelchairs."

While they waited, Gardner turned to Mike. "Go on, tell Sunny about our band."

Mike laughed again. "We were the Cosmic Blade. I played bass, and Gardner here had a wall of drums. Remember how we used to start 'Gimme Some Lovin'?" He began fingering chords on an air guitar. *"Ba-da-da-da-dooomph, ba-da-da-da-dooomph . . ."* Gardner immediately started wailing away on an imaginary drum set. Sunny couldn't help noticing that he was seriously out of time with Mike— and that he quickly tired.

"Spencer Davis," Gardner wheezed.

"A long time ago," Mike said.

A young woman in a blue uniform came in, and began

the process of transferring the patients from bed to wheel-chair. Gardner Scatterwell was slow and awkward. "Damn stroke has really fouled me up." His tone fell somewhere between explaining and complaining as he struggled into the chair.

Ollie was even worse. Pain not only made him clumsy, but also made him afraid to shift his weight at all. But at last both were in their chairs. Gardner looked up at Mike. "Would you mind wheeling Oliver?"

He grinned at Sunny. "At my age, and in my condition, I've got to grab any chance I can get to be with a lovely woman."

Shaking her head but smiling, Sunny took the handgrips on the wheelchair. "Where to?" she asked.

He directed them around the nurses' station and down one of the other hallways. Although it had the same floor and paint job, this corridor seemed a little narrower—older.

This must be the wing I saw coming up the walk, Sunny thought. Glancing over her shoulder, she saw Mike looking around with interest as he followed along with Ollie's wheelchair. Ollie sat in a dejected huddle, ignoring it all.

"Just keep going, right to the end, and then you make a left," Gardner said.

Sunny followed his directions past a series of semipri-vate rooms, finally coming into a combination sunroom and cafeteria, where a small collection of older folks—mainly women—clustered in wheelchairs and walkers around a younger man playing guitar. They were all sing-ing "Pennies from Heaven." Sunny, Mike, Gardner, and Ollie all waited in the doorway until they finished and rewarded themselves with a little applause.

"Got room for a couple of late kids, Luke?" Gardner called as the clapping died away.

"Always," the guitarist replied with a smile. He was a guy about Sunny's age, with a big mass of shaggy, curly brown hair that spilled down into a big, shaggy beard. A proud nose poked out of all that hair, and a pair of warm brown eyes beamed at them.

Like melted chocolate, Sunny couldn't help thinking.

The man shifted his shoulder under the colorful strap on his acoustic guitar as he beckoned them into the circle around him. "Luke Daconto," he identified himself. "Musical therapist. Tunes and therapy, at your service. So, Gardner, you brought me a couple of new recruits?"

"Yeah, it's a little too quiet for us down in the rehab wing," the older man replied, introducing Ollie, Mike, and Sunny.

"Well, let's see if we can come up with a cheerful song." Luke's fingers seemed to dance along the guitar's fretboard as if they had a mind of their own.

Ollie suddenly perked up. "That's 'Smoke on the Water.'"

"Guilty," Luke admitted. "You can't always be playing 'You Are My Sunshine.' How about this?"

He launched into a spirited version of "When I'm Sixty-Four." Some of the older audience members didn't know the words, but Gardner Scatterwell joined in. So did Mike, and then Ollie. Finally Sunny picked up the chorus. She noticed one woman who wasn't singing, but still tapped out the rhythm on the armrest of her wheelchair. Luke played a selection of tunes from several generations, from hits to standards to children's songs. It was kind of silly, but Sunny found herself chiming in with as much gusto as the older members of the audience. The grand finale was "On Top of Spaghetti," where Luke did a sort of call and response routine. It was obviously a favorite of the regulars in the group, drawing hearty applause.

"I'm afraid that's it for today," the guitarist eventually said. "Thanks to all of you for coming. I'll be back here in a couple of days. And especially thanks to Oliver, Mike, and Sunny. I hope I'll see you again."

"Count on it," Mike said heartily, and then looked embarrassed. After all, he was only a guest.

Gardner Scatterwell laughed. "Well, I need someone to wheel me in here. You volunteering, Mike?"

As they rolled back to Room 114, Sunny was glad to see that Ollie looked a little more animated. "He seems like a nice guy."

"Hell of a guitarist," Gardner said. "Did you listen to those little snatches of song he plays between the sing-alongs? Folk, jazz, rock, classical . . . this kid would have been a big help on the Cosmic Blade, right, Mike? Why'd the band ever break up anyway?"

He continued with funny anecdotes about the high school band's musical career until they reached the room—and a mean-looking heavyset man leaped up from the visitor's chair to loom over Ollie.

"Where the hell have you been, Barnstable?" the man demanded in a gravelly voice that was all too familiar. This could only be Mr. Orton. "What are you trying to pull?"

3

The one certainty that Sunny had found in her work relationship with Oliver Barnstable was his uncertain temper—or rather, the certainty that sooner or later he would erupt over something. An unworthy part of her was just glad that this time around, she wasn't the one he was unloading on, but the unpleasant Mr. Orton.

"What does it look like I'm doing?" Ollie the Barnacle demanded. "Dancing *Gangnam Style*?" His normal red color came flooding back to his face as he pointed at his injured leg. "I busted this, and they doped me up to keep me out of it while they screwed with my leg—screwed in it, actually. So I haven't paid much attention to our deal, Orton. I'll get to it when I get to it."

"Then you should have read this more carefully." Orton jerked a thumb at the overstuffed envelope still sitting on

Ollie's hospital table. "If you had, you'd know that the option for that parcel of land you want has a time limit on it. Go over the time limit, and you'll have to renegotiate the whole agreement. And I promise you, the longer you jerk me around on this deal, the more you're going to end up paying."

With that, Orton stomped out of the room, leaving Ollie to chew his lips in silence for a moment. Then he turned to Sunny. "Have you got the number for my lawyer?"

Luckily, Sunny had that one memorized. She recited it to Ollie, who punched it into his bedside phone. The conversation was brief and definitely unpleasant, with Ollie demanding his counsel get up to Bridgewater Hall as soon as possible. He hung up still angry. "We'll have to go over this damned contract," Ollie said as if it were all Sunny's fault. "I'll want you here in the morning to pick it up."

Before he could complain any more, a woman in a white lab coat entered the room. From the way she walked, Sunny suspected this was a woman who didn't put up with much. She didn't look more than ten years older than Sunny, though a few gray strands were beginning to appear in the brown hair she wore pulled back. Her skin was pale, her cheekbones high, and her lips were full—or would be if she relaxed them from that tightly pursed expression— and her eyes were a stony gray, set on either side of a proud beak of a nose.

"Evening, Doctor," Gardner Scatterwell said, his voice sounding like a fawning grade school student.

The doctor paid no attention to him, nor to Sunny and her dad. "I am Dr. Gavrik," she announced to Ollie in a slightly accented voice. "I have read your charts from the hospital and will perform an examination now."

With a few brusque movements, she got Ollie back into bed and then pulled the curtains around them. "Your blood pressure is much higher than it has been at your other readings," they heard her comment from behind the gaily patterned fabric.

"He just had a rather tense business discussion," Mike called in explanation.

For just a second, Dr. Gavrik's face appeared from behind the curtain, her expression withering. "Did I ask you for a diagnosis?" she all but hissed at him.

Mike glanced at Sunny and his own face reddened.

I suspect the blood pressure reading just went up on this side of the room, too, Sunny thought, but she said nothing and neither did her father.

The doctor vanished behind the curtains again for several minutes. When she reappeared, briskly moving the privacy curtain back to the wall with a rattle of hooks against the ceiling track, she seemed the model of serene professionalism.

"Except for the blood pressure, all the other exam results are normal. I'll have the nurse check your pressure twice more this evening. I expect it will be acceptable. Then, tomorrow, you will be evaluated by our therapy department, and they will prepare a treatment plan for you. Good evening, Mr. Barnstable."

With a nod, Dr. Gavrik headed for the door, leaving the room in silence.

Despite a wince of pain from the exertion, Ollie pulled himself up to make sure that the doctor was well and truly gone. Even then, he kept his voice low as he turned to

Mike. "What kind of joint have you gotten me into?" he demanded. "Doctors like that—they bury their mistakes."

"Doctors like who?" Sunny asked.

"You know—foreign ones." Ollie kept his voice low and his eyes on the doorway. "Anything goes wrong, they can always go back to wherever they came from."

"I can't believe—" Sunny began, but Gardner Scatterwell suddenly spoke up.

"She'll never win any bedside manner awards, but I can assure you, Dr. Gavrik is an excellent physician," he said. "Most of the people in this ward are basically trying to get themselves better, so health is less of an issue. But in the time I've been here, I've seen Dr. Gavrik save the lives of several permanent residents."

Now I see why they call Gardner the mayor of the rehab ward, Sunny thought. *He even talks like a politician.*

Gardner waggled his eyebrows. "Besides, when you get to know her, you'll find she's a very attractive woman."

Sunny rolled her eyes. *Maybe too much like a politician.*

"I guess Dad and I ought to be heading home," she said.

"Yeah," Ollie the Barnacle said. "Check in at the office tomorrow morning, then come here and collect these papers."

Sunny and her dad said good-bye to Ollie and Gardner, then headed down the hallway. Mike was silent as they walked past the nurses' station and then toward the front door.

"You okay, Dad?" Sunny asked. "That doctor didn't upset you, did she?"

"I was thinking of something else." But Mike didn't

elaborate as they got to Rafe the guard's desk. While her father paged back through the sign-in book, Rafe smiled at Sunny. "Well, it looks as if you survived the Curse of Portia," he said.

Mike looked up. "Is that Dr. Gavrik's first name?"

That took the wind out of Rafe's sails, reducing him to "Er, ah . . ."

"This is my dad, Mike Coolidge," Sunny introduced them. Then she went on to explain the rumors about Portia acting as the fickle finger of death.

Mike snorted and shook his head. "I'm getting gladder and gladder I didn't come to this place when I was sick. It's beginning to sound like a home for the feeble-minded."

"Just a place where a lot of lonely folks have no place to go and nothing much to talk about," Rafe said. "It's like little kids telling ghost stories."

"Yup—definitely happy that I can get out," Mike mumbled, scrawling his name in the appropriate spot. Sunny signed out, too, then said good-bye to Rafe.

"Have a good evening," Rafe replied.

As they stepped out the door, Mike said, "That's a nice boy."

"Dad." Sunny gave him an exasperated look. "You don't have to worry about setting me up."

"I was just thinking that maybe Will Price could use a little competition," Mike turned an innocent blue gaze on her. "They're even in a similar field. Will's a cop, and this fellow is in security."

"Rafe's also a lot younger than I am," Sunny pointed out.

"Oh, that all evens out in, say, twenty years."

Wonderful, Sunny silently groused. *He's already got me married and sitting beside the fire for twenty years.* "What's got you thinking like this?" she asked.

"I've just been mulling over something Gardner mentioned," Mike confessed. "He asked why the band broke up. You know, I met your mother through that stupid band. She used to stand right up front when we played." He smiled at the memory. "There were usually three kinds of people you'd find up front. The ones who couldn't dance, the ones who wanted to look cool, and the ones who really enjoyed the music. Your mother loved music—not that I need to remind you of that, with your name."

Sunny nodded. With a name like Sonata, it hadn't always been easy when she was younger. Kids are the ultimate conformists, and anything even a little bit different tended to get picked on. But she'd come through reasonably all right. *It's too bad I lost Mom just when I was finally getting comfortable with the name,* she thought. She'd thank her for it now.

"So she knew your friend Gardner, too, huh?" Sunny said. "You know, there's a fourth reason for people to hang around in front of a band—groupies."

"I think that's why Gardner got into music," Mike told her. "I had to give him a poke in the snoot when he started sniffing around your mother while she was going out with me. It's definitely what broke up the band."

"Dad!" Sunny couldn't believe what he was saying.

But Mike merely nodded and gave her a shamefaced grin. "I'd forgotten about all that when I saw him today. It was almost fifty years ago, for the love of mud. I'd just hear about him in passing. Seemed as if he was always going off places, sometimes for years at a time. Mexico, Nepal . . . I suppose he could tell you some stories."

"Well, at least you seemed friendly enough now," Sunny said. "I guess the two of you have gotten older and wiser."

Mike just shrugged. "Older, at least."

He got in his truck, she got in her SUV, and they both headed home.

*

Shadow had checked all the rooms in the house—all except one, where the door was closed. So he'd given up for the time being and come back downstairs. He woke from a nap at the rattle of keys in the lock and strolled over to investigate the newcomers. Would it be Sunny—which would be cause for a warm welcome—or the Old One, her father, who would just get a cursory sniff?

It turned out to be both of them. He twined around Sunny's legs as they headed for the room where the two-legs kept the food.

Shadow's nose told him that Sunny and the Old One had been in the same place. Some of the smells clinging to them were familiar—they reminded him of scents he'd encountered when he'd been taken to be treated for sickness or hurts. But he also got a whiff of many Old Ones, smells of sickness.

When Sunny knelt to pet him, Shadow detected another scent on her hands. He smelled cat!

For a second, he was disconcerted and nearly pulled away. Instead, he found himself avidly sniffing her fingers as she gently stroked through his fur. Sunny made happy sounds and spoke to the Old One, who grumbled in reply. His rumbling only got louder when Shadow approached to sniff at him, too, though he quickly returned to Sunny when he didn't find the interesting cat scent on the other human.

Even when Sunny stopped playing with him and began preparing a meal, Shadow stayed close, breathing in the dissipating scent. Definitely a She. Strange. He'd smelled plenty of cats in his wanderings. What made the scent of this female so interesting?

*

Shadow acted a bit oddly during supper, climbing several times into Sunny's lap to sniff at her hands.

"You did wash 'em before you touched the food, right?" Mike asked.

"Dad!" Sunny gave him a look.

"Well, the furball keeps checking them out. And you said it was a female cat you were petting." Mike's bright blue eyes fixed Shadow with a dubious stare. "Are you sure he's been, like, fixed?"

"It was one of the first things Jane Rigsdale checked when she became his vet," Sunny assured her dad. "I don't exactly think Shadow could fake that."

"All right, all right, just asking." Mike switched the topic. "I'm glad we invited Helena over. Be nice to see her."

Sunny knew her dad had been missing his lady friend, who'd been out of town over the weekend visiting her daughter in Boston. And, of course, Sunny knew Mike had an ulterior motive. Helena Martinson was sure to bring her award-winning coffee cake. "You're just glad to have some dessert tonight," she scolded. "Don't go crazy on the cake."

Mike raised his hands in mock surrender. "Okay, okay. The food police have spoken."

"Speaking of police, I invited Will over, too," Sunny tried to sound casual. That date for pancakes had never materialized over the weekend. Will had been preempted for something on Saturday morning, and he stayed out of touch on Sunday. Since he'd switched to the day shift this week, she'd invited him over tonight. "Don't worry," Sunny assured Mike. "If there's not enough coffee cake to go around, he can share my piece."

That sort of mirrored her problem with Will. Just like the coffee cake, there weren't enough available males to be found in a small town like Kittery Harbor. Sunny should be glad to be seeing a guy like Will. But she wondered if it wasn't getting a bit . . . well, dull. Pancake breakfasts, coffee cake. It didn't sound like a healthy diet, for the body or for the soul.

Mike didn't seem to have that problem with Mrs. M. His face was eager as they cleared the dinner plates and cleaned them. Then he set a pot of coffee brewing and got out the good china cups and cake plates. The coffee was just about done when the doorbell rang.

Mike moved with an extra spring in his step to answer it—although he almost sprang back when he opened the door to be greeted with a joyful "woof!" A biscuit-colored dog had his paws halfway up Mike's thigh as he stretched to try and lick at his hands.

That pup just keeps growing, Sunny thought as Helena Martinson struggled with the golden Lab's leash.

"Toby, get down! Where are your manners?" the petite woman scolded. She had a figure women decades younger would envy, and even her hair had merely gone from blond to something more like platinum. Mike had to bend down to receive her kiss, but he obviously thought it worthwhile. He didn't even notice the dog romping around his legs. Mrs. Martinson gave Mike Toby's leash and walked down the hall with a rueful smile. "Toby is still a bit of a handful," she said, handing Sunny a small box that held her famous coffee cake.

"If he keeps growing, you'll be able to ride him over," Sunny replied.

Mike released Toby from his leash, and the dog headed immediately into the living room, sniffing the air and whining because he couldn't find his friend Shadow. Sunny glanced back toward the kitchen, but the cat had definitely made himself scarce. He'd probably put in an appearance when the guests were leaving—Sunny was never sure whether it was an attempt to be sociable or if Shadow wanted to make sure the dog was definitely gone.

The bell rang again, and Sunny went this time to find Will Price at the door. He wore a pair of khakis and a natural cotton short-sleeved shirt, which should have gone over well on his rangy form with its summer tan. But the light colors only brought out a bright redness under his tan, a redness that only increased on his nose and cheeks, although the area around his eyes was noticeably paler. Wherever he'd spent the weekend, he'd been wearing sunglasses.

"That looks like a pretty good burn," she told him, not feeling too much sympathy. So this was why he couldn't see her?

"Ben Semple invited me out on his boat for some fishing Saturday morning," Will said, naming a cop colleague.

"We were stuck out there longer than I anticipated—without any sunblock. Ben got it even worse—he's fairer than I am." Will's regular features, usually so calm and competent, twisted in embarrassment. "I spent Saturday afternoon and all of Sunday in the tub, trying to soak this down."

"Well, I can't tell if you're blushing, so it didn't quite work." Shaking her head, Sunny led him to the living room, where Mike and Mrs. M. were already ensconced with coffee cake. After commenting on Will's sunburn, they turned to Ollie Barnstable's mishap. When Mike mentioned bumping into Gardner Scatterwell after all these years, Will looked a little surprised. "I met the man while doing some fund-raising for my old school," he said. "Scatterwell graduated about thirty years ahead of me, but I was sent to try and tickle a donation out of him, along with a lot of rich folk up in Piney Brook."

"Lord knows, Gardner would have the loot," Mike chuckled. "I remember—"

But Helena cut off his flood of reminiscence. "I never warmed to Gardner," she interrupted, "and I'd prefer not to hear about him."

Mike was taken aback but quickly switched tracks to talk about the prickly Dr. Gavrik. Sunny waited until she and Helena were alone in the kitchen to put in her two cents. As a major linchpin in the Kittery Harbor gossip network, typically Mrs. M. would be eager to hear the latest news, even about people she didn't necessarily like.

Especially about people she didn't like, the cynical voice in the back of Sunny's head suggested.

"I hope Dad didn't upset you, mentioning Gardner Scatterwell. They were in a band together back in his high school days—although Dad says that ended when Gardner got too interested in my mom."

"A chronic condition for him," Mrs. Martinson muttered as she put plates in the sink. "I didn't grow up around here, so I never encountered the Piney Brook crowd until I moved into town with my late husband." She shook her head. "'Scatterwell' was an appropriate name for Gardner. He said it was because some ancestor must have been good at sowing seed on a farm. What he was good at was sowing wild oats—long after he should have grown up. You've heard the saying, 'Shirtsleeves to shirtsleeves in three generations'? Gardner did his best to make that come true. His father made the family fortune, and he found ways to throw it away."

"Sounds like a lot of people who've got more money than brains," Sunny said.

Helena shot her a sharp look. "But not enough of a reason to dislike the man? Then how about this—true to form, he once got me alone in the kitchen during a party and told me how much he loved me."

Sunny shrugged. "You've always been an attractive woman."

"Yeah, but then he tried to show the depths of his devotion by shoving his tongue down my throat." Helena Martinson made a face. "He knew I was married, for heaven's sake. And if you remember my Raymond . . ."

Sunny recalled Mr. Martinson as a big, stocky guy who'd obviously adored his petite wife and gorgeous daughter (who was a few years older than Sunny). He'd had to put up with a lot of teenaged boys around the house, but he was pretty easygoing, even tolerating the guys who'd buzzed around Helena like moths drawn to her hot-mom flame—pretty much the same way Shadow tolerated Toby coming over.

"I recall a lot of guys who had crushes on you," Sunny said.

"Boys." Helena made a dismissive gesture. "Gardner was old enough to know better. And if Ray had found out, Gardner would've had his head handed to him."

"What did you do?" Sunny couldn't help asking.

"I pushed him away, told him his passion wasn't requited, and made sure I was never alone with him again." Mrs. M.'s lips twisted in a sort of smile. "He moped around for a couple of weeks, trying to convince me he was heart-broken, then went off to make some other woman's life miserable. You could follow it like the phases of the moon. Usually his so-called deathless passions lasted about six weeks."

"So you have no interest in tracking him down at Bridge-water Hall and rekindling the flames?" Sunny teased.

Helena's answer caught Sunny off guard. "I'm very happy with what I have with your father. Someday I hope you can enjoy the same thing." She glanced at the kitchen door. "Even if the man in your life lets himself get roasted like a turkey."

Sunny determinedly turned the conversation away from herself and Will. "Dad told me he gave Gardner a poke in the snout in their go-round," she said. "Is he the one who knocked it off-kilter?"

"No, but I guess I shouldn't be so surprised to hear that someone did." Helena sighed. "His nose was fine when I knew him. Gardner Scatterwell was a very handsome man—and knew it. That was one of his problems." She moved aside to let Sunny add the cups and saucers to the dishes in the sink, and then turned on the water. "I don't think I'd like to see what became of him."

They finished with the dishes and went back outside, where Mike and Will were discussing the woes of Red Sox Nation. Helena Martinson chatted a little more, then she rose to get Toby's leash. As if by magic, Shadow suddenly appeared, just as Sunny had anticipated. Toby gave a loud bark of delight and loped over to the cat. Shadow's tail lashed around, demonstrating his discomfort, but he put up with the dog's clumsy overtures. To show there were no hard feelings, Shadow even accepted a brief petting from Mrs. Martinson. Then she clipped the leash onto Toby's collar, and they left into the night.

Will soon followed her example. When Sunny turned from the doorway, she found only Shadow behind her. Mike had graciously left the living room to give some privacy for a good-night kiss.

After the door closed, Sunny sat down on the floor and stretched out her hands to Shadow. "You were a very gracious host," she teased him. "Especially with Toby." He climbed into her lap, pursuing her hands with his nose.

"I think it's time to give that up," Sunny told him. "I've washed my hands a couple of times, plus doing the dishes. All you're going to smell is soap."

Shadow gave her a sidelong look with those gold-flecked eyes of his, then reached out with both paws to capture her other hand.

Mike returned to reestablish himself on the couch. "So what were you and Helena gabbing about in the kitchen?"

Claire Donally

"Just girl talk," Sunny replied. She wasn't about to pass along what Mrs. Martinson had told her.

Her dad gave her a sly smile. "Maybe about a good-looking young security guard?"

"Dad." It took everything Sunny had to keep the word from drawing out into the exasperated whine of her teenaged days.

"I know, I know, you think he's too young." Mike waved her dirty look away. "It's just a coincidence that Helena has had younger guys making sheep's eyes at her as long as I can remember. Of course."

If she argued, Sunny knew her father would just hang on to the subject like Toby with a toy bone. "Whatever," she said darkly.

Mike nodded in self-satisfaction and began working the television remote.

"Probably looking for a rerun of *Father Knows Best*," she muttered to herself.

*

The next morning, Sunny got up earlier than usual. She came downstairs fully dressed and made a quick breakfast—somewhat hampered by Shadow, who insisted on rubbing his way around her ankles in a complex pattern. At last, however, Sunny managed to say good-bye to her dad and her cat and set off for the office. If winter threw ice and snow in a commuter's way, summer brought tourists to clog the roads. When Sunny discovered that the reason traffic had slowed to a crawl up the hill above town was because some yo-yo was shooting pictures of the scenic vista, she was mightily tempted to see if a nudge from

~44~

her Wrangler could send the tourist's rental car down the rougher end of the slope.

Even with the delay, however, she got into the office ahead of her regular time. Sunny checked the answering machine and cranked up the computer. No smoke signals warning about business or Internet troubles. So she locked up the office again and went back to her SUV.

The trip to Bridgewater lived up to all the hype she wrote for the MAX tourism website—the countryside was rolling and verdant at this time of year, especially when she hit the country roads, and a clear sky spread above. She arrived at Bridgewater Hall, parked, and walked through the baronial entrance. The security guard didn't live up to the grandeur this time around—he looked as if this was his first job out of high school. His uniform didn't fit. Sticking up from the collar on a skinny stalk of a neck, his head looked like a particularly unlovely plant. Small, dull brown eyes barely looked at her as the guy said, "May I help you, ma'am?"

"I'm here to see Mr. Barnstable in Room 114."

The guard needed to consult a separate binder to establish that such a patient was in residence. Then he finally pushed the sign-in book her way.

At last she headed down the hallway to the nurses' station, though it was empty—as was Ollie's room. An aide in blue surgical scrubs offered help. "Mr. Barnstable is in therapy. Go back to the desk and take the second hallway."

Sunny followed the directions down a hall with a lot of wheelchairs—many folded together and apparently stored along the walls of the corridor. A few, though, were occupied. She quickly spotted Gardner Scatterwell beside an open door. Gardner waved her over. "Good to see you,

Sunny." Then he glanced up at the man standing behind his chair. "You've got to meet this delightful young woman, Alfred. Sunny, my nephew Alfred."

"Alfred Scatterwell." The guy had to be somewhere around Sunny's age, and he looked like Gardner—sort of. He had the same beaky nose (though his was straight) and the same glassy blue eyes. He had more hair than his uncle, and it was darker, but he was already losing it. And where Gardner was portly, Alfred was tall and skinny, except for an outsized potbelly. It gave him the look of an anaconda working hard at digesting a swallowed sheep—even to the slightly dyspeptic expression on his face as they shook hands.

Dyspeptic . . . or distrustful?

"I'm trying to track down my boss," Sunny explained. "He's Gardner's roommate."

Alfred seemed to relax a little at that.

"Now you feel better?" Gardner's voice held a faint mocking note. "He was afraid you'd turn out to be another unfortunate attachment to be mentioned in my will. Alfred is the family's all-purpose heir. He's determined to restore Grandfather Scatterwell's fortune the old-fashioned way—by inheritance."

Alfred's face set in the pattern of someone who'd heard the same joke over and over and was long past finding it funny.

"Ah." Sunny couldn't think of anything to say to that. Time to change the subject. "Do you know where Ollie is?"

Gardner jerked a thumb at that doorway. "He's in for PT. Some call it physical therapy, I call it painful torture. I'm waiting to see who'll be putting me through my paces."

Even as he spoke, a woman came out. "Mr. Scatterwell."

She was not unattractive—the bone structure was there in her face, behind the wire-framed glasses she wore, but she wore no makeup and her thick gray-streaked brown hair was pulled back in a no-nonsense ponytail. Her figure was disguised by a bulky sweat suit, and she walked with a slight limp.

Gardner looked at the woman and recoiled theatrically. "Oh, no, it's Elsa, the She-Wolf of Occupational Therapy! Take it easy on me, please, Elsa. I'm still recovering."

Elsa gave a weary sigh. "You've been recovering for several months, Mr. Scatterwell. We should be seeing more results by now."

That got a different reaction from the older man. "So you've been working with me for several months now? Which means you've been paid during that time—while I've been contributing very generously to your salary and all the others?"

"If you want to discuss administrative issues, you should speak to Dr. Reese." The woman's voice became so careful, it was toneless.

"Hank Reese is an old friend of mine," Gardner Scatterwell said. "We were boys together. That's one of the reasons I came to this overpriced torture chamber."

"It *is* overpriced, Uncle," Alfred chimed in. "When you had to spend a couple of days back at the hospital, Dr. Reese charged four hundred dollars a day just to keep your bed here."

"More money that won't be coming to you." The cheerful guy Sunny had met yesterday was completely gone now. Money really seemed to bring out the worst in Gardner. "But I'll be staying here as long as I need." He glared at both Alfred and the therapist. "As long as I want."

"I'll see if I can get you a different therapist," the woman said, heading back to the door. She almost collided with Sunny, who was just trying to get away from the developing scene.

"Sorry," Sunny said, stepping through and to the side.

"I'm Elsa Hogue." The therapist lowered her voice with a glance over her shoulder. "If you have any influence with Mr. Scatterwell, I'd appreciate it if you could explain that he needs to take this therapy more seriously."

"I'm sorry again," Sunny said. "I don't have any influence around here. I'm looking for my boss—" She broke off when she spotted Ollie in the large, crowded room. He stood, after a fashion, crouched over a rolling walker. His face was pale and damp with sweat, and his knuckles were white as he clutched at the handles. A husky physical therapist walked at his side, keeping a sturdy grasp on the seat of Ollie's sweatpants. Bringing up the rear came a kid, a summer volunteer probably, pushing a wheelchair.

A security blanket, Sunny realized. He obviously can't walk very far, but this setup encourages him to stay on his feet as long as possible.

At that moment, Ollie looked up from taking a step and saw Sunny. He was in the middle of moving his bad leg and staggered, nearly falling back onto the chair. His face was a mask of humiliation and fury as he bawled, "Get out!"

4

The large room went silent, all of the people stopping in the middle of their various exercises to stare at Ollie after his outburst. All that attention didn't improve his mood, but at least he moderated his voice—slightly—when he spoke again. "Why'd you even come here?" he demanded. "I left the package with the nurse."

Who of course wasn't around when I arrived, Sunny thought. "I'll go and get it now," she said, heading back outside and just as glad not to have a room full of people gawking at her. *Let Ollie handle them in his own inimitable way,* that cynical side of her brain suggested.

Gardner Scatterwell and his nephew were still in the hallway, but they'd obviously heard Ollie's outburst. "I'm afraid Oliver is a bit out of sorts today—he was up late,"

Gardner explained. "He and his lawyer were going over those papers well after the normal lights-out."

Having nothing to say to that, Sunny just nodded and headed for the nurses' station. Now, of course, there was a nurse on duty, who passed over the thick envelope. Sunny checked inside and found a note in Ollie's nearly indecipherable handwriting. It instructed her to make copies for his files and his lawyer, then express-mail the originals to Mr. Orton. She headed down the hallway and to the parking lot. No sense risking any more grief from Ollie. She'd get on the job right away.

The scenery was as lush and pleasant on the way back as it had been on her outward journey, but Sunny's mood ruined the drive to Kittery Harbor. She then spent most of the morning taking care of that monster document, rounding out her time with routine office tasks.

When she answered the phone just before lunchtime, she was surprised to hear Ollie's voice on the other end of the line. "Look," he said gruffly. "I—um—I have to apologize. You caught me—this therapy stuff is rougher than almost anything I've ever had to do."

"I know that, Ollie. When my dad was sick, he had a real fight to get back on his feet. And look at him now."

"Yeah." Now Ollie sounded embarrassed. "He called to say he was coming up. The old-line folks in town, people like my dad, would do stuff like that, even if they weren't really friendly with someone in the hospital or whatever. I'd hate to have him hear that I'd treated you badly. I didn't mean what I was saying."

"Well, he won't hear about it from me," Sunny promised.

"Um. Good. There's something else you can do for me. Check in the files for a couple of folders." He described what he wanted—several real estate transactions. "These are other deals I've done with Orton. I want to compare them with the one you just copied."

"Fine, Ollie." Sunny looked longingly at the sandwich she'd just arrayed on her desk. "When do you need this?"

"We'll do it like we did yesterday," Ollie said. "You can leave the office a little early, and when you're finished up here, you can go home."

With a longer trip, longer business, and no overtime, Sunny's unpleasant reporter alter ego piped up.

Still, she agreed, took another note, and hung up. After lunch, she dug the keys out of her desk and went to the bank of tall cabinets that lined the back wall of the office. She took the precaution of copying all the files that Ollie had specified and putting the originals back where they came from.

Don't want him yelling at me if Jell-O gets spilled on them.

When Sunny arrived at Bridgewater Hall this time, she got a much more enthusiastic welcome. Rafe Warner was on duty now and greeted her with a smile and some chat as she signed in. And who should appear from behind the security desk but Portia, sniffing Sunny's ankles and then peering around them as if she expected someone else to be standing there.

I don't think she's looking for Dad, Sunny thought. *I think Shadow sent a message on me—and Portia's certainly answering.*

She spent a little time trying to pet Portia, who seemed

more interested in twining around her ankles. So in the end Sunny gave up and headed down the hallway to the rehab wing. Checking with the nurse, Sunny made sure that Ollie had finished his second therapy stint of the day and then went on to Room 114. There, she discovered both visitor's chairs were occupied. Mike Coolidge sat beside Gardner Scatterwell, and Luke Daconto, the guitarist from the other day, sat with Ollie.

"Well, this is unexpected," Sunny said.

"I had a bell-ringing class upstairs and decided to stop by on my way out," Luke said. "Considering Mr. Barnstable's interest in music, I'm trying to convince him to take some guitar lessons when he's feeling better."

"Trying to drum up business," Ollie said suspiciously.

"I didn't say I wanted to teach you," Luke replied with a good-natured smile—at least that's what Sunny thought was going on under all that foliage on his face. "I'm just saying you could easily pick up an inexpensive guitar and find someone to get you started."

"I was interested in music, as you put it, around the same age those two"—Ollie gestured at Mike and Gardner—"had their half-assed band."

"It's never too late to start," Luke insisted.

"You think?" Ollie looked hopeful for a moment, then shook his head. "I dunno. When I was sixteen, I saw a guitar in a music shop window—a Gibson. I never wanted anything more, but it was way out of my dad's price range. Three hundred dollars, if I remember right."

His eyes went to the ceiling, looking at something only he could see. "I spent a year doing shifts at the Sweet Shoppe for my dad, mowing lawns, shoveling snow . . . I even folded people's wash down at the Laundromat for minimum wage, which was about a buck-ninety in those days. And when I finally pulled together enough money—"

"You went to the store and the guitar was gone," Mike finished for him.

But Ollie shook his head, an almost heartbroken look on his big, round face. "I couldn't bring myself to spend so much money on something so—frivolous."

"I think you set your sights too high," Luke offered. "You should have gotten yourself a secondhand acoustic guitar—something inexpensive—and seen how it felt to play."

"That's what I did," Mike said. "Got my Rickenbacker at a pawnshop in Portsmouth for seventy-five bucks."

"Really?" Luke swung around to look at Sunny's dad, his eyes shining with interest. "Do you still have it?"

Mike shrugged. "Up in the attic maybe."

"If it's in good shape, you might be amazed at how valuable it's become now," Luke said eagerly. "Some Rickenbackers from that era go for a couple thousand dollars now—maybe more."

Mike gawked for a second, then said, "Really? That old bass may be the best investment I ever made."

While they were laughing, another visitor entered the room—a four-footed one.

"Portia, what are you doing here?" Sunny asked, kneeling to pet the calico cat. "Did you follow me?"

"Probably following Shadow," Mike muttered, not happy to find another cat barging into their lives.

Portia amiably gave each of the seated visitors a sniff, then launched herself into a leap that landed her in Gardner Scatterwell's lap.

"Whoa!" Luke said.

Gardner smiled, reverting to the nice old man Sunny had first met. "Hello there, kitty," he said as Portia pushed her head under his hand.

"Hey, Sunny," Mike asked, a little malice glinting in his bright blue eyes, "isn't that the cat you told me about? The one who, after she visits patients, they wind up kicking the bucket?"

"Are you that cat?" Gardner stopped in the middle of petting. Portia just stared at him and purred. "I've heard stories. Some of the ladies who sing along with Luke are afraid of you."

"There must be a logical explanation," Luke said.

Sunny gave her father a look for bringing up the subject in the first place.

"Of course there is," Gardner said, ruffling Portia's fur. "The fact is, the mortality statistics here are a trifle high lately. My nephew Alfred found that out looking on the Internet somewhere. He's trying to get me to move to some place with a lower death rate—and lower financial rates, of course. I think any home for the elderly is going to have its ups and downs, and they shouldn't blame pretty kitties if a bunch of old folks decide to die in a clump."

"Myself, I'm not so trusting of cats—they're always hungry," Mike said with suspicious mildness. "The one in your lap there, she may only be waiting for you to get ripe."

That outrageous comment got some shocked laughter, especially from Luke.

"What's going on in here?" a blue-clad aide asked from the doorway, but the smile on her broad, plain face belied her strict tone of voice. "Sorry, folks. Just wanted to check and make sure everyone was okay." Once Sunny got past the scrubs, she realized the aide was little older than a kid. She proved it as she turned to Sunny. "Could I get you a chair, ma'am?"

If any more of the staff calls me "ma'am," I'm going to think I should be living here. "No thanks," she said aloud.

"Camille here does a wonderful job, taking care of Ollie and myself, not to mention a dozen or so other inmates," Gardner said. "I'm sure you know Luke Daconto, Camille. This is an old friend, Mike Coolidge, and his daughter, Sunny."

"How do you do." Camille looked as though she'd be more at home working on a farm than in a health-care setting. Her big, sturdy form would be perfect for hauling around big bags of fertilizer or seed. She had a wide mouth and a diminutive nose, framed by an unflattering pageboy cut. Her best feature was a pair of soft hazel eyes, which glanced shyly around the strangers in the room. But she was quite competent when she said, "Mr. Scatterwell, you raised the top of your bed and slid all the way down."

"I used to be a very good downhill racer—although that was some years ago," he said.

As she stepped forward, Camille spotted the calico cat in Gardner's lap, and her smile got wider. "Mam'selle Portia, what are you doing in this neck of the woods? Are you scaring too many of the people upstairs?"

"So you've heard the stories, too?" Gardner said.

The aide nodded, extending a blunt-fingered hand for Portia to sniff. "And I think it's a shame, blaming a sweetie like Portia."

"Do you need help?" Luke asked, but Camille shook

her head. Her big, strong hands grasped the bed pad under Gardner, and with him pushing with his legs, she quickly had him pulled up to a more comfortable position. Portia went along for the ride with no problems whatever.

I don't know if Shadow would do that, Sunny thought. *On the other hand, he might like it.*

"Are you okay, Mr. Barnstable?" the aide asked, turning his way.

Ollie shook his head. "I'm arranged just fine. No problems."

"Okay, then." With that, Camille left.

"Nice kid," Mike said.

Gardner shrugged. "I suppose so."

Guess he's not about to fall in love with her, the reporter who lived in the back of Sunny's head quipped.

Ollie operated his bed to sit up higher, wincing as he moved to a new position. "Did you bring those files?" he asked Sunny.

"I hope you're not going to spend another night going over papers," Gardner said.

Ollie paused, the stack of files that Sunny had just passed to him in his hands. "I didn't keep you up, did I?"

Gardner shrugged. "I don't sleep as well as I used to. Part of it is just age. And I guess you'd call it post-stroke nerves. When I went through the attack, the diagnosis and treatment and everything, it was like being shot out of a cannon, no time to think about anything. Now that I can sit back and consider—it's enough to give you the shakes sometimes."

"Isn't the doctor giving you something for that?" Luke asked.

Gardner made a face. "She feels I have enough meds for the time being, and I think she has a point."

Ollie looked up from the papers he'd already spread across his hospital table. "Did you bring the other thing I asked for?"

"Oh, right." Sunny went back to her satchel and dug out the bag of potato chips. "Salt 'n' vinegar—that's what you wanted, right?"

Ollie eagerly reached for the snack bag of chips, then frowned. "Couldn't you get a bigger size?"

"Did you want me to use petty cash for food?"

For a second, he seemed almost ready to say "yes." But then he must have realized what a precedent that would set. Instead, he began struggling to get the bag open. "Stupid damn things. It's bad enough that the food here is so bland."

"Let me help," Luke offered, grabbing hold. He tried to yank the top seam open. Instead, with a loud *pop!* the bag seemed to explode, showering Ollie with chips and chip dust.

"Oh, God, I'm sorry," Luke apologized, offering Ollie the tiny box of tissues beside the bed.

"Clean up on Bed Two," Mike snickered.

Ollie glumly tried to rescue as many chips as he could, too crushed by the loss of his snack to comment.

Gardner picked up the control for his bed. "Once those crumbs get under you, they'll drive you crazy," he said. "I think we'd better buzz for Camille . . . and hope that she won't mention it to Dr. Gavrik."

Camille came back in, and after Ollie got cleaned up, the time passed pleasantly enough—a little business, a little conversation. Gardner told a tale from his travels, and Luke contributed a story from his life on the road. By the time she and her dad headed down the hallway to the guard's desk, Sunny was in a pretty good mood again.

"Good evening, sir." Rafe Warner smiled as Mike came up to sign out. "Hi, Sunny."

"Evening," Mike said, absentmindedly reaching for the pen. Then he jumped back when he realized there was a cat clinging to Rafe's arm. "The place is crawling with them," Mike muttered.

"And who is this?" Sunny asked as she came up. The cat seemed a little shy, so she didn't make any overtures.

"This is Patrick," Rafe explained. "He's Portia's brother. I'm afraid he's been sick for a while, so he's been sticking pretty close to me."

Patrick was a handsome cat, with white patches on his black fur. Sunny had heard some people refer to the color scheme as a tux. "He's getting better, I hope?"

Rafe nodded. "But slowly."

Mike glanced dubiously at the cat as he signed himself out. "Nothing catching, is it?"

Rafe surprised them by answering, "Cancer. Poor Patrick had to go through chemotherapy."

Now Mike gave Patrick a long, thoughtful look. "I've had friends who went through that. Guess all I can say is good luck, Patrick."

"Thanks, sir." Rafe gently petted Patrick as Sunny signed out.

"I hope he'll be okay," she said. Mike was already ahead of her, opening the big door.

When they were outside, Sunny grinned at her dad.

"Still so eager to have Rafe as a son-in-law?" she teased. "Love him, love his cats."

"Hmmph," Mike said, considering that unpleasant prospect.

Sunny decided to push the subject. "And speaking of prospective sons-in-law, how about Luke? He's more my age, and a very nice guy, even if he can't open a bag of chips without disastrous results." He even had a nice, dark tan—probably thanks to his Italian genes. No sunburn that Sunny could spot.

"A musician?"

From the tone of his voice, it might as well have been, "An ax-murderer?" Sunny thought.

"Why not?" she said, rubbing it in. "Isn't that what you wanted to be, back when you were with the Cosmic Rays?"

"The Cosmic Blade," Mike corrected. "And I quickly gave that up."

"Mom loved music," Sunny pointed out.

"And your mom knew how hard it was to make money from music," Mike replied testily. "She was always giving lessons to pay for that piano we got."

"Sorry, Dad." Sunny took his arm, genuinely penitent for upsetting him. "I was just teasing."

For a second, Mike looked at her and then shook his head. "You had me going for a little while."

"So I guess I'm stuck with Will for the time being." She put her head on Mike's shoulder with a wicked grin. "Unless Gardner Scatterwell offers to make me a rich widow."

"If he ever became my son-in-law, I guarantee you'd

soon be a widow," Mike said in his sternest voice, but he was grinning, too.

*

When Shadow arranged himself for his afternoon nap, he'd draped himself along the top of the sofa. That way he could keep a drowsy eye on all the comings and goings along the street. So, even before Sunny and her father parked, Shadow was at the doorway. The Old One, as usual, held no scents of interest. But Sunny . . . he worked his way around her ankles, inhaling deeply. The mysterious She had marked Sunny very thoroughly.

For a second, Shadow wondered if he should worry about that. He'd been in a lot of homes during his wandering days—before he'd found Sunny and decided to settle down. Sometimes, in those other places, when a new pet came in Shadow had found himself out on the street. Then he caught a whiff of that intoxicating fragrance again, and he stopped thinking at all.

Even when Sunny almost tripped over him, he couldn't stay away. The scent kept drawing him. While she prepared food and even while she ate it, Shadow couldn't keep himself from under her feet.

She actually scolded him, and the Old One rumbled at him, too.

But Shadow couldn't stay away.

*

Sunny began to suspect there might be a problem when Shadow arranged himself across her feet under the dinner table and just lay there, breathing deeply and purring.

She reached down to stroke his fur, but he didn't even raise his head to be petted.

Of course, I never got my hands on Portia today. She concentrated on my ankles—and now, so is Shadow.

He only stopped pestering her when she went up to her room and changed from the khakis she'd been wearing into a pair of shorts. And then he disappeared while Sunny and her dad watched some television in the living room.

Sunny decided on an early night, heading up the stairs to her room and yawning. Maybe she could make up some of the sleep she'd lost this morning.

She opened the door to her room and froze. Her khakis, which she'd hung from the back of a chair, were now on the floor in a heap. And lying on top of them, his head on the hems, was Shadow.

"Well, I guess I'm not wearing them again this week after all," Sunny said. But the surprises weren't over. When she tried to pull the pants out from under him, he looked up and actually hissed at her.

"Okay, buddy," she told the cat, "you can have them for tonight. But after that outburst, don't think you're getting into bed with me."

*

Sunny had a dreadful night, her dreams confused and disturbing. She stood at the doorway to a church—or was it the splendid entranceway to Bridgewater Hall? Sunny wasn't sure, but she knew she was in a wedding gown. Her father stood beside her, a look of disapproval on his face. She was getting married—but to whom?

Rafe Warner came up, dressed in his guard's uniform. But he walked by, into the church. So did Luke Daconto, carrying his guitar case. Gardner Scatterwell came rolling up in a wheelchair pushed by Alfred. Both of them smirked at her as they went past. Then came Will Price in his constable's uniform. But he only looked at her sadly as he went into the church, too.

So who was the groom?

A limousine pulled up, and the chauffeur hustled round to open the door.

Shadow hopped out.

Sunny tried to say something, but there was no time. Shadow ran past her, and then the organ music started and her father took her arm.

And all the way down the long, long aisle, Sunny watched as Shadow kept going from bridesmaid to bridesmaid, sniffing their ankles.

Then the wedding bells began to peal.

No, wait a minute, that wasn't the sound of wedding bells. It was the telephone. Sunny's eyelids seemed gummed together, but she finally got them open. Woozily, she groped around for the phone. The bedside alarm read a few minutes after four.

"H'lo?" she managed to croak into the phone. If this turned out to be a wrong number—

"Sunny, that you? It's Ollie—Oliver Barnstable." His voice was tight and trembling. "I need you up here right away. Something's going on. Gardner is dead."

5

"Wh-What? Ollie? What happened? Hello?" Sunny realized she was almost shouting into the phone, but she got no answers. Ollie had already hung up. And when she dialed his number at Bridgewater Hall, she couldn't get through. Instead, a recorded message came on, telling her that residents' phones were not available from ten p.m. until nine a.m.

"Of course," she muttered, staggering out of bed and heading for the bathroom. She almost stumbled over Shadow, who'd been awakened either by the ringing phone or by her end of the conversation. He hopped around her, obviously picking up on her anxiety.

"What is it? What's going on?" Mike appeared in his doorway as Sunny stepped into the hall. Oh, wonderful. The ruckus had roused him out of bed, too. Sunny bit her lip, trying to decide on an answer. Early-morning alarms upset Mike, especially since over the past year he'd usually been the cause, awakening at ungodly hours suffering from angina attacks. But a phone call at four in the morning—he knew that meant bad news.

Finally, she decided to give it to him straight. "That was Ollie calling from Bridgewater Hall. Gardner Scatterwell passed away." Slowly, the rest of what Ollie said percolated through her brain. "He said there was something wrong, and he wanted me up there right away."

Sunny blinked. "Or did I dream that?"

"The phone definitely rang," Mike told her. "So I guess the rest of it must be true, too. Can you call Ollie back?"

"No. I tried, but the system won't let me call back for another five hours or so." Sunny shook her head. "What am I supposed to do?"

"I suggest we wash up, have some coffee, and head up there." Mike took it for granted that he would come, too. Sunny silently blessed the Kittery Harbor Way.

After they'd showered, dressed, and had a quick bite to eat, Sunny and her father got into her Wrangler, and they set off for Bridgewater Hall. They made good time in the predawn darkness; at this hour, traffic was almost nonexistent.

As they pulled into the parking lot in front of the nursing home, Sunny saw a lot more cars than she'd expected. *Either the night staff uses the visitor's parking,* she thought, *or . . .*

Then she realized one of the cars—parked at a sloppy angle in front of the door—was an official Sheriff's Department vehicle. For a moment, she wondered if Will had responded to the call. Then she shook her head. He was on the day shift now. That didn't start for hours yet.

Looks as if "or" is the answer I was looking for. She carefully made sure her Wrangler was parked between the painted lines, and then she and Mike headed for the front entrance.

The elaborately carved door was locked, but Mike pounded on the heavy wood with his fist. After a moment, Sunny heard rattling, and then the door opened a slit to reveal Rafe Warner's surprised face staring at them.

Down by Rafe's ankles, Portia and Patrick peered out, too.

"Sunny! Mr. Coolidge! What are you doing here?" the guard asked.

"I got a call from Ollie—Mr. Barnstable," Sunny explained. "He sounded pretty upset, and when I tried to call him back, I couldn't get through. So we figured we'd better come up in person to make sure he's all right."

"Mr. Barnstable's all right." Sunny couldn't help noticing the slight emphasis that Rafe put on Ollie's name.

"But Mr. Scatterwell isn't?" she said. "That's the message I got over the phone."

Rafe sighed. "Mr. Scatterwell—" He shook his head.

"Can we see Mr. Barnstable?" Mike broke in. "He sounded as though he needed some calming down."

The usually obliging Rafe found himself on the spot. "I don't think—it's not the policy—"

"Can you call in to his room and see what he wants?" Sunny suggested.

Rafe shrugged. "Why not?" he muttered, "They've enough other people banging around in there." Then he abruptly shut up, obviously regretting his words. "I'll make the call, but you'll have to stay outside, okay?"

He closed the door. Sunny turned toward the lightening

horizon and asked Mike, "Do you think we'll get in before the sun actually comes up?"

"Can't say," Mike replied. "Although I've got to wonder—does the sheriff send a car over whenever somebody kicks off in one of these places?"

The door opened wide, and a visibly relieved Rafe Warner beckoned them in. Obviously, the decision was off his shoulders. "Room 114," he said. "You know the way."

In late-night mode, Sunny and her dad discovered, most of the corridor lighting in Bridgewater Hall apparently got switched off.

Guess that makes sense, Sunny thought. *Most of the residents should be sleeping.*

But it did make for a shadowy, slightly spooky trip down the mostly silent hallway. There was a little more light at the nurses' station, where the skeleton crew for the floor seemed to have huddled into a knot, the aides and nurses staring as Sunny and her dad passed by.

Unlike the other patient accommodations, light poured from the doorway of Room 114. Gardner Scatterwell's bed wasn't merely empty, it had already been stripped. But as Rafe Warner had suggested, there were lots of folks inside. Sunny didn't recognize the tanned, lean man with the thinning blond hair and the gold-rimmed eyeglasses. But she certainly knew Dr. Gavrik, looking unexpectedly dressy for the early hour in a pale jade suit. Then, as he turned at their footsteps, she found the third face in the room all too familiar.

Frank Nesbit was the sheriff of Elmet County, the head of local law enforcement . . . not to mention being Will Price's boss. No matter how rich he was, Gardner Scatterwell's death didn't merit that kind of attention. Not unless there was a smoking gun involved.

Nesbit's green Sheriff's Department windbreaker looked crisp and official, and his trademark silver mustache was as immaculate as ever, but his hair was mussed, and he had bags under his eyes. Not the kind of image he'd want up on local billboards during election season, telling voters how he kept Elmet County safe.

"Do you really want her in here?" The sheriff's voice took on a pleading note as he turned back to Ollie Barnstable.

"Well, you're not doing me much good." Ollie's voice was flat. "If you won't look into it, who will?"

A light went off over Sunny's head. Frank Nesbit might be a lawman, but at heart he was a politician, and Ollie was one of his few supporters down in Kittery Harbor. Mike and all his friends were staunchly anti-Nesbit. They'd even brought Will Price, the former sheriff's son, back to the county as a town constable in hopes of unseating Frank in the next primaries.

She remembered how Ollie had once shown her a plastic courtesy card from the Sheriff's Department, something that Mike had disparaged as a "get out of jail free" card. But Ollie had apparently played it as a "make the sheriff appear" card.

"Meester Barnstebble." It sounded as though Dr. Gavrik's attempt to restrain her temper made her accent thicker. "You are upset, I can see. It is a difficult thing, to have a person die."

"In the next bed!" Ollie put in.

She nodded. "In the next bed. But you understand that Mr. Scatterwell was not well. He had not regained full function after his stroke. And there was always the possibility of another stroke, causing further damage—even death."

"He was perfectly all right when he went to bed." Ollie's tone was gruff, but under that, he begged for an explanation.

Dr. Gavrik could only shake her head. "Do you know what they call strokes now, Mr. Barnstable? 'Brain attacks.' Like a heart attack, a person can seem perfectly healthy, even record a healthy electrocardiogram, and then go home to a fatal episode."

Ollie slowly nodded. "That's what happened to my father."

"It can be a terrible surprise, happening without warning." The doctor spread her hands in a "what can I say?" gesture. "Mr. Scatterwell, though, had some warning. He already had a stroke. And although I can understand you're upset, I cannot stand here and let you suggest that this facility let him die."

"I'm not suggesting that at all." But if Ollie intended that as an olive branch, he undid that with his next words. "I think someone killed him."

That got a sputtered chorus of "Mr. Barnstable!" from the three authority figures in the room—plus an "Ollie!" from Sunny.

Mike, though, stayed silent. "It sort of makes sense," he finally said. "Gardner was a guy who traveled all over creation raising hell. And now, the first time he's stuck in one place, it's lights out for him."

Dr. Gavrik appealed to the tall stranger. "Really, Dr. Reese, do we need to listen to this?"

So this is Hank Reese, Gardner's boyhood friend in high places. Sunny gave the man a long, hard look. *He*

doesn't seem so broken up that his good buddy is dead.
More like embarrassed, I'd say.

Ollie, however, had given up on the older and wiser heads in the room. He turned to Sunny. "So here it is. They're trying to tell me that a patient kicking off in this joint is something that happens at least once a week and twice on Thursdays. Maybe that's so in the wards where they keep the old crocks. Didn't Gardner mention that the mortality rate was high here?"

Dr. Reese drew himself up to his considerable height. "I beg your pardon?"

"Apparently his nephew Alfred found the data somewhere on the Internet," Sunny explained.

"But this is the rehab ward, where the people expect to get better and go home. How often do you have people popping off in here?"

Reese had to fumble for an answer. "We've had several patients who had to be returned to hospitals for various reasons."

"And how many in this ward died in the middle of the night?" Ollie demanded, then shook his head at the lack of an answer. "That's what I thought. When it happens in the bed next to mine, I want to know why." He turned to Sunny. "And I want you to find out."

"Me?" Sunny had to wonder if Ollie weren't having an anesthesia flashback. "What makes you think—"

"It's not the first time, is it? I've seen you figure out who killed those other folks," Ollie pointed out. "Just do what you did with them."

Sunny really didn't like where Ollie was going here. "I didn't have much of a choice in those cases." Yes, she'd been involved in a few police investigations, but it had been a question of self-defense basically—protecting people she was close to from being accused of crimes they hadn't committed.

"You work for me." Ollie's implication was clear. Either she agreed to play detective, or she wouldn't work for him anymore—not a good thing in an awfully tight job market. Once again, she wasn't getting much of a choice.

"Let me get his straight." Mike suddenly spoke up. "You want my daughter to do the sheriff's job."

"I don't think we have grounds here for an official police investigation," Sheriff Nesbit said, stung. "Or even a reason for the medical examiner to proceed."

Dr. Gavrik nodded forcefully. "Mr. Scatterwell had a preexisting condition and was already under my care. The cause of death is obvious. Any doctor would feel justified in signing a death certificate in such a situation."

"So you're just going to sweep everything under the rug and ignore what happened?" From the tone of Mike's voice, this story was just going to grow—and it wasn't going to make Frank Nesbit look very good.

"I'm not saying that," Nesbit hurriedly replied. "In fact, I'd be willing to detail Constable Price to assist Ms. Coolidge in determining the circumstances of Mr. Scatterwell's death."

Sunny opened her mouth to object that everyone seemed to take it for granted that she'd whip out her magnifying glass and start looking for clues. But then she shut it with the feeling that she'd somehow gotten stuck on a train zooming off, already leaving the station of normal rationality behind. How else could she explain her boss threatening her job if she didn't start snooping? And to tell the truth, she felt that little flutter deep inside, a reporter's gut feeling that she might be on to something—although she had no idea exactly what that something might be. And there was the added appeal that she'd be dong it with Will.

However reluctantly, Sunny had to hand it to the sheriff. The man was a political animal. He'd just figured out how to placate one supporter (Ollie) by having a political rival (Will) personally investigate the death of someone from the wealthy enclave of Piney Brook. Whatever Will did, he'd make waves in that entitled community, closing some of the deep pockets he'd need to tap to finance a Will Price insurgency. Two birds with one stone.

Considering Nesbit's offer, Ollie transformed into the master of the deal.

"Sunny and Price will need access to people and records here—not to mention the assistance of the administration."

Dr. Gavrik's lips compressed so tightly, they seemed to disappear. "This sounds to me like an attempt at blackmail by a patient who, perhaps, should find another facility for his recuperation."

Ollie turned to Reese. "If there's any attempt to throw me out of here, I'll be a patient who definitely sues this facility. And I can make sure there's a lot of publicity about it, too."

Dr. Reese gave a small shudder. But his voice was steady as he said, "We might consider an arrangement along the lines you're suggesting. However, we cannot violate patient confidentiality. You'll all have to sign confidentiality agreements. Whatever Constable Price and Ms. Coolidge discover will be turned over to the sheriff. If he still finds no grounds to proceed, that will be the end of it."

Ollie glanced over at Sheriff Nesbit, who shrugged. "Sounds reasonable to me."

"One more thing." Now Reese was in full negotiating mode. "We can't have an endless fishing expedition going on. There should be a time limit. I suggest one week."

"I can live with that," Ollie replied.

Mike took Sunny by the arm and drew her outside in the hallway. "They're making a lot of conditions in there that *you'll* have to live with."

"What can *I* do about it?" she asked. Whether it was the early-morning wake-up call or the shock of Gardner Scatterwell's death, the whole situation still struck her as dreamlike, unreal. Her brain couldn't seem to process it.

"You can tell them all to go to hell," Mike advised, his voice low.

"And lose my job?"

"So quit," Mike said. "You don't owe Ollie anything."

"Yeah, but Ollie is a big noise around Kittery Harbor—around the whole county. I'd have a hard enough time getting another job in this economy. With him against me . . ." She shook her head. "It would be hopeless." She frowned. "Besides, you heard them—they're going to throw Will into this whether I agree or not."

"So?" Mike asked. "He's a cop, after all. A professional. This is his job."

"But I got to know Gardner," Sunny said, "at least a little."

Besides, her own professional instincts were rousing now. *I've got a few ideas about why someone might have had it in for him,* she thought. *I got an earful from Mrs. Martinson about what went on behind that nice-guy front he put up, not to mention seeing him in action with that therapist*. It might be a thankless job. It might be a wild-goose chase. Gardner might have simply died of a stroke. But . . .

"Like it or not, we'll find ourselves involved. Will's going to be talking to us, asking questions," Sunny finally said. "I think I'd rather be an investigator than just a witness."

They returned to the room. Sunny stood at the foot of Ollie's bed. "If I'm going to do this, we need to have some ground rules," she said. "The big one is, we're not doing this to prove you right, we're just trying to get to the bottom of an unexpected death. If we find that Mr. Scatterwell died of natural causes, you'll be all right with that."

Ollie scowled, but said, "Okay—I'm pretty sure you'll find otherwise."

"The other deal breaker is, our investigation must be independent. You can't tell us what to do."

Now Ollie really scowled, but he reluctantly nodded. "I'll expect regular updates, though. No surprises."

"I'll do my best," Sunny told him. "Finally, you'll have to get someone else to mind the office. This is going to be hard enough, working against a deadline. I can't do this and work at MAX full-time, too."

"You're just an office worker?" Sunny was amazed at how much disdain Dr. Gavrik managed to put into those five words.

"An office worker who managed to solve a couple of murders," Mike replied, silencing her and anyone else who planned to object.

Ollie shrugged. "It's summertime. There are enough college kids floating around. Take one on as an intern."

And that's how highly he prizes the work I do for him,

that cranky reporter's voice in the back of Sunny's head said. *I can be replaced by some kid off the street.*

She sighed. "Of course, I'll be available if some catastrophe happens." Somehow, she knew one would. "And I still get my paycheck while I'm doing this, right?" Sunny could have kicked herself as soon as the words were out of her mouth. At the very least, she should have tried to stick Ollie for time and a half.

"Of course," he said.

She took a deep breath. "Then I agree."

"So you'll have one week from today to answer Mr. Barnstable's suspicions," Dr. Reese said.

Sunny shook her head. "One week from tomorrow. I've got to arrange coverage for the office, besides getting things set up." She stifled a yawn. *Not to mention catching up on some of the sleep I've been cheated out of.*

Ollie had a self-satisfied smirk on his face, looking more like himself than he had since his accident. Dr. Gavrik hissed angrily into her boss's ear, but while Reese looked as if he'd just swallowed a very unpalatable pill, he wasn't raising any objections. Mike looked honestly worried, while Nesbit just stroked his trademark mustache with an expression Sunny had seen on Shadow's face—the cat who ate the cream.

"What do you say we get a move on, Dad?" She was just as glad to get out of there.

By the time Sunny and Mike got home, they just beat her wake-up alarm. She dashed up the stairs to turn it off, then came down to the living room and sat in an armchair, closing her eyes. The good thing was, she was already washed, dressed, and fed. The bad thing was, she really missed those hours of sleep she'd lost. If she kept her eyes closed, she might not be able to open them.

A heavy weight landed in her lap. She opened her eyes to find herself almost nose to nose with Shadow. He had a paw on each collarbone, his gold-flecked eyes peering worriedly into hers.

"Are you concerned because I'm upset, because we've been running around so early . . . or because you're afraid I'll forget to feed you?" she asked with a laugh.

Shadow relaxed against her, his deep purr rumbling against her T-shirt.

"Right," Sunny said, running a hand along his back. "Feeding it is."

A moment later, Mike came into the room, a cup of coffee in his hand. "Figured you'd need this to fuel your way into town."

"Thanks, Dad." Sunny gratefully accepted the cup and took a sip. Hot and sweet, with lots of milk. Between the caffeine and the sugar, it should keep her going until she got the office coffeemaker percolating.

Mike hovered over her chair. "You won't be doing this alone, Sunny. I'll beat the bushes and see what I can find out about Gardner. I can ask Helena to do the same."

"Leave Mrs. Martinson to me," Sunny told him. "She's not exactly fond of your old buddy Gardner." She put the cup on the end table and reached up to catch his hand. "And thanks again, Dad. I always knew I could depend on you."

With that, she devoted herself to lowering the level of coffee in her cup without scalding her mouth. Then she

Claire Donally

rinsed the empty cup in the kitchen sink and set out some food for Shadow. But as Sunny went to the front door, she was surprised to find Mike right behind her.

"It's still early," he said, heading for his own pickup. "Figured I'd hit the track and get a jump on the day."

He waved as he headed out for the old high school, Sunny going to downtown Kittery Harbor. When she arrived at her office, she found Will Price leaning against the door in full uniform. His blues looked good on his long limbs and wiry build and even seemed to diminish the sunburn on his strong features. Although he was taller than Sunny, his relaxed posture put them almost on a level. Too bad those gray eyes with their brownish-gold flecks held such an enigmatic expression as he straightened up, his arms still folded across his chest.

"So," he said, his voice mild, "I arrive at work today, and they tell me that I've been detailed to an unofficial investigation with you at a local nursing home." His eyes, so disturbingly like Shadow's, looked hard into Sunny's. "What have you fallen into this time?"

"I didn't fall, I was pushed." As she unlocked the door and let Will in, Sunny briefly described the scene in Ollie's room. Just the memory of the early hour made her yawn.

"So Barnstable thinks this is a suspicious death, but nobody else agrees with him."

"I'll be the first to admit it might turn out to be natural causes," Sunny replied. "On the other hand, are the doctors responsible for the guy going to admit anything? And you know Frank Nesbit."

One of the reasons that Will had been called back to Elmet County was the suspicion on the part of a lot of citizens that Nesbit was keeping the county safe—and himself reelected—by fudging the local crime statistics. Assaults became harassment, felonies fell to misdemeanors. Now, after years of a spotless record, Nesbit had a murder on his books thanks to Sunny. If Ollie hadn't held his feet to the fire, the sheriff would probably have ignored Gardner Scatterwell's passing, except maybe to press some flesh at the wake.

Still, Will wasn't about to jump on Ollie's bandwagon. "I understand Gardner Scatterwell was a stroke victim."

Sunny nodded. "He was recovering from a stroke, staying at Bridgewater Hall for therapy." She hesitated, remembering how easily Gardner had tired. "I wouldn't say he was in the best of shape, but he looked all right when I left them yesterday evening, and Ollie says he was fine at lights-out. Then, somewhere between three and four a.m., Gardner died. We'll have to get the gory details from Ollie. I didn't want to ask him any questions with the doctors watching over my shoulder."

"We'll also have to try and persuade the family to go for an autopsy." Will made a face. "That won't be easy. Legally, this isn't a suspicious death. I'll bet the facility will issue a death certificate. Do you think we'll get any help from any of the relatives?"

"As far as I know, the next of kin is a nephew, Alfred Scatterwell," Sunny said. "Gardner kind of ragged on him as the family's 'all-purpose heir.' Alfred is also a bit of a cheapskate. I heard him moaning about the expense of rehab at Bridgewater Hall, especially since he claimed the place had a high mortality rate. He wanted Gardner to move somewhere less pricey."

Will's expression didn't get any more cheerful. "So he's unlikely to go for the expense of a private autopsy, especially if it might delay his inheritance."

Sunny shrugged and spread her hands in a gesture of hopelessness. "Them's the breaks. But it might give us something in the way of a money motive."

"I'd be happier with a little more in the way of facts. We don't even have a clear idea of cause of death." He frowned, thinking. "We'll have to dig into Scatterwell's life, see if we can find other people with motives, and then find out if they had the opportunity get to him at the facility."

"I can tell you he was a ladies' man," Sunny offered. "The way I heard it, he fell in love with someone every six weeks or so."

Will nodded. "He liked grand gestures but could change his mind pretty quickly. I know that from personal experience."

"He got in some kind of trouble with the law?"

"No, this was about money. Remember? I mentioned meeting Scatterwell while doing some fund-raising for Saxon Academy."

Saxon Academy had been the "snob school for boys" during Sunny's high school days. If you went out with a guy from there, you were assured of a well-heeled date, at least. Not that Sunny had ever snagged a Saxon guy. Getting to know Will, she'd discovered that he'd gone to Saxon, a couple of years ahead of her. Practically speaking, he might as well have been on another world.

"Hey," Sunny said with a grin, "they turned my old

school into a community center. Too bad we didn't have any well-heeled donors with school spirit."

Instead of laughing, Will looked a little embarrassed, as if he had to explain things. "Your dad and some of the other folks in town thought it would be good to show that I was interested in the community." He sighed. "Especially around Piney Brook."

"That's where the money is." Now Sunny began to understand. "If you wanted to mount a campaign for sheriff, it would be good to know those folks, and maybe wave the old school flag to get some contributions."

"You sound just like your dad and his political pals," Will said, not making it sound like a compliment. "But it's also true that the old school could use some help. They're trying to go coed, and that means building a lot of extensions."

"Like adding little girls' rooms?" Sunny laughed.

"Try locker rooms and gym facilities," Will replied. "Scatterwell was Class of '66, way before my time, but he made a very generous pledge when I approached him—not enough to get a gym named after him, but the most I was able to persuade any of the Piney Brook folks to part with. Then, of course, he got sick and yanked it all back."

"You can't exactly blame him," Sunny said. "Bridgewater Hall is a pretty expensive setup. I heard his nephew complain that they charged four hundred bucks a day to hold on to the bed when Gardner had to go back to the hospital."

"I don't begrudge the man spending money on his health." Will shook his head. "But he might have explained instead of just never sending a check. I had people looking at me pretty funny for a while."

"Are you sure you didn't go sneaking into his room with a pillow?" Sunny asked.

"You're right," Will replied with mock seriousness. "Maybe I should recuse myself."

"Recuse, hell," Sunny told him. "Who's going to help me investigate this can of worms?"

"What do you figure our first step should be?" Will asked.

"Talk to Ollie," Sunny quickly responded. "See what he can tell us about what happened this morning."

"Right." Will rose to his feet. "Well? Shall we?"

Sunny tilted her head at him. "You might want to change your outfit."

"Why?" Will looked down at his uniform.

"My dad has what they call 'white coat hypertension'— his blood pressure goes up when he goes to the doctor," Sunny said. "I'm afraid we may encounter some people with a similar problem—'blue coat muteness.' Just a guess, but maybe you've encountered it."

"Yeah, yeah, don't rub it in." Will headed for the office door. "I'll go home and change. What'll you be doing?"

"I'll be on the phone to Ken Howell," Sunny answered. "He uses a lot of summer interns to get the newspaper out. I'm hoping he'll have someone dependable enough to let me get out of the office."

6

By the time Will returned, Sunny had gotten Ken to loan her a young woman spending an unpaid summer working in the office of the *Harbor Courier*. The intern had walked over to the office, and Sunny was busily bringing her up to speed on the duties to keep MAX going. "Remember, Nancy, whatever you do, don't install any upgrades on any components in the system. As soon as that happens, it fouls up the way everything else works."

As they went over the remainder of the points in the checklist Sunny had worked up, she noticed that Nancy kept glancing over her shoulder at Will. Lounging against the wall of file cabinets in sunglasses, a tight gray Henley shirt, and a pair of black jeans, he made a pretty good distraction.

Sunny finished with Nancy's orientation, then left her to go through the morning's e-mails.

"Okay, I'm ready," she told Will. "You're looking pretty casual." She fingered the short-sleeved jacket she wore with matching slacks—simple, but businesslike.

"You've heard of good cop–bad cop? We'll try well-dressed cop versus scroungy cop." Will grinned. "Once you're out of uniform, crime-busting has no dress code."

Rolling her eyes, Sunny stepped outside to her Wrangler while Will climbed aboard his pickup. They drove up to Bridgewater Hall, arriving around eleven in the morning. That turned out to be lucky timing, as they encountered a volunteer just rolling Oliver out of the therapy room. Ollie held a rolling walker balanced on the footrests while Elsa Hogue walked beside the wheelchair, talking. Even though the therapist wore another dumpy-looking sweat suit, she seemed to move more naturally, even smiling at Ollie. "It gets easier the longer you work at it," she assured him.

"Thanks," Sunny heard Ollie reply. "It's nice to know I can do *something* right."

He smiled hopefully as he looked up at Elsa. But his expression instantly hardened when he spotted Sunny and Will. "About time you got here," he said gruffly.

"I had to get things squared away," Sunny told him. "Is there somewhere we can talk?"

Elsa spoke up. "If you call down to the coffee shop, you can reserve a table, and they'll have Mr. Barnstable's lunch waiting when you get there. It's a nice, quiet place where you can order a meal and chat."

"Thanks," Ollie said. "That's very nice of you to tell us."

"And have you tried the gardens?" Elsa went on.

"They're really beautiful this time of year." She smiled down at Ollie the Barnacle and tried to look strict. "Just make it back by one thirty—Jack has big plans for you today."

"With advance warning like that, I might not come back at all," Ollie said.

"I know it's hard, especially to start, but I think you're one of the patients who takes the work seriously." Elsa frowned. "Some don't, and they never regain full function again."

Ollie nodded. "It's tough. The little I did yesterday just about knocked me out," he admitted.

She patted his shoulder. "It really does get better. Believe me." Then she turned to leave. "Now, let's see if I can convince Mrs. Jaspers of that."

Will took over the wheelchair from the volunteer, and Sunny directed him down the hallway. "So, Ollie, do you want to try this coffee shop?"

"Yeah," Ollie said. "I don't think it's a good idea to hang around in the room anyway. They had somebody coming in with all kinds of disinfectant sprays when I was leaving."

Will glanced at Sunny, his expression showing that his worst fears had come true regarding their potential crime scene. He could only raise his shoulders in a hopeless shrug. "They've probably contaminated the place already." He glanced down at Ollie. "Maybe it's better to let the fumes evaporate before you go back in."

They stopped at the nurses' station, and a helpful nurse made the call to the coffee shop for them. "Take the hallway to the front door and make the first turnoff," she said when they asked how to find the place. "You'll pass the entrance to the auditorium, and a little farther on you'll find the coffee shop. You can't miss it."

For Sunny, the words "coffee shop" evoked loud, crowded places that served quick, cheap eats, with linoleum-topped tables and waitstaffs rushed off their feet. But Bridgewater Hall's so-called "coffee shop" reminded Sunny of one of those tearooms of yesteryear—a throwback to an age of more gracious living. It was small, just a dozen or so tables, but each one was decked out with a white tablecloth; embroidered banquettes surrounded slightly larger tables; and for the lone or rushed eater, a few tall chairs faced a highly polished mahogany counter.

"Nicer than a lot of the eateries in town," Sunny said.

"A better bar, too," Ollie muttered, taking in the lunch counter. "I wonder if I could get a beer here."

An older woman with permed white hair approached them with some menus. "Is this the Barnstable party? I can seat you here over by the window." She led the way to a table with a splendid view of the gardens. Will parked Ollie's wheelchair facing the window, and he and Sunny sat down flanking him.

"Elsa wasn't kidding," Sunny said. "It looks lovely out there."

"Yeah, yeah," Ollie griped, already done with small talk. "What kind of progress have you made?"

Sunny was about to protest that they hadn't had time to do anything yet, but Will jumped in with, "I tracked down Alfred Scatterwell and gave him a call." This was news to her. "He was definitely not happy to hear that you had doubts about his uncle's death, but he agreed to speak to us tomorrow morning," Will reported.

Ollie grunted and turned to Sunny, but she started talking before he could ask any embarrassing questions. "What we really need to hear is what happened this morning. Start from the beginning, and tell us what you saw and heard."

Before Ollie could start, the permed manageress returned to take their orders. "You're our first customers of the day," she said, nodding toward the empty tables around them. "You beat the rush."

Sunny and Will both ordered the hamburger platter. Their choices arrived quickly, along with Ollie's lunch. Sunny looked at her boss's slivers of meat in a reddish sauce. "What is it supposed to be?" she asked, lowering her voice. "Pulled pork?"

"According to the menu I signed off on, it's turkey tetrazzini." Ollie unenthusiastically poked at it with his fork. "They give you a lot of choices for each meal, but one always seems to be baked fish. On paper, this looked the least bad." He raised a forkful to his mouth and began chewing.

"So how is it?" Will arranged the tomato and onion slices on his burger and took a bite.

"Better than yesterday's Salisbury steak. I guess a lot of the old folks' teeth probably aren't up to anything more solid than ground or chopped-up meat. I just wish that they didn't always seem to have run out of salt in the kitchen." He watched greedily as Sunny sprinkled salt and pepper on her fries, then dumped a blob of catsup on the side. "I could kill for one of those fries."

"Are you allowed to have them, though?" Will asked.

Ollie's expression fell somewhere between annoyed and heartbroken. "They gave me some with the Salisbury steak. Eighteen, to be exact. I counted each one as I ate it."

Well, the visitors obviously get a more generous portion of French fries. Sunny turned her plate toward Ollie, who reached over to grab a fry—the biggest one, of course—dunked it in the catsup, and then just about inhaled it.

"Well, they don't stint you on the food," Will said, not turning his plate to share. "I see green beans, pasta, bread, coffee, milk, and both fruit and Jell-O."

"Yeah." Ollie's eyes followed Will's burger as he brought it up for another bite. "I'm just a lucky fella."

"So tell us what happened." Sunny wanted to get this meeting back on track before Ollie made a grab for her pickle.

"Specifically, why do you think something's wrong?" Will put in.

"I didn't want to say it in front of the doctors." Ollie leaned forward in his wheelchair, his voice low. "They'll say I was crazy, or dreaming, or blame the pain pills. I've been cutting down on them, but I do take one the last thing at night. Makes it easier to sleep."

"I can understand that," Will said. "But what did you see?"

"It was more like what I heard." Ollie shifted uncomfortably in his wheelchair. "Somebody was definitely in the room, with Gardner. I don't know if what I heard woke me up, or if my eyes just popped open, and that's why I heard it. But I know I woke up all of a sudden, in the dark, and I heard rustling and low voices over by Gardner's bed."

"What were they saying?" Sunny asked.

Ollie shrugged. "I couldn't make it out. Just a mumble of voices, then a cough—that was Gardner, I think. And then . . ." Ollie groped for a word. "It sounded like someone smacking their lips. I know, that doesn't make much sense. But at the time I thought, *Gardner's been here awhile and knows everybody. He's got connections. Maybe somebody's smuggling in a glass of something for him*. He told me once that given the choice, he'd prefer a snifter of brandy to a pain pill. And frankly, I agreed."

"It certainly might make you cough," Will said.

"And you might smack your lips afterward," Sunny added. "But it's something *you* wanted, so you could be projecting. Or you might've been dreaming."

"That's not the kind of thing I usually dream about." Again, Ollie paused, trying to put his feelings into words. "It felt . . . real."

I don't think I want to know what Ollie usually dreams about, Sunny thought, and then found her mocking inner voice chiming in. *Says the woman who had a dream about marrying her cat.*

"I debated speaking up but decided against it." Ollie shrugged his heavy shoulders. "I mean, whatever was going on, Gardner was doing it on the sly. I figured if I heard it going on for a couple of nights, I'd ask him about it quietly. Now I wish I'd made a stink—at least found out who was with him."

"That might not have been the smartest thing," Will told him. "If it was a killer, what do you think would have happened to you?"

Ollie opened his mouth as if he were about to speak, then shut it with a snap. "I didn't think of that."

"So what did you do?" Sunny asked.

"I closed my eyes and must have drifted back to sleep. The next thing I hear, Gardner is moaning. I sat up and

got a light on. He tried to talk, but I could barely understand him. Said his face was numb. When he tried to get
the beeper for the nurse, he couldn't handle it. I don't know
if you noticed it, but after his stroke, he was weaker on his
left side. Now his right side wasn't working right, either."

He shook his head. "I called the nurse, and while I was
doing that, Gardner puked. He was choking on the stuff
when the nurses arrived. They worked on him, and then
Dr. Gavrik charged in. Within a couple of minutes, they
were calling for an ambulance. The paramedics came and
rushed him off." Ollie sagged back in his chair. "From
what I heard, he was gone before they even got him in the
ambulance."

"And you started raising hell," Sunny said.

A bit of Ollie's normal hard edge came back. "I told
everyone who'd listen that something was wrong. That
Gavrik woman wanted to give me a tranquilizer, but by
then I'd already called Frank Nesbit." He smiled grimly.
"Sometimes it's handy to have the sheriff's home number."

Will leaned across the table. "Did you tell him what
you heard before Scatterwell's attack?"

"I didn't get the chance," Ollie said. "Dr. Gavrik was
all over me, and then they brought in the muckety-muck,
Reese. He runs this joint." He drew in a deep breath and
let it out slowly. "I was lucky enough to convince Frank
through other means."

Political means, Sunny thought.

"Do you think this is enough for Nesbit to open an
official investigation?" Ollie asked.

"I figure he's already got me—us—on the hook," Will
quickly said, frowning. "According to your agreement,

he's the one who sits in judgment as to whether there's a case or not."

"Well, yeah," Ollie said. "But—"

"And you know that he doesn't like to admit that crimes ever happen in his jurisdiction," Will went on.

Ollie looked so woebegone, Sunny let him have the rest of her French fries. Apparently, chewing helped his thinking process. "Do you know if it's usual for stroke victims to throw up?"

Will shrugged.

"My dad's doctor, Dr. Collier, may be able to help," Sunny suggested. "His practice treats heart ailments and strokes."

Sunny looked at Ollie's plate. In spite of his complaints, he'd made good inroads on most of the food there. The turkey was completely gone.

It didn't seem like there was much else to discuss about the case, so Sunny asked how Ollie's rehab therapy was going. "Elsa had me working while I sat down," he said. "She wants me to work my upper body and arms so I can deal with this thing." He reached for the walker they'd put off to the side. "Now I can look forward to an hour of PT— or as Gardner used to call it, painful torture. I don't know which is worse, the pain from my leg, or the fear of falling."

The reminder of Scatterwell's sometimes sharp tongue stirred a memory for Sunny. "Did Gardner ever say anything about Elsa Hogue?"

Ollie stared at the unexpected question. "No. Why should he?"

"Just wondering. Did he have a nickname for your physical therapist?"

Grinning, Ollie nodded. "He called him Jack the Gripper, from the way he steadies people by holding on to the seat of their pants."

"Well, that one makes sense." Sunny glanced around to see that the room was starting to fill up. It looked like the customers were mainly long-term residents and members of their families. "Maybe we should get a move on. Looks as though they could use the table."

Sunny and Will settled their bills and then set off for the rehab ward, wheeling Ollie along. When they reached Room 114, the pungent smell of disinfectant leaked out into the hallway. Ollie vigorously fanned his hand in front of his nose. "Maybe we should go straight to the therapy room."

"Just give me a minute." Will stepped inside. Gardner's bed still remained stripped, and the drawers on the chest at the foot of his bed all stood open.

"They don't waste much time, do they?" Ollie muttered to Sunny. "A real sentimental bunch."

Sunny just nodded. It seemed odd to erase Gardner's presence so thoroughly, considering that the administrator here was an old friend of his. *Or so Gardner believed when he was alive,* she couldn't help thinking.

Will came back out. "Looks like the Ritz, compared to some of the state police barracks I've lived in," he said with a grin. "Generally, they kept out the snow but were a bit on the Spartan side."

He took command of the wheelchair again, and they headed back to the therapy room. Jack the Gripper (as Sunny would now forever think of him) stood just inside the door. He had to be in his forties, shorter than Will but with a lot more muscle on a stocky frame, his reddish-blond hair gelled up in spikes.

If somebody had to hold up Ollie the Barnacle, this would be the guy to do it, Sunny thought.

"You can cancel the search party," the therapist told the volunteer who was just leaving.

Then he looked down at Ollie with a smile. "How are you doing today?"

"As well as can be expected after having turkey tetrazzini for lunch," Ollie told him. Catching the man's inquisitive glance at his companions, Ollie said, "Sunny Coolidge here works for me. She and her friend Will took me out for lunch."

Sunny had expected a different introduction from Ollie, but apparently he thought people might speak more freely if they didn't know that she and Will were snooping around. Well, maybe it was better to keep their investigation on the down low—at least as long as they could.

"Jack Quentin." The therapist extended a powerful hand to Sunny.

"We'll leave you to it," Sunny said, sure that Quentin and probably a lot of other people remembered the uproar from Ollie when she'd come into this room just yesterday. She patted Ollie on the arm. "Be in touch with you soon."

"Yeah." Ollie gave her a look. "Let me know what you hear from that doctor."

"Will do," Sunny promised. Then she and Will got out of there.

Will waited until they reached the parking lot before speaking. "If there had been a glass beside the bed, it's gone now. And after the bucket-and-mop brigade got done in that room, I don't expect there's any trace of physical evidence left." Cold anger made his face all sharp angles. "I didn't think it was worth getting Ollie all riled up, especially when he's apparently hoping we can stay undercover."

"Thanks—I could do without another tantrum." Sunny didn't mention whether she expected it from Ollie or Will.

Will didn't holler, but he obviously had someone to blame. "At least Nesbit could have asked the folks here to hold off until I'd gotten a look around."

"Do you think he's stacking the deck against us?" Sunny scowled at the idea. She hadn't expected this job to be easy, but people didn't have to go out of their way to make it harder.

"We should have probably taken that as a given," Will said with a sigh. Then he began to look more thoughtful. "If this is standard operating procedure, Bridgewater Hall seems to make the dear departed disappear awfully quickly."

"That could make sense among the older residents," Sunny said. "It might upset them, being reminded of absent friends." She shrugged. "Maybe they're trying to be businesslike, getting things ready for the next customer."

"Or maybe there are some guilty consciences at work, who don't want to leave any evidence of incompetence or malpractice lying around," Will suggested.

"When Alfred Scatterwell was trying to get his uncle to shift to a less expensive facility, he claimed that the mortality rate at Bridgewater Hall was higher than average,"

"That would be a good reason to make any evidence

disappear, wouldn't it?" Will said. "Especially if someone screwed up Scatterwell's treatment."

"Ollie didn't notice anything go wrong while they were working on Gardner," Sunny objected. "But maybe we should file the facility's mortality rate under motive. When I first met him, Gardner Scatterwell seemed like kind of a cheerful boob, rich and clueless. Then I saw his not-so-nice side, the way he treated his nephew and Elsa Hogue. If he found out that something wasn't up to snuff at Bridgewater Hall, I have a feeling he wouldn't be above a little blackmail."

Will nodded. "The problem with blackmail is that it rarely stays little. Someone could have decided to get rid of Scatterwell instead of paying up."

Behind them, the door swung open and a tall, distinguished figure stepped out into the sunshine. But Dr. Henry Reese missed a step when he saw them. "Good afternoon, Doctor," Sunny said. "This is my partner in this investigation, Constable Price."

Reese didn't offer to shake hands, but it looked as though Will was pretty used to that. "Actually, Dr. Reese and I have met before," he said. "He's another Saxon alum from the class of '66 that I tracked down for fund-raising. The name didn't spark anything, but I definitely remember the face."

The chief administrator of Bridgewater Hall showed no trace of recognition . . . and not much in the way of manners. "You'll have to excuse me," Reese said, frozen-faced. "I have an appointment." He headed for his car as if he were afraid that Will might tackle him.

*

Shadow was not happy. He'd managed to get out while Sunny and the Old One were both busy, which was good. But the sun was hot, and even the shady patches were uncomfortably warm. He'd tried all the windows, even the ones to the Dark Place underneath the house, again without any luck. The only loose screen he found was for the little house behind, where all the boxes lived. That didn't help at all.

He'd lain down to think about it but had fallen asleep instead. When he awoke, the patch of shade he'd picked for his rest had moved away. Shadow stood. He felt hungry, and his food dish was inside the house—inside the house he couldn't find a way into. He sat on his haunches, looking up. There were windows he hadn't been able to reach from the ground, windows on the second floor.

If I could fly like a bird, I could go up and look.

But that was a stupid thought. He pushed it away.

There was another way up, of course, but it meant climbing. Shadow could see the route. Up the trunk of the tree behind the house, out on that branch, and that would bring him to the roof, where the upstairs windows jutted out. Could he do it? There was only one way to find out.

Shadow went to the tree and leaped up, his claws catching in the bark. At least he didn't fall. It was hard work and unpleasant, hanging by his claws, forcing his way up . . . hard and thirsty work, too. He thought longingly of his water bowl, hidden in the kitchen . . .

Something flashed past him. Instinctively Shadow ducked and slid back several inches, scrabbling frantically to keep a hold. He didn't like to think what it would be like to fall from this height. It was many-many times the length of his whole body. He continued his ascent, and the flash came again—this time with a peck! Shadow clung precariously to the tree trunk, trying to look around. It was a bird, the stupid bird he'd chased. Now it was chasing him, darting at him, trying to keep him from climbing.

Stupid, stupid *bird,* he thought, freeing one paw while digging in with the rest of his claws as best he could. When she came diving at him this time, he swatted out with the paw that wasn't clinging to the tree bark for dear life. It didn't hit the bird, but it did scare her away.

It scared Shadow, too, as a chunk of bark tore loose, nearly sending him tumbling to the ground.

His claws scraped long scratches, but he managed to hang on. After that, it was like a bad dream, toiling end-lessly upward, watching out for sneak attacks. Shadow was so distracted, he almost missed the branch he was aiming for. But once there, it was more like walking than climbing, and that dumb bird stopped bothering him.

Shadow made it to the roof. It hadn't seemed to slope so steeply when he'd been looking at it from the ground, but he could walk on it—if he was careful. He carefully skittered along to the nearest window. It was open, and he saw Sunny's room, but he couldn't budge the screen.

This is getting very, very bad, he thought. If he couldn't get in, he'd be stuck up here on the roof. The sun was beat-ing down, and the shingles were burning hot under the pads on his paws.

Shadow scrambled along to the next available window. He let out a mew of relief. The glass was up, and this screen was older. It rattled when he touched it. Extending his claws, he scratched at the frame around the screen. It moved!

It took patience, but he carefully shifted the screen until he could get a paw around the edge. Then things got easier. Shadow tugged and pushed at it until he had a space large enough for his head, his shoulders . . .

Bursting through, he flopped down into dimness. He was in!

And then, sniffing, he realized which room in the house this was—the one room he rarely, if ever, wanted to be in . . .

*

Sunny watched Henry Reese pull away in his late-model Mercedes. "I'm surprised you didn't ask about why the room got cleaned," she told Will. He shook his head. "No use crying over spilled milk—or in this case, disinfectant. I'd prefer to talk directly to the cleanup crew first, and then work my way up to the big boss." He glanced at his watch. "In fact, I might do that now unless you want to set up something with your dad's doctor."

Taking that as a hint, Sunny got out her cell phone and called her dad. When she explained why she wanted to talk with Dr. Collier, Mike got enthusiastic. "Let me call the doc and see if I can get you in. This is his short day— he should be finishing his office hours, but it's still a while before his tee time." Mike gave a brief snort of laughter. "It's kind of a sad thing when you're at the doctor's so much, you know his schedule."

Mike called her back within minutes.

"Okay, the doc says he can see you right away," he reported. "You're pretty close to his office, too."

Dr. Mark Collier was at Cardiovascular Associates of Elmet, which operated from a small medical building on the outskirts of the county seat, about eight miles from Bridgewater Hall. When Sunny and Will arrived, they were brought in immediately to Dr. Collier's office. He was a trim man with salt-and-pepper hair, glasses, and a no-nonsense expression. The only clue that he might be off duty was the fact that he'd loosened the tie he wore with his cream-colored short-sleeved shirt.

"Sunny," he said, rising to shake hands. After she'd introduced Will, the doctor motioned them to the seats in front of his desk. "Mike tells me you've got some questions about strokes." He grabbed his phone, pressed a button, and said, "Craig, can you come in for a moment?"

Another doctor, similarly dressed but with whiter hair, came in.

"This is my partner, Craig Snow," Dr. Collier said. "He's the vascular part of Cardiovascular Associates. Craig, these people have some questions about a possible stroke."

"Early this morning, a patient died at Bridgewater Hall," Will began, describing the symptoms that Ollie had seen. He was brief, to the point, and very coplike.

Dr. Snow obviously caught that. "Are you an investigator, Mr. Price?"

"I'm a Kittery Harbor town constable," Will replied, "assigned to help Ms. Coolidge look into this death."

"I'm not going to comment on any questions of treatment," Snow warned. "That wouldn't be proper."

"We're just trying to get some basic information," Will said, relaxing his cop mask.

"Okay. Well, basically, there are two types of strokes. In one case, something in the blood—a clot, usually—blocks a blood vessel feeding the brain and causes damage to brain cells."

"Much like the heart attack your father suffered, Sunny," Dr. Collier said. "Except his blockage caused damage to the heart muscle."

Dr. Snow nodded. "In the other general type of stroke, a weakened vessel ruptures, literally bleeding into the brain, and the pressure damages brain cells."

"When Dad had his heart attack, you gave him stuff to thin his blood." Sunny frowned. "Does the same thing happen with strokes?"

"For ischemic strokes, the ones caused by blockages, yes," Dr. Snow replied.

"But if a person thinned the blood and it turned out to be the other kind of stroke, that would make them bleed more," Will pointed out.

"I wasn't in the room," Snow said stiffly. "As I said, I cannot comment on treatment."

"Well, based on what you heard, do you think Gardner—the patient—had a stroke?" Sunny asked.

"Considering that I'm working from hearsay, a layperson's observations, without test results or personal examination . . . but I can at least say that the symptoms are not inconsistent with a stroke."

"There was one other symptom," Sunny said. "He began vomiting. Is that unusual for a stroke?"

"Vomiting is not unknown," Snow said. "In fact, some

studies now suggest that vomiting can be a sign of a more severe stroke."

Will absorbed that, then said, "So, considering that the patient had had a stroke previously, there's no reason that this attack wouldn't most likely be considered another stroke."

"As you say, most likely."

"Are there any drugs or substances that might create the same symptoms? Something that might look like a stroke?"

Dr. Snow shook his head and rose from his chair. "I really don't—"

"Arsenic," Dr. Collier interrupted. "It's an oldie, but there's a reason why people stay with the classics." He smiled at the aghast expression on his partner's face. "Some of us enjoy reading or watching mysteries, and some don't. I do."

"I think I'm done here." Dr. Snow gave them all a disapproving look and left the office. Collier laughed.

"Sometimes it's not a bad thing to have a careful doctor," Will said.

"It doesn't hurt to consider possibilities." The cardiologist shifted back in his seat. "Snow's the expert, of course, but basically any drug that has a neurological effect could possibly be mistaken for a stroke. There are certain kinds of shellfish poisons, even a drug used to treat breast cancer."

"Is there anything that could be swallowed?" Sunny asked, remembering Ollie's story about being awakened.

"Some of the heavy metals, perhaps," Dr. Collier replied. "Mercury, lead, cadmium, they all have toxic and neurological effects. But they're usually eaten or breathed in. You can get cadmium from cigarette smoke—the lungs absorb it better than the stomach. Arsenic, though, that's been a favorite since before the Renaissance. Its symptoms mimicked cholera, which was widespread up to the 1800s, when arsenic got the nickname 'inheritance powder.' And it's still used today—an old reliable." He got a little more serious. "It would require special tests—tests that a medical examiner might not perform if he thought the cause of death was a stroke."

"Just for the sake of argument, let's say the patient we described was being cared for by you and your partner. Given the situation, would you be asking the medical examiner to do those extra tests?"

Dr. Collier silently regarded him for a long moment, and then finally said, "No."

Will gave him a glum nod. "That's pretty much what I was thinking, too."

7

Sunny and Will thanked the doctor for his help and left the office. "So, natural causes or foul play?" she said. "It looks as if we're coming right down the middle."

"It would have been nice if he'd gotten something clear-cut," Will admitted. They walked into the parking lot for the medical building and stood between their two trucks. "Guess we might as well head back to Bridgewater Hall and talk to the people who cleaned out Room 114."

When they got back to the facility, they found Rafe Warner working the security desk. He was uncharacteristically silent as Sunny signed in. But as she turned away, words seemed to tumble out of him. "Is it true that you're investigating how Mr. Scatterwell died?"

There goes our chance of keeping this quiet, Sunny thought.

"Where'd you hear that?" Will demanded.

"People say things." Rafe's eyes roved the area, checking for anyone who might overhear. "Folks in the office say Dr. Reese has them working on a big document for you to sign."

The damned confidentiality agreement! Sunny had forgotten all about it.

"I can't say anything about that." She kept her voice low, too. "But we'll want a look at the log to see who came in and went out last night."

"That'll be up to Dr. Reese," Rafe said nervously.

"And he'll agree." Will gave him a wolf's smile. "That's in the big document, too."

Then he asked for directions to Housekeeping, which Rafe was willing enough to give, but talking to the crew that cleaned Gardner's room got them nowhere. The maintenance people weren't withholding—they just didn't know anything.

"We go in whenever anybody passes away," a guy in janitorial greens explained. "We don't do anything while the other person is in the room. That upsets them. But once they're away, we clean and clear out as soon as possible."

He leaned forward. "This time around, the patient had puked. So we cleaned up after that, and did a specially careful job." He allowed himself a small smile. "They don't like germs around here."

Sunny and Will left the office. "Well," he said, "should we go give Ollie a lack-of-progress report?"

"Hey, we found out a couple of things," Sunny replied. "Can we help it that they're things he won't want to hear?"

When they arrived at Room 114, though, Sunny was surprised to see Luke Daconto just leaving.

"Thought I'd stop by," he said. "Mr. Barnstable was pretty bummed to lose his friend."

"Not just Ollie," Sunny told him. "I'm sure you'll miss Gardner, too."

Luke lowered his eyes. "Yeah. It's kinda rough. He was a great guy."

It seemed as though Luke wasn't as plugged in to the rehab center grapevine as Rafe Warner. He obliviously shook hands with Will. Obviously, here was another person that Ollie hadn't let in on the investigation. *Is Ollie being cagey, or did he just get hit with Reese's confidentiality agreement?* Sunny thought. She introduced Will, not mentioning that he was a constable. *If that's the way Ollie wants to play this, I'll go along.*

They chatted for a moment, and then Luke moved on.

If Ollie had been bummed out before, hearing their report didn't cheer him up much. He sat up in bed, listening with a frown on his face. But when they finished, Ollie said, "I've got a suspect for you."

"Someone here? Someone who knew Scatterwell?" Will asked.

Ollie shook his head. "Stan Orton."

"The man you did the real estate deal with?" Sunny stared at her boss.

"The guy who threatened me—and then I beat him on that contract," Ollie told her. "I think he got Gardner by mistake."

"You think Orton snuck in last night?"

"Of course not." Ollie gave her a withering look. "He sent somebody, somebody who works here. At first, he probably just hired them to spy on me. That's when whoever it was must have overheard me talking with Gardner about brandy."

Will looked doubtful. "So it's someone who knew who was talking while they were eavesdropping, but couldn't recognize who was who in the dark?"

Ollie made an impatient gesture. "Okay, maybe two people—one from the day shift, one for the night."

"And they'd be willing to poison you?" Sunny couldn't keep the doubt out of her own voice.

"No, no, Orton wanted to punish me, not kill me. It was probably something to make me sick as a dog. But if Gardner got it instead, well, he was in pretty bad shape. Maybe what would have just made me sick was enough to kill him."

Sounds like the kind of story you'd find on the lamer cop shows, Sunny thought, but she kept her mouth shut.

Will, who had more professional pride, looked ready to argue. "Ollie—"

"We'll take it under advisement," Sunny said. The last thing they needed was to provoke a fight with her boss.

"It's not like you've got a theory of your own," Ollie griped. "So get out there and dig into Orton. Maybe he's pulled a dirty trick or two before. And don't sign anything with these people. I've got my lawyer going over their so-called agreement."

"Okay," both Will and Sunny promised. They said good-bye to Ollie and got out of there before he opened another can of craziness on them. As they walked down the hall, Will lowered his voice, looking up and down the hallway. "Do you know where the john is around here? I know Ollie's room had one, but I didn't want to stay in there."

Sunny spotted Camille the aide walking toward them, and directed Will's question to her. "Four doors down on the other side." The girl pointed.

Will thanked her and hurriedly headed away.

"There was quite a lot of excitement here early this morning," Sunny said when they were alone.

Camille nodded. "Poor Mr. Scatterwell."

Sunny decided to do some gentle information gathering. "Do you lose a lot of patients from this ward?"

Camille shook her head. "It happens more in the resident wards, where people are older and sometimes frail. But here? This is the first I know of. But then, I've only been here a couple of months. Bridgewater Hall took me on right after I finished my training."

"Do you like the job?"

An embarrassed smile appeared on Camille's plain face. "I wanted to help people—and make a living. Everywhere I looked, they kept saying that health care was one of the only growing career fields. So I went for a training course, and at least I got a job."

"Is it all it was cracked up to be?" Sunny asked.

Camille gave her a shrug. "It's kind of a look into a different world. Most of the people here, I'd say they have money. Not like where I grew up."

"So are the rich really different?" Sunny grinned. "That's what one writer said."

"They're used to having people take care of them, I'd say." Camille looked a little put on the spot. "Some of them are nice. Your friend Mr. Barnstable isn't that bad, once you get past the grumpiness."

"He's my boss," Sunny said. "And if you say he's being nice, I've got to find out what kind of pills you're giving him."

"He's . . . honest," Camille said. "That usually happens when people are sick or in pain." Her smile slipped a little. "Not with Mr. Scatterwell, though. He liked people to think he was a nice guy, but he wasn't."

Sunny nodded. "I saw a little of that."

"He was really sick, but he wouldn't do the work to get better." Camille seemed upset at the waste. "But even though he was badly off, he still liked to chase women. Not that he'd be able to do anything if he caught them." Scorn turned into something else on her face. "If you weren't pretty or rich—"

Like Camille, for instance, Sunny thought.

"You might as well be a piece of furniture," Camille finished.

"That doesn't sound very nice at all," Sunny said.

Camille shook her head. "It could be worse if he noticed you. Ms. Hogue found that out."

"The occupational therapist?"

"She kept trying to get him to do more, and he didn't want to." Camille lowered her voice. "He got really mean, calling her names, telling her she wouldn't have a job, that his big buddy Dr. Reese would fire her—I even caught him feeling her up when he thought no one was looking."

Camille looked a little wistful. "Ms. Hogue used to look really pretty, but the longer she worked with him, she stopped wearing makeup, or nice clothes, she just sort of hunkered down."

"Couldn't she have gotten Mr. Scatterwell assigned to someone else?"

"She tried, but he went over everybody's head." Camille's tone got more guarded. "Things haven't been the same around here since Dr. Reese took over. With Dr. Faulkner, you felt as if the boss cared. But with Reese, well, he and Rafe Warner have been at each other's throats."

Why would it matter what the security guard thought? Sunny wondered.

When Camille saw the baffled expression on Sunny's face, she explained. "Rafe is the shop steward for the union, and Reese wants to tear up the whole contract."

I'm beginning to wonder what kind of an investigator I am, Sunny thought. *All this intrigue going on in front of me, and I don't catch any of it. I guess if Rafe is at war with Dr. Reese, no wonder he's getting news of what goes on in the administrator's office.*

"And it's getting worse." Camille's voice sank to a whisper. "When Rafe's cat Patrick got sick, Dr. Faulkner said that because he's a therapy cat, Bridgewater Hall would cover his treatment. But Dr. Reese said it wasn't in writing, and he's not paying for vet bills."

A light over one of the doors down the hallway began blinking.

"That's one of my patients needing help." Camille excused herself and hurried to respond.

Sunny turned back to find Will standing beside her. "Uncover any clues?" he asked with a smile.

"No, but we dug up a lot of dirt—I'll tell you once we're outside."

They headed around the nurses' station and down the long corridor to the front door. When they got to the security desk, Sunny asked Rafe, "Where's Portia?"

"Patrick wasn't feeling all that well, so Portia is keeping him company." He pointed in the corner behind him. Sunny leaned over the chest-high security desk to see a cat bed in the tiny space. Patrick sat up, his head hanging and his fur out at all angles while Portia carefully and gently groomed him with her tongue.

"Does he often have bad days?" Sunny asked.

"It comes and goes," Rafe replied. "The vet says that with chemo, the cure can feel as bad as the disease. But Patrick's hung in there, and so have I."

Sunny noticed that Rafe wasn't in a uniform shirt today, but a plain, short-sleeved number starting to fray at the collar. *Hanging in there, but looks to me like you might be having trouble making ends meet,* Sunny thought. She and Will signed out but got a surprise when they opened the door. Mike was about a step away, reaching for the handle.

"Thought I'd stop by and see how Ollie was doing," he said.

Sunny smiled. *The Kittery Harbor Way strikes again.*

"Luke Daconto was in to see him, too," she said. "I'll see you at home for dinner, Dad." Sunny gave her dad a quick kiss on the cheek, and then she and Will went to their trucks.

"I'm dying for a cup of coffee. Do you know some place in the area that won't cost us an arm and a leg?" Will asked.

"Another mistake," Sunny sighed. "I should have held Ollie up for an expense account." She got out her cell phone and called the MAX office. Nancy answered, sounding reasonably cool and calm.

"Hi," she said when Sunny identified herself. "Everything went pretty well. Quitting time is coming up soon."

"Remember to lock up the office," Sunny told her. "But

first, I want you to check our restaurant database for any places near Bridgewater or Levett."

Nancy quickly gave her the names of a couple of places. One struck a bell.

"Thanks," Sunny said, and then turned to Will. "There's a sandwich place that opened this summer. They're supposed to make a mean panini, and the coffee's good."

She gave Will the address, and soon afterward they pulled up in front of a small strip mall. The shop was small but clean, and the staff was enthusiastic. Sunny and Will both came out with paper cups of coffee.

Will sipped his and let out a sigh. "Ah, the four cop blood types: A, B, O, and Morning Mud." While he got his caffeine infusion, Sunny passed along what Camille had told her.

"Sounds as though this therapist was having a real problem with Scatterwell. If what the aide says is true, he'd actually progressed to physical harassment." Will frowned.

"But I guess she wouldn't get very far making a complaint if Gardner had a friend at the top of the pile." Sunny silently contemplated her cup of joe for a moment. "A person could get mighty desperate in a situation like that."

"Then there's Reese himself," Will suggested. "Apparently he was brought in as a new broom, expected to cut operating costs. How do you think the staff has reacted?"

"Camille said it's not the same," Sunny said.

Will nodded. "And maybe the care isn't as good. That would explain the spike in the mortality rate." He frowned down into his cup.

"Nothing wiggling in there, I hope?" Sunny peered over.

"Just a nasty little thought niggling at my brain," Will

told her. "Your friendly aide essentially said that there's labor strife going on at Bridgewater Hall. What if some of the union people are taking it too far?"

"You think they're killing patients?" Coffee slopped out of Sunny's cup, landing on the hood of Will's truck. She dabbed at the splotch with her napkin, trying to hide how upset she was. "From what I see, most of the people in that place are like Camille. They want to help people."

"But if they get stepped on often enough, maybe they don't go the extra mile anymore." Will gave Sunny his napkin, too. "There's something else. You say that Scatterwell wasn't very backward about telling people how tight he was with Reese. What if someone picked up on that and decided to make a public example out of old Gardner?"

"Striking at Reese through Gardner? Sounds kind of extreme."

"It would rub Reese's nose in the problems going on in the facility," Will argued. "And maybe there's a personal side to it, too."

Sunny looked at him, not sure she wanted to hear what Will had in mind. "How?"

"You told me that Reese went out of his way to screw over your friend Rafe."

"He's not my friend." For a second, Sunny felt like she was arguing with her dad. "He just seems like a nice guy."

"Who has a sick cat that might die if Rafe can't keep up the payments for chemotherapy," Will said. "Did you see his shirt today?"

Unwillingly, Sunny nodded her head.

"I'd say he's pretty close to the edge. Maybe he wanted Reese to find out how it felt to lose someone close to him."

"But to kill someone?" Sunny objected.

"A not very nice person." Will's lips tugged into a sort of smile. "I've seen how people act around their cats. You can't call it strictly rational."

She gave him a look. "So what do you want to do about it?"

"I'll ask some friends to check and see if Rafe Warner or Elsa Hogue has ever turned up on the Sheriff Department's radar screens," Will said. He stepped around to open the door on Sunny's Wrangler for her. "We still have Alfred Scatterwell to see tomorrow," he said.

She nodded. "The guy with the money motive. I vote that if he offers us anything to drink, we say no."

"I should say not," Will told her. "If he offers us anything to drink, we take a sample before pouring the rest down the drain."

*

Sunny arrived home to find an empty driveway. *Guess Dad's still visiting with Ollie,* she thought as she parked and walked to the door. No sooner did she step into the house than a four-footed rocket came flying from the living room to orbit around her ankles. Shadow circled her once, then twice, and then drew away, looking almost affronted.

"What's your problem?" Sunny asked as she walked down the hallway to the kitchen.

Sunny opened the refrigerator and began rummaging in the chiller compartment for salad makings. She brought out a head of romaine lettuce, some tomatoes, a container of mushrooms, a couple of leftover carrots, some radishes, and a jar of marinated peppers. As she closed the door and stood up, she found herself face to face with Shadow, who had somehow gained the high ground on top of the fridge. He lay with his paws primly together, giving her a reproachful look.

"I haven't forgotten to feed you," Sunny told him. "I just want to get supper ready." She washed the vegetables in the sink, tore the lettuce leaves into smaller pieces, chopped the vegetables, and placed all the rabbit food in a large wooden bowl. All the while, she was aware of Shadow's eyes on the top of her head.

"Dressing," she said, getting a packet of low-sodium Italian and mixing it with water, olive oil, and balsamic vinegar. Shaking it vigorously in a bottle, she put it aside and looked at the cat.

"All right!" Sunny burst out. "Dinner for you. Happy now?" She went to the cabinet and got a can of Shadow's regular food, pulled the pop top, and dug the delicious chicken and tuna dinner into his bowl. It had to be delicious, it said so right on the can. Then she refilled his water bowl.

But Shadow remained on his perch, silently regarding her.

"Fine, fine, have it your way." Sunny ignored the cat, and dug around in the freezer section for more dinner fixings. The previous weekend, Mike had fired up the grill and cooked up a mess of boneless chicken thighs, which he'd had marinating in the refrigerator for two days before. Sunny had packaged all the leftovers, two to a freezer bag, and frozen them. Now she pulled out a bag with a pair of bigger pieces of meat, put them in a microwavable bowl, and nuked them on *Defrost*.

When Mike came home a little while later, Sunny

heated the chicken in the microwave and tossed the salad with the dressing she'd made. Splitting the greens between two bowls, she sliced the hot chicken, put it on top, and doused it with the remaining dressing.

"Looks good," Mike said as he came into the kitchen and took a bottle of lemon-lime fizzwater out of the fridge.

Sunny got the glasses, and they sat down to eat. She glanced around the kitchen, noting that Shadow no longer guarded the top of the fridge but was finally paying attention to the food she'd laid out for him.

But while she—and Shadow—ate, Sunny noticed that he kept looking over at her as if something was wrong.

*

Shadow kept giving Sunny puzzled glances. This wasn't fair, not after all he'd gone through today, nearly killing himself climbing that tree, nearly getting killed by that crazy bird, getting trapped on the roof, and finally escaping . . . into the Old One's room. He knew the Old One usually kept his door tightly closed, just to keep Shadow out. Shadow didn't mind because it also kept the scent of the Old One in. He feared he'd be stuck in there, and Old One smells weren't particularly interesting or pleasant. The scent of the human's sickness was fading away, which was good. But the Old One had one pair of shoes that let off such a terrible stink, Shadow was surprised that Biscuit Eaters weren't showing up to roll on them.

He'd had a bad time for a while but the door hadn't latched, and he'd managed to get it open, escaping out into fresh air. The first thing he'd done was go downstairs to the kitchen and drink some water. Then he'd taken a nap.

And then, when Sunny came home, he'd rushed to her with an eager nose, hoping to erase all the bad things that had happened, the unpleasant smells he'd endured, by sniffing around her. She carried the same scents that he'd detected for the past few days, scents of illness and, in this case, a particularly nose-twisting odor he hadn't liked. She also smelled of car, and the He who was often around her, and several kinds of food.

But the scent he really wanted, the scent he'd been looking forward to . . . there wasn't a trace! For days now, Sunny had brought back traces of the mysterious She. The thought of filling his nostrils with that intoxicating aroma had brought Shadow at a run, only to be disappointed. Was the She teasing him? Or was Sunny?

He sullenly made the cat food disappear, all the while doing his best to give Sunny a cat's version of a dirty look.

*

The next morning, Sunny dressed with a little more care than usual. Maybe it was silly; she'd crashed New York's swankiest enclaves of the rich and famous as a reporter. But today she was heading for Piney Brook, the fanciest neighborhood in her old hometown, to beard Alfred Scatterwell in his den, or stately home, or whatever. That seemed to call for special armor. She got out the dusky blue lightweight suit she saved for the biggest interviews. Will seemed to have had the same thoughts, turning up in dark gray slacks, a slightly lighter shirt, and a sport coat with a very fine houndstooth pattern. "Do you mind riding with me?" he asked. "I've got a couple of things to discuss before we tackle Alfred."

As they drove over, Will said, "I got some files from my friends this morning—figured the night shift was the best time for them to go and look."

"Anything that helps us?" Sunny asked.

He shook his head. "Nothing on Elsa Hogue, not even a traffic ticket. Her husband passed away about seven years ago—severe heart attack. Rafe Warner was involved in a confrontation once, but it won him a commendation, not an arrest. He once apprehended a guy who grabbed a tourist's wallet in a restaurant and headed for the door. Warner put him on the floor and kept him there until the cops arrived."

"So he's a good citizen," Sunny said.

"A good citizen who has no problem putting a bad guy down," Will replied. "I added Alfred Scatterwell to my wish list, just to see if anything came up. He's never been accused of a crime, but he's been a complainant in several cases, usually for assault."

Thinking of Alfred's attitude when she met him, Sunny wasn't exactly astonished.

"Of course, given the present administration's stand on crime statistics, the charges all became harassment," Will went on.

"Which is probably what they were in the first place," Sunny said. "Alfred strikes me as the kind of guy who'd claim assault quickly to defend his dignity."

"You mean have other people—like the cops—defend his dignity." Will drove on for a moment, then said, "Would it surprise you to hear that Gardner Scatterwell, on the other hand, had been in some kind of trouble stretching back to his high school days?"

"What kind of trouble?"

"Drunk driving, disturbing the peace, harassment—female division, this time. It all stayed pretty low-level, fines and suspended sentences, probably due to him having expensive lawyers. Usually there were fairly long gaps between charges, so I guess he tried to behave himself."

"Probably he took his bad behavior out of town. My dad mentioned that he often traveled," Sunny said.

They were getting close to Alfred's address, but as Sunny looked out the window, she didn't see the picture of gracious living she'd expected. The houses were nice and well kept, but they weren't much bigger than the one she lived in, and they were rather close together. "Wait a minute, I know this neighborhood," she burst out. "My dad used to call it 'the servants' quarters.'"

"Sort of Piney Brook by extension." Will grinned.

"A dump, by Piney Brook standards. If this is where the Scatterwells come from . . ." It took Sunny a minute to find the words. "Well, let's just say they put the 'pretend' in 'pretentious.'"

"Oh, this is just Alfred's place," Will assured her. "The old family manse is a big, dilapidated pile right on the banks of the Piney Brook itself. That's where Gardner used to live, although he closed the place up when he wound up in Bridgewater Hall."

"I wonder if Alfred looks forward to moving up to the big house," Sunny said.

Will grinned and sang, "'Movin' on up . . .'"

They stopped in front of a house not that different from its neighbors. Sunny wasn't expecting Jeeves the butler to appear when they rang the doorbell, but the apparition that answered went way too far in the opposite direction. In a knit polo shirt and plaid Bermuda shorts, Alfred Scatterwell definitely hadn't dressed for the occasion. Seeing his knobby knees and scaly elbows was bad enough, but his potbelly seemed to bobble with every step.

"So you found the place," he said. "What do you want?" Apparently while he was only the all-purpose heir, Alfred had held himself back around his uncle. Now that he expected to rake in Gardner's money, Alfred was letting his true nature out.

"First, we'd like to offer our condolences—" Sunny began, but Alfred waved her off.

"You saw how well the old man and I got along. Do you really think I'm bereaved?"

Smelling the brandy on his breath, Sunny had another description in mind.

"I think you should be concerned about the way your uncle died," Will firmly told him. "There are some unusual circumstances."

"The people at Bridgewater Hall told me Uncle Gardner died of a stroke, and his personal physician concurred," Alfred replied. "Considering he had a stroke three months before, how unusual is that?"

"There's a situation you're not aware of." Sunny told Alfred the story Oliver Barnstable had recounted to her and Will.

Scatterwell looked incredulous. "You're taking the word of that flabby-faced loudmouth? The man is on pain medication, for heaven's sake."

"You yourself complained about the mortality rate at Bridgewater Hall," Sunny pointed out. "Don't you feel any responsibility to find out what happened?"

"I felt responsible enough to the family fortune to look into the possibility of suing for malpractice." Alfred shook his head. "The outlay in lawyer's fees didn't match the uncertain chances of winning a settlement."

Sunny didn't know what to say to that. She looked over at Will, who was eyeing Alfred as if he'd encountered a strange specimen. "Mr. Barnstable raised enough concern that we're looking into what happened to your uncle." Will tried to appeal to Alfred's penny-pinching side. "It needn't even cost you anything. If you just approached the medical examiner and asked for some test—"

"Why should I?" Alfred interrupted. "If there was a policy with a big payout, the insurance company may want to quibble, but I don't. My uncle always sneered at me for inheriting family money. But what did he do? He received the lion's share of my grandfather's estate and spent his life wasting it. There aren't many Scatterwells left, thanks to people like Uncle Gardner who never had children. If I can amass enough money, invest it intelligently, there may be something for the next generation—and we could repair the mansion that's going to rack and ruin. I was down in the big house yesterday trying to see if we could use any of the public rooms for a memorial. They're all going to need work."

Sunny couldn't get over this attitude. "So you'd wink at murder to get your inheritance?"

"I reject any culpability for my uncle's death." Alfred drew himself to his full height. He might have looked impressive, if he'd been dressed better and his belly didn't jiggle. "But if—*if*—someone hurried his demise along, it stopped him from wasting money on that overgrown home for the senile." He glared at Will. "Just as his stroke stopped him from throwing money away on a high school he'd barely thought of in the last fifty years or so. When you called yesterday, I knew I recognized your name—so I looked in Uncle Gardner's papers to find the connection. What did you do to get his money, sing the school song?" Alfred put his hand over his heart and croaked, "'Saxon, Saxon, onward, upward,'" his expression looking as if he wanted to spit. "Oh, yes, I went there, too. A few years before you did. Family tradition, sending the males to that ridiculous place. And I hate to disappoint you, Mr. Fundraiser, but they won't get one thin dime from me."

He finally led them into the house from the doorway, along a hallway toward the living room. "I was from the same family as Uncle Gardner, went to the same stupid schools. But for my entire life, he lorded it over me, mocked me, belittled me. Well, he's not so superior now."

Alfred pointed at the coffee table, which held a waxed cardboard box with a metal handle, the sort of thing that might accompany a large order of take-out Chinese food. "It's just like that old joke he liked to tell—all men are cremated equal."

8

A slow, red tide crept up Will's neck to his face. "You wasted our time when you'd already cremated your uncle?"

"I wanted to find out what your investigation had turned up," Alfred coolly replied. "From what I heard, I have nothing to worry about."

"You mean, worrying about a murder charge?" Sunny asked. She figured it was worth one last chance to try and shake up Scatterwell a little. "Maybe you could tell us where you were between, say, ten p.m. and four a.m.?"

"I was home, alone, watching a DVD and then sleeping in bed." He smiled. "The sound sleep of the innocent." From his mocking tone, Alfred might as well have been channeling his uncle's nasty side. "Good luck to you. I'd say you'll need it."

Sunny watched Will's hands slowly close into fists at his sides.

We'd better get out of here before Alfred winds up adding another assault complaint to his record. She put a hand on Will's elbow. "No use wasting any more time," she said. "Let's go."

It was a long walk back to the street, especially when they heard Alfred chuckling behind them. "I'd love to shove that laugh back down that smug jerk's throat," Will muttered. "Along with a couple of teeth."

"Getting mad isn't going to get us anywhere," Sunny warned, then smiled. "Getting even might. You know, it's amazing. I had my doubts about this investigation. But all of a sudden, I wouldn't mind proving that Gardner's death was a murder, especially if it meant taking down some smug jerk for the crime."

They climbed into Will's pickup. "Now that you've had a moment to cool down, do you really think Alfred is a suspect?" Sunny asked Will.

He stabbed his key into the ignition aggressively. "Well, he destroyed any possible evidence of foul play by cremating Gardner's body. I wonder if he was already arranging that when I called him yesterday morning."

Sunny nodded. "That's definitely a mark on the suspect side of the ledger." She glanced at him. "Do you think Alfred actually committed the crime?"

"If I were Gardner, I certainly wouldn't take a drink from him in the middle of the night." Will frowned, chewing on that for a moment. Then he said, "Of course, from what you've told me about Gardner Scatterwell, maybe he didn't think that Alfred had the stones to try and kill him." Will continued to think it over. "Of course, Alfred didn't have to be the actual doer. He could have paid to have it done."

Sunny blinked. "You mean that now you're agreeing with what Ollie suggested? That somebody at Bridgewater Hall could've been tempted by money?"

Sunny suddenly remembered Rafe Warner's frayed shirt and went silent.

"The one thing I keep hearing about the wonderful world of health care is the low salaries—especially the farther down the ladder you go with the caregivers," Will continued. "Alfred seems to have at least a piece of the Scatterwell fortune. I think he might be able to offer a price that someone on the staff couldn't refuse." He shook his head. "I wish we could look into where Alfred's money's been going, but I don't think we could talk Nesbit into doing some forensic accounting."

Sunny grinned. "Who needs Nesbit? We can get Ollie digging into good old Alf and the Scatterwell fortune. He's good at following the money, and he has financial contacts all over the state. The day that Gardner died, he had me bringing files of earlier deals he'd done with Stan Orton. I bet he's doing the same sort of investigation into Mr. Orton's finances."

"Probably to see if Orton demanded money back from his bumbling assassin." Will turned the key. "Okay, that gives us two reasons to check in at Bridgewater Hall, getting Ollie to tap into his money contacts and seeing who on the staff might have been bribed." He grinned. "By Orton or anybody."

As they drove up, Sunny used the time to check in with

Nancy. She was relieved to hear that no problems had developed at MAX. *Let's hope it stays that way,* she thought, but then changed her mind. *Maybe one, small, reasonably easy problem,* she hedged. *Just so Ollie doesn't think he can dump me and hire Nancy at half my pay.*

Arriving at the nursing home, they decided to tackle the question of susceptible personnel first. That meant a visit to the administrator's office, which turned out to be on the second floor and took advantage of the bay window next to the main entrance.

"Do you have an appointment with Dr. Reese?" the secretary outside his office door asked. Since she had a computer screen facing her chair, she probably had the answer in front of her eyes.

"I'm pretty sure he'll see us," Sunny told the woman. "Or those confidentiality agreements he's had you working on will be pretty useless."

She quickly got on the phone. "He'll see you now," she said, rising to open the door. But Reese beat her to the punch, swinging the door open from his side and gesturing Sunny and Will into the office.

When they explained that they wanted to see who'd been working the night that Gardner had died, Reese frowned. "I don't think—" he began.

"I can't imagine anything in the employee attendance records that could affect patient confidentiality," Will broke in.

"And if you're worried about the labor problems, we'll certainly do our best to stay out of them," Sunny chimed in.

Reese sank back in his desk chair, his face gray. "Do you think I like playing the bad guy here?" he demanded in a hoarse voice. "There was a reason why the board forced Faulkner out and brought me in. This facility has been losing money for the last two years. We've had to dip into the endowment, and if we keep doing that, it's just a matter of time before we have to close the doors. Yes, I'm asking people to sacrifice. But the alternative would be no jobs at all."

"Have you explained that to the union?" Sunny asked.

"I don't dare." Reese leaned across his desk. "If they hear that we may close, the more well-heeled families will pull their loved ones out of here. That will just accelerate the downward spiral." He paused for a second, clearing his throat. "Of course, I'm telling you all of this in confidence."

Boy, Sunny thought, *he's really depending on those confidentiality agreements—especially since we haven't signed them yet.*

"In the meantime, employee morale is diving, and your mortality rate is going up," Will pointed out. "Is there a connection?"

"None that I can find." Reese dug out a handkerchief to mop his suddenly sweaty face. "We have a monthly mortality review, and there's nothing out of the ordinary. Every facility dealing with the elderly has spikes and sometimes valleys in their statistics." He sighed. "It's just unfortunate that it's happening now."

"Maybe more unfortunate than you think," Will said, telling Reese their suspicions about a staff member's possible involvement.

"You think that one of the staff was bribed—that one of our people—" He broke off, staring blindly into space.

Probably imagining the headlines, and what would happen after they came out, Sunny thought.

"At this point, let's call it an unnerving possibility." Will used a soothing voice. Sunny had seen cops use it to coax suspects into confessing crimes. "It would be better if we checked it out to exclude innocent people."

Reese caved. "Rafe Warner has the relevant records." He gave them a pleading look. "Just don't tell him what they're for."

Sunny figured it was kinder not to mention that Rafe was already aware of their investigation.

When they got downstairs to the security desk, they found Rafe Warner out of uniform. He smiled at Sunny. "I'm here early. When the weather's decent, I like to grab a sandwich in the coffee shop and eat it out in the garden."

"Sounds nice," she said. "Can we join you?"

A few minutes later, they sat on a bench outside in the garden, a large area with graveled walks meandering around bushes and trees, with plants and plenty of flowers wherever Sunny looked. The day was clear and warm, with the afternoon sun beating down heavily.

"The trick is to find places with shade and a breeze." Rafe took a careful bite of his chicken salad sandwich and washed it down with a sip of soda. "And you've got to watch out, because we get a lot of bees around here. The flowers draw them."

"Rafe," Will said, "we just had a meeting with Dr. Reese."

"Oh?" Rafe's eyes grew guarded.

"He gave us the okay to check the records for the night that Gardner Scatterwell died." Will looked closely at the security guy as he spoke.

"I'll still have to check with him, of course." Rafe looked as though his sandwich didn't taste so good anymore.

"That's exactly what you should do," Sunny told him. She paused for a moment, trying to phrase her next question so it wouldn't sound like an accusation. "I know you're pretty busy on the door during the early part of your shift, but things must get kind of boring overnight, don't they?"

"Oh, no," Rafe replied. "I have screens to watch from the video cameras outside, and I do at least one set of rounds, clocking in at stations all over the building."

Something else to check, Sunny thought.

"Did you notice anything odd the other night? Anybody out of the ordinary?"

"You mean, anybody I want to put the finger on." Rafe put his sandwich down and pulled out a cell phone. After dialing, he said, "Hey, Dee, it's Rafe. I need to talk to the doctor." He waited a moment, then said, "Afternoon, Dr. Reese. I'm here with Miss Coolidge and Mr. Price—"

That was as far as he got. Then he sat listening in silence. "Okay, I understand. Yes, sir."

He shut his phone and put it in his pocket, frowning. "I'll give you the records when we get back inside," he said. "As for who was here—well, the whole late-night shift, of course. They're spread pretty thin, but most of the patients are fast asleep anyway. So who else? Elsa Hogue worked late. So did Luke Daconto."

"What was he doing, giving midnight concerts?" Sunny said in bafflement.

"All the therapists have paperwork." Rafe shrugged. "Ask them about it."

"Anyone else?" Will asked.

"One funny thing," Rafe said. "They paged Dr. Gavrik but weren't sure whether she would show. It was her day off.

Dr. Reese came bombing in and told me to get the number for the on-call doctor, but then Dr. Gavrik arrived. It was around three in the morning, but she didn't drive up in her car. I saw it on one of the security camera screens. She got out of a town car. And you know how people look when they jump out of bed? She didn't look that way."

Will leaned forward on the bench. "You mean, she looked like she'd already been awake?"

"She looked like she'd been out," Rafe said. "She was wearing a good suit, which she doesn't usually do when she comes in here."

Sunny slowly nodded, remembering the light jade number she'd noticed on the doctor. She'd thought it was awfully dressy for that time of night, but Rafe had been more observant. "It was rumpled, as though she'd been sitting in it for a long time. Longer than just a ride in a town car." He shook his head, looking a little less sure. "And something else. When she came in, I thought I saw some kind of airline ticket in the pocket of her jacket." He touched his chest. "Up here. But when she left, it was gone."

Will glanced over at Sunny. "You think she could've taken a red-eye flight in from somewhere?"

She shook her head, confident in the knowledge gained from working at MAX for more than a year. "Not one that came in through Pease. The latest arrivals there are around ten thirty at night."

"And you're sure about the time?" Will asked Rafe.

"It was definitely after three a.m. That's when Mr. Scatterwell got sick."

Sunny shared a look with Will. *Well, there's something else to check.*

Rafe finished his soda and crumpled up the paper wrapping from his sandwich. Sunny noticed that half his sandwich was still in there. Had this conversation killed his appetite, or was he penny-pinching, saving something for later?

"Technically, I don't start for a couple of minutes," the guard said, "so I'll get the sign-in and make copies for you."

They went to the security desk, and Rafe brought out a loose-leaf binder. "I'll help photocopy," Will offered, walking off with him.

Making sure nothing gets lost along the way, Sunny realized.

She stood waiting by the guard's station when a familiar figure in ginger and black fur crept into sight. "Portia!" Sunny leaned down to run a gentle hand between the cat's ears. "How are you today?"

Portia seemed upset—maybe she'd picked up on Rafe's feelings when he stepped behind the desk. She wasn't happy climbing all over Sunny's feet. She stretched up to rest her paws on Sunny's knees, meowing.

Sunny sighed. "All right." She picked up the cat, who snuggled in her arms, butting her head against Sunny's shoulder to demand more head scratching.

Another outfit that will have cat fur all over it. Sunny smiled at the rueful thought. *And one of my nicer summer outfits, too.*

Still, she did her best to comfort Portia, who finally lay bonelessly in her arms, purring.

Rafe laughed when he returned with Will. "She's shameless."

"Which one?" Will asked, shaking his head. "Sunny or the cat?"

He watched with an exasperated smile as Sunny transferred Portia into Rafe's arms.

"Are we going to go to Ollie's room?" she asked.

"Sure," he replied, folding the photocopies in his hand into thirds to fit in his back pocket. "Unless you intend to find another cat to play with. It seems to be turning into a habit for you these days."

"Hey, come on, Portia was upset. She's sensitive to things."

Will rolled his eyes. "She certainly picked up on who was likely to be the soft touch around here."

As they walked down the hallway to the nurses' station, they encountered Luke Daconto carrying his guitar case. "Sunny!" He smiled, then grew a little serious. "If you've got the time, do you think you could bring Mr. Barnstable to our little sing-along today? I can tell he's still upset about what happened to Mr. Scatterwell, and, well, maybe we could cheer him up."

Will just shrugged. "Anything to get Ollie into a better mood," he said.

"Okay," Sunny told Luke. "Just give us a few minutes to chat with him first."

I guess it's my lot in life, helping out upset creatures—cats, bosses, whatever, she thought.

They arrived in Room 114 to find Ollie sitting in his wheelchair—and nursing a bad mood.

"Are you having pain in your leg from sitting too long?" Sunny gave him a worried glance.

"I'm suffering from a pain in the butt named Stan Orton," Ollie growled.

"I figured you'd be looking into him." Sunny shot a *See? I was right!* glance at Will.

"I found out that he snookered me on that real estate contract." Ollie sounded really annoyed with himself. "No wonder he kept pushing me to seal the deal. He didn't own that parcel of land, he only had an option on it, and it was due to expire. If I had known and waited, I could've dealt with the real owner and gotten what I wanted for chump change."

He shifted in his chair with a deep groan. Sunny wasn't sure if the pain came from his leg or his wallet. "Instead, I just found out that I paid that creep Orton eight times what he paid for the option."

"Maybe I have something that will take your mind off that," Will offered. As he told Ollie of their run-in with Alfred Scatterwell and the games he played, Sunny saw her boss pay more and more attention.

"So we need someone to take a very close look at the guy," Will concluded.

"Like I did with Orton—even if I left it a little too late!" Ollie scowled, but slowly nodded, his expression showing he was a hundred percent on board with the project.

"And if you find some way to make a profit of your own, well, I wouldn't mind you skinning that cat." Will looked over at Sunny, who winced. "If you'll pardon the expression."

I'm just amazed at the idea of Ollie using his nasty powers for good, her wisecracking alter ego put in. She changed the subject.

"We bumped into Luke Daconto in the corridor," she told Ollie. "He was bringing his guitar to that sing-along thing he does, and he specifically asked me to invite you to come. Would you like to go?"

Ollie shrugged his heavy shoulders. "I'm already in the wheelchair, and *Judge Judy* is just about over."

Sunny took command of the chair and wheeled Ollie toward the solarium. Will walked alongside. As they came closer, they heard Luke noodling away on the strings, one of those snatches of songs he did between sing-alongs.

"That's the intro to 'California Dreamin','" Ollie said, glancing up at Will.

"You really know your music." This was a side of Ollie that Sunny had never seen before. Luke was happy to see them arrive, his white teeth showing through his beard in a smile.

"Since we have a couple of guys here today, what do you say we go with something more manly?" Luke strummed his way into "Show Me the Way to Go Home," and Ollie picked it up immediately. His singing voice was deep and surprisingly powerful.

"Let's take it around again," Luke said, still strumming. Now everybody in the room was singing, even the lady who Sunny had previously seen just beating the time with her hand. When she heard Will chime in, Sunny smiled.

The song ended to rousing applause. "Good singing," Luke complimented the group, then looked over at Ollie. "Very good singing, Ollie."

Ollie grinned a little awkwardly, patting his belly. "Back in the day, they used to tell me I had an opera singer's diaphragm."

"I wish I had that," Luke confessed. "Some gigs I've played, I've gone hoarse trying to put a song over to a crowd that's busy talking."

He played a couple more moldy oldies that Sunny's grandfather would have known, then he swung into a completely unexpected rendition of "I'm Gonna Be (500 Miles)" complete with a phony Scots accent. The older members of the audience fumbled with the song, but picked up on the chorus. Ollie enjoyed bouncing his voice off Luke's.

For a finale, Luke suggested that Sunny, Ollie, and Will try a little harmony on "You Are My Sunshine" while the others sang as a chorus. It took a little while for Ollie to learn to moderate his voice, but when he did, the song sounded pretty decent.

"Thank you, everybody," Luke told the group. "Really great job."

The little old lady who tapped in time to the music turned to Ollie. "You really have a beautiful voice. Do you sing in a choir?"

"Uh, no," Ollie replied, abashed. "I just sing for fun."

The ladies started moving off in their walkers and wheelchairs, but Will approached Luke as he put his guitar in its case.

"It's pretty sad, what happened to Ollie's roomie," Will said. "And it just seemed to happen out of the blue."

"Yeah." Luke kept his eyes on the case, making sure the clasps snapped shut. "That's the thing about strokes. You never expect them."

"Sunny was pretty shocked to get the news. She'd been visiting with Gardner that afternoon, and he seemed his usual self."

Sunny wanted to give Will a kick, but she followed his lead, giving Luke a sad look.

"You saw him pretty often," Will went on. "Did you think he was getting better?"

Luke looked up from his guitar case to meet Will's eyes. "I'm a music therapist, so I'm not the guy to talk to about Gardner's physical progress. You should talk to Jack and Elsa about that—or even Dr. Gavrik. All I can say is that I'm glad that Gardner seemed happy in the time before he passed away."

"But he didn't seem weaker or sicker lately, did he?" Will pressed.

Luke looked from Will to Sunny and back. "Why do you ask?"

"It's just that we had an odd conversation with Gardner's nephew, Alfred."

"Ah." It was hard to tell with that big, bushy beard, but Sunny thought she caught a brief flicker of distaste from Luke at the mention of Alfred's name:

"Yeah, he talked a lot about the Scatterwell name and the Scatterwell fortune, going to the right schools and knowing the right people." Luke's lips definitely twisted under all that facial fur.

"But he didn't really talk much about his uncle, except for the inheritance," Will continued.

"I don't think they got on that well." Luke could only shake his head. "It's a shame, really. From what I heard, it's not as though they had a lot of relatives."

"I guess family feeling doesn't mean much to Alfred." Will watched Luke carefully as he said, "He just had his uncle cremated, barely a day after Gardner died. We went over to see Alfred, and he already had the little box in the middle of his living room table."

"That's . . . kind of quick, isn't it?" Luke looked as though he wanted to say something else but reconsidered it.

"We thought the same thing. Makes us wonder if Alfred was covering up anything that might have happened to Gardner. I heard you were around kind of late that night. Did you see anything out of the ordinary?"

"I saw a lot of paper that night." Luke gave them a sheepish look. "Playing guitar and singing with the residents is the fun part of the job. But I also work with a lot of people, getting them to play simple instruments. We have a bell chorus, and other musical programs, and I'm supposed to write reports on all of it."

He shrugged, patting his guitar case. "I'm a music maker, not a report writer, so I'm usually pretty far behind. But this new administrator is very results oriented. A little bird told me that if I didn't get up to date, there'd be trouble. So when I finished the day's work, I holed up in an office and ground out the paperwork to make Dr. Reese happy." Luke grimaced. "I put in, like, a whole extra shift on that nonsense. Didn't get done until sometime after midnight. I was glad to get home—my neck was hurting from bending over the computer keyboard." He sighed. "And then I heard about Gardner."

"Did you do a report about him?" Sunny asked.

Luke's reply was a sad laugh. "No. Gardner was a freebie. I'm supposed to work with the permanent residents, keep their spirits up over the long haul. Gardner wasn't a client." Luke paused for a long moment. "He was a friend."

9

"**Gardner will be** missed," Ollie said as Luke hefted his guitar case.

Luke smiled and patted Ollie on the shoulder with his free hand. "I know, Mr. Barnstable. Just hang in there. Try and sing a little more."

"Thanks, Luke," Ollie said. "I'll look forward to it."

"I hope I'll see you, too," Sunny said, earning herself a look from Will.

Luke headed off with his guitar, and Will went to take the handles of Ollie's wheelchair. But Ollie waved him off. "What the hell were you doing?" he demanded in a low, venomous voice. "Why were you giving that kid the third degree?"

"For one thing, that was hardly the third degree," Will replied. "I just asked him a couple of questions. We know he was here late, after lights-out, which is when you told us Gardner had his mystery visitor."

Ollie looked as though he wanted to argue but was aware that he was awfully short of ammunition.

"Second, at this point our strongest suspect is Alfred Scatterwell. So I wanted to see how Luke felt about Alfred, how he'd react when I talked about him, especially the cremation. I'll admit I hit him a little hard, but I hoped to shock a reaction out of him."

"And did you get what you needed?" Ollie asked.

Will's expression changed a little. "I'm not sure. He was a tad off, not forthcoming. I think Luke was going to say something, but changed his mind."

"Maybe he was going to curse out Alfred," Ollie suggested, "but didn't because Sunny was here."

"I can't say—but he did censor himself about something," Will said.

No one had anything else to add, so they just talked around the subject, making mundane conversation as they rolled along to Room 114. Once they were inside, Ollie said, "Sunny, could you call for an aide? I'll need some help getting back into bed."

She did as Ollie asked, and moments later, Camille the aide came in.

"Why don't you give us a couple of minutes while I get Mr. Barnstable straightened away here," she suggested.

Sunny and Will stepped out into the hallway, where Will proceeded to give her the fish eye. "What's the idea of you telling that Daconto guy you hoped to see him again?"

For a guy who'd rather spend a weekend getting sun-

burned than going out with me, he's pretty quick on the jealousy trigger, she thought, but decided it wasn't worth going into that. Instead, she said, "Luke's one of the nicer people in this place. I'd definitely rather see him again than, say, Dr. Reese." She shuddered. "Or Dr. Gavrik. She can really be nasty."

"I've been thinking of the good doctor," Will said. "Specifically, what Rafe the guard had to say about the way she turned up on the night Gardner died."

"That's right—he thought she'd been flying. She didn't change her clothes, which is weird because any flight into Pease would have gotten her home hours before she was paged." Using her tourist-information knowledge, Sunny considered other nearby airports. "Portland doesn't have any red-eye flights. The latest arrival there is before midnight. Maybe Boston?" Sunny frowned. "Of course, maybe she flew in a lot earlier and was hanging around someplace. Otherwise, Logan Airport would have the latest flights in the area. Wherever she came from, Gavrik rode in a town car. Maybe that could tell us something."

He nodded. "I've got an old buddy from my state trooper days who moved over to the Boston Police. Suppose I ask him to check the car services down there and see if any of them made a run from, say, Logan to Bridgewater? It's almost a hundred-mile trip, so that should make it a fare to remember."

"That's a good idea," Sunny replied. "No way am I confronting that woman without something I can hit her over the head with. Metaphorically speaking, of course."

"On the other hand, Rafe might have a reason to try and distract us with the doctor," Will said. "We're getting to the end of our first full day here; that means only six to go. Time keeps ticking away."

She nodded. "Much as I'd like to concentrate on Obnoxious Alfred—or the nasty doctor—we still have other people to question. I'm going to tackle Elsa Hogue tomorrow. And I think *I* should do it. Sounds like she had a hard enough time with Gardner. I think she'd react better to a sympathetic female ear."

"Fine with me," Will said. "I'll spend the night going over those attendance lists that Rafe copied up." He smiled, but with a little malice. "You can play with your cat."

They went to sign out. Rafe nodded his good-bye, but Portia was more demonstrative, jumping onto the top of the desk and rubbing her face against Sunny's shoulders.

When Will and Sunny stepped out of the rest home, they discovered that the weather had changed. A dome of dead air, hot and soggy, had settled over the area. Merely getting from the grand doors of Bridgewater Hall to Will's pickup left Sunny's suit wilted and sticking to her. Will yanked off his coat and opened the top two buttons of his shirt.

"Now I remember why I didn't wear this outfit later than the end of May." Sunny caught the front of her knit top between her thumb and forefinger and tried to pull it away. It still felt plastered to her. Will moved on ahead, climbing into the cab of the pickup, starting up the engine, and closing the windows. Sunny joined him to find the air-conditioning on, but not making much headway against the warm air trapped inside. They didn't do well against traffic, either.

When they got onto the interstate, the usually brief ride seemed to drag on forever.

At last they turned onto Wild Goose Drive and followed the gently curving road to Sunny's house. She thanked Will for the ride, and mentioned she'd take her Wrangler tomorrow. "Maybe we'll be able to cover a little more territory."

Will nodded. "You want to talk to the Hogue woman. I'll see if I can get in touch with my friend in Boston tonight."

"I'll also talk to Mrs. Martinson again and see if she can come up with any dirt on Alfred Scatterwell . . . and Henry Reese." Sunny paused for a moment. "Are any of your police friends veterans? Recent veterans, I mean? Maybe it wouldn't be a bad idea to get a picture of what Rafe Warner is like when he's not behind the security desk at Bridgewater Hall."

Will slowly nodded. "That's probably something we should follow up. I'll try to talk to some of the guys tomorrow. And you were right—we should have hit Ollie for expense money. Coffee and doughnuts don't come cheap."

They waved good-bye, and Sunny made her way through the thick air into the house. She could feel the air-conditioning on in the living room. When she looked in, she found Mike half-lying on the couch, his eyes closed, looking like a wrung-out washrag.

"I got caught in this lousy weather and got home as fast as I could," he complained. "For a while there I wasn't sure if I was breathing or sipping water through a straw."

"You're sure you're okay?" Sunny asked worriedly.

"Yeah, I just feel tired," Mike told her. "Give me a little more time here in the cold air to revive."

Sunny went up to her room to peel off her suit. She left

it on the bed and quickly changed into a pair of shorts and a T-shirt.

When she returned downstairs, she found Mike watching the end of the weather report on television news. "It's going to be miserable like this tomorrow," he reported. "Maybe I'll try to get in an early walk, or go up and do it in one of the malls. Otherwise, I think I'm going to stick close to home."

"I wish I could do that, too," Sunny said. One thing was certain—no dressing up tomorrow. A nice tee and a pair of light cotton pants would have to do.

She looked around the room. "Where's Shadow?"

"He got out of here when it started getting cool. Maybe he decided it was unnatural to have that kind of indoor weather in summertime." Mike shrugged. "You'd think he'd be happy for a chance to enjoy some cool air, stuck in a fur coat the way he is." He gestured vaguely toward the rear of the house. "Try the kitchen."

But when Sunny arrived there, she didn't see Shadow, not even on top of the refrigerator, where she'd expected to discover the cat hiding out.

Looking in the fridge, Sunny shook her head. They were running low on supplies. But even her brief exposure to the weather had killed her appetite, and she was willing to bet her dad felt the same way, too. She gathered a large can of tuna from the bottom shelf, a Vidalia onion, and an avocado that had been taking its sweet time getting ripe. She chopped up some of the onion and mashed the other ingredients together with some lemon juice, a hint of oil, and a shake of pepper. After washing some romaine leaves, she arranged them on two plates and then scooped a healthy dollop of the tuna-avocado mixture in the middle.

Although Mike praised the salad—after first asking, "What is that?"—he just nibbled, making the most of the saltless saltines Sunny had added to the table, and drinking a couple of glasses of seltzer. To be honest, Sunny didn't do too much better.

She kept checking for Shadow, looking toward the entrance to the kitchen, down the hallway and the foot of the stairs, even out the screen door, which she began to suspect Shadow had learned somehow to manipulate. If so, he'd be in trouble now. They'd shut the storm door to keep the air-conditioning in. Finally, Sunny tried the ultimate Shadow lure, getting up and rattling some cans of cat food together. But the cat declined to appear.

"Do we want to save this?" Mike's words jangled through her distracted thoughts. She turned to find him frowning at their plates, still generously piled with the salad. Obviously his traditionally thrifty Maine upbringing was at war with the world of unknown food.

"We'll put it in one of the bowls with the lids that seal tightly," Sunny said. "Hopefully, it will keep till tomorrow. I guess we should also make a list and do some shopping." She grinned at her dad. "In case it doesn't keep."

They did the dishes, and Mike got a pencil and paper, heading to peruse the refrigerator and make a shopping list. Sunny trudged upstairs, the air feeling warmer with every step. *I really ought to get my suit brushed and hung up*, she thought, stepping into her room. Then she froze at the foot of the bed.

Shadow lay sprawled facedown across her suit jacket and pants, all four legs spread wide, his eyes shut, his whole body inflating with deep inhalations.

"What are you *doing*?" Sunny demanded, trying to yank the clothes from under him. "I'll end up with three times as much cat fur—"

She broke off with a cry of pain as Shadow leaped up, hissing and lashing out with his claws.

Sunny stared at the three furrows torn through the skin on the back of her hand, at the dark red blood welling up, a drop falling down on the dusky blue suit below.

Belatedly, she brought the wounded hand up to her mouth and then ran for the bathroom.

*

Shadow lay in a stupor of pleasure, breathing in the two most wondrous scents in the world. Every time he filled his lungs, he tasted the fragrance of Sunny . . . and also the aroma of the mysterious She that permeated the soft cloth. He exhaled and drew the scents in again until he thought his lungs might explode.

It was bliss. He didn't know how long he'd lain here, luxuriating, indulging his nose. He'd been fast asleep, lying in the shadowy coolness under Sunny's bed when she first returned home earlier, and he'd slowly awakened when she came into the room and moved around for a bit. By the time he emerged, she was gone, but on the bed he'd discovered this wonderful source of aromas that made his senses swim. He was vaguely aware that he was hungry, but what was hunger compared with the chance to wallow in these sensations?

Oh, he'd encountered the herb that drove other cats crazy, the sharp-smelling stuff put inside toys that caused cats to meow, or run around chasing invisible prey, or roll and sniff.

But this was different.

Maybe the closest sensation to what he presently enjoyed would be the times a cat would lie, belly exposed, gazing foolishly up at the ceiling.

But he wanted to warm this soft cloth, make the scents within the fibers rise to fill his nose and mouth, to cling to it and keep it forever . . .

And then, the jarring shout, the sensation of this wonderful cloth being jerked out from under him, it had shattered his nerves like an unprovoked attack. And when he was attacked, he responded in kind. He hissed, lashed out with his claws. Yes! They struck and tore. That would teach the interloper!

But now he came out of his daze, his overpowered olfactory senses bringing information to his brain.

The One who had interrupted his bliss, the One he'd attacked . . . it was Sunny! And worse, he could smell blood, her blood! How could he have done this?

Shadow stood rooted on the bed, his spirit falling into desolation as Sunny recoiled from him, blood on her paw. She brought it to her mouth to lick, then turned and ran away. The cloth that had entranced him lay wadded and disregarded at his feet. The stink of blood overcame the alluring scents that clouded his senses.

Leaping to the floor, he raced to the doorway and stood staring out into the hallway. The door to the room of tiles was closed, and Shadow could hear the sounds of rushing water.

He couldn't get to Sunny, and even if he were able to, what could he do? Lick away her hurt? By now he'd known her long enough—well enough—to remember that she hadn't liked it when he tried to help with other hurts. And those weren't his fault! This time . . .

Shadow crouched till his head was barely above the floor, a low moan coming up from inside him as painful as when he retched up bad food. He'd seen cats lose homes for scratches like that.

How could this have happened? Didn't Sunny realize the torment she put him through, bringing those strange, disturbing . . . intoxicating scents home with her?

Couldn't she smell?

*

When Sunny returned to her bedroom, Shadow had disappeared again. She spread the suit jacket on the bed and got the handy-dandy lint remover that Mike had ordered from the ad on TV. After a couple of runs over the bloody area, the plastic roller was covered in cat fur. Sunny ran it under water, dried it, and went to work again. When the fur was gone from the area, she took the jacket into the bathroom.

"At least it's permanent press," she muttered as she started the cold water. Rummaging in the medicine cabinet, she found the old shaker of salt that had sat in there lord knew how many years, to use for gargling with salt water to treat a sore throat.

Sunny wet the area around the stain, then sprinkled salt on the spots and began rubbing them together. She kept at it until she couldn't see the stain anymore.

It would have been a lot easier if she could have used both hands. But she had to be careful with her right, the one where Shadow had drawn blood. Sunny had carefully washed the gashes, spread on antiseptic ointment, and then covered them with gauze and some tape. They felt okay, but she had to be careful not to soak the pad in the water and start all over.

At last she held up the jacket, peering at the damp fabric for the stain. "Gone, I hope." Sunny went back to get the pants and then brought them both to the basement for a gentle cycle through the washing machine.

"Decided to give these a wash," Sunny told her dad, popping her head into the living room. "With this sticky weather, they need it." Which was true, even if it wasn't the full story.

She saw him looking at her bandage. "Little accident upstairs." No sense giving Mike something else to complain about when it came to Shadow. She stayed downstairs while the suit was in the washer, and when she took the jacket out, the stain seemed completely gone. After running the suit through the dryer, Sunny breathed a sigh of relief. She couldn't spot the spot at all. Putting jacket and pants on a plastic hanger, she started climbing the stairs from the basement. About halfway up, she realized a pair of eyes were watching her from the doorway to the kitchen.

"Shadow?" She almost whispered his name. He gave a brief, very quiet mew.

When she got up to the kitchen, he backed away from her, keeping his eyes on her face, almost as if he were afraid. "Oh, Shadow," she said, "what happened?"

She hung the suit on one of the knobs for the kitchen

cabinet. Shadow didn't even glance at it. He only had eyes for her. The only thing dimming the moment was that his stomach suddenly rumbled.

"That's right, you haven't eaten." Sunny replenished his water bowl and got a can of cat food. He watched her make the preparations but still wouldn't come close.

"I hope I won't regret this," Sunny muttered, kneeling down beside the bowl and scooping up a bit of wet food on her left forefinger. Then she leaned toward him, extending the finger. Step by slow step he approached and delicately licked her finger clean.

"Now go eat the rest," she told him gently, retreating to one of the kitchen chairs.

It was a slow process—Shadow spent more time glancing at her than he did concentrating on his food. But when he was finished, he got up and followed her out to the living room.

Mike was watching a mystery show, and Sunny settled on the floor, leaning back against a chair. They chatted for a little while, and Sunny asked if he would enlist Mrs. Martinson's aid in getting the skinny on Alfred Scatterwell.

"I don't see why not," Mike said. "Helena may not have liked Gardner, but Alfred is a whole other kettle of fish to stick a spoon into."

Right then, Shadow appeared beside her left thigh, pressing his furry body as close to it as he could.

Are you trying to say that you're sorry, or are you just huddling for warmth? As usual, Sunny's wisecracking side had to have the last word—even if no one knew it but her.

But she gently reached down and petted her cat all the same.

*

The next morning, Sunny woke to find Shadow plastered against her under the covers—although that might have been due to the fact that she had her air-conditioning unit on. She gave Shadow a careful hug, then got up and went to the bathroom. Peeling off the gauze, she flexed her hand and frowned. It hurt a little, but the real problem was that she didn't want anyone to know that Shadow had scratched her, and the healing slash marks were too easily identified.

Guess I'm going to be wearing gauze for a while. Sunny could only shrug.

She took a shower, put on a new bandage, and got dressed in lighter-weight clothes this time around.

When she got downstairs, she found a note from her dad, saying he'd set off for outlet-land to do his walk in air-conditioned comfort. He also warned her to take an umbrella, since the weather was supposed to break late in the afternoon, but there was a chance of showers. Sunny went to the phone, called Bridgewater Hall, and asked for Elsa Hogue. The occupational therapist said she'd be busy with clients, but agreed to meet with Sunny a little later in the morning.

Sunny had almost finished breakfast by the time Shadow came creeping in, the picture of subdued contrition.

"There you are." Sunny had already cleaned and refilled his water bowl. Now she put some dry food in the other one. She knelt down to arrange the bowls, and Shadow came closer, his gold-flecked eyes seeming larger than usual as he gazed up at her.

"I can see you feel badly over what happened." He made a little noise of distress and nudged her hurt hand. "What got into you?"

He licked her fingertips, something he'd never tried to do before.

"Okay, okay." She scratched his head between his ears. "You're forgiven. Just don't start this humble act with Dad. He'll think you're sick and start pestering me to take you to Jane Rigsdale for a checkup."

*

Sunny drove up to Bridgewater Hall after the morning rush, which allowed her to avoid all traffic. With the windows down, the forced breeze kept the heavy, sultry air from feeling too horrible.

She signed in at the security desk and walked down to the rehab wing, arriving early for the appointment she'd made with Elsa Hogue.

And who was Elsa working with but Ollie Barnstable, urging him on with some good-natured banter as he complained about the number of reps he had to do, lifting a weighted bar. "Oh, we always ask you to do more than you want to do," Elsa told him with a smile, "but never more than you *can* do."

Ollie didn't notice that Sunny was there until he finished his session. When he did, his face tightened, his eyes going from Sunny to Elsa.

Yeah, you didn't have any trouble with us going after

Alfred, or Mr. Orton, or Dr. Reese, Sunny thought. *But investigating means bothering people you like, too—like Luke Daconto . . . or Elsa.*

Sunny patted him on the shoulder. "You're doing wonderfully," she told him. "I'll be in to see you after I speak with Elsa." Lowering her voice, she whispered in his ear, "I'll be gentle."

Then, to Elsa, she said, "Is there somewhere private where we can talk?"

They wound up outside in the garden. As they passed through the door, Sunny saw a notice warning residents about going out in extremely hot weather.

"I think we'll live," Elsa said, following Sunny's gaze. Sunny could tell that since Gardner Scatterwell was no longer on the scene, the woman had changed. She'd let her hair down, falling softly around her face, and though she still wore her glasses, Sunny detected traces of makeup. And instead of the sloppy sweats Sunny had seen her in on the first day, today Elsa wore what looked like a tailored safari suit, the arms of her jacket rolled up to reveal well-toned arms.

"Is there something you need to tell me about Mr. Barnstable?" Elsa's expression grew sympathetic. "You see a lot of men like him in rehab. They feel their body has betrayed them. They hurt. They're scared. That's pretty much standard. Usually it's just a question of volume."

"He gets loud when he's frustrated," Sunny admitted.

"But he's settling in now," Elsa said. "He's working hard, and if he keeps it up, he may find himself better off than before."

Sunny thought of her own dad, taking regular exercise,

eating more healthily—even if she had to argue with him about it. *Wait a minute, we're getting off the track.*

She shook her head. "I have to ask you some questions about Gardner Scatterwell. Oliver and several other people here at Bridgewater Hall have asked me to look into the circumstances of Mr. Scatterwell's death."

Elsa's expression became haunted. "All I can tell you is that Gardner Scatterwell was a vile sort of person. He began acting inappropriately almost as soon as I began working with him."

"He had a reputation as a ladies' man when he was younger," Sunny offered. "I'm told he fell violently in love about every six weeks."

"'Violently,'" Elsa echoed in a bitter voice. "And it went on for more than six weeks. But then I suppose the pickings were slim around here." She seemed to shrink in on herself. "He used to touch me when he thought he could get away with it."

She looked Sunny in the eye. "Maybe I do the man wrong. He seemed cheerful and charming with everyone else. Strokes sometimes have psychological effects. If so, I took the brunt of a very nasty split personality." From the look on Elsa's face, she didn't really believe that possibility. "Or maybe it's a family trait. Alfred Scatterwell always claimed he was a very different man from his uncle, but he had the same cruel streak . . . or self-absorption to the point where it amounted to the same thing."

Sunny wondered what had prompted Elsa's low opinion, but after her few encounters with the younger Scatterwell, she couldn't imagine Alfred improving with longer acquaintance. She decided to keep the conversation focused on Bridgewater Hall.

"But Gardner was your real problem. And you couldn't do anything . . ." Sunny prompted.

"Because of his friendship with Dr. Reese. That's why I was working late, getting my reports in order. I needed to maintain a good level of performance, because I've been looking for another job."

I didn't expect that, Sunny thought. *But I guess it's the only option Elsa had.* Out loud, she said, "It must be difficult, leaving a facility with such a strong reputation."

"Not really," Elsa shook her head. "Several therapists have left already. We're all independent contractors, you know."

"No, actually, I didn't know that. You aren't in the union?"

"Sometimes I wish we were," Elsa said. "It might give us a little more bargaining power. As it is, we find ourselves working longer hours for less pay and fewer benefits. As do a lot of people these days. I guess that's why Dr. Reese feels so free to press us—so far he's pushed one person into retirement, and two others to new facilities."

"And you were ready to vote with your feet, too," Sunny said.

"I like this place, my colleagues, and most of my clients, but it's not enough."

I guess I can see why, Sunny thought.

"To go back to the evening in question, did you see anything unusual?" she asked.

Elsa shrugged. "I was working in our office. We're sort

of in our own little world, between the clients' rooms and our facilities."

"You were here after lights-out for the patients."

The therapist nodded. "But I didn't see . . . Oh, wait. I went to the nurses' station in hopes of getting a cup of coffee or tea, and bumped into Luke Daconto, who was there for the same reason. He's a very sweet young man. The residents love him."

She started to smile, but that faded away. "I'm sure a lot of people thought highly of Gardner Scatterwell, too. So many were shocked and saddened when he died."

Elsa's face was almost blank as she turned to Sunny. "But I was just . . . relieved."

10

"**One more question** I have to ask," Sunny said as she absorbed what Elsa had to say. "I spoke to Luke Daconto as well. He mentioned being warned about Reese and the need for reports. Did that happen with you, too?"

Elsa nodded.

"Where did it come from? The head of therapy?"

She shook her head. "We don't report to the same person—different kinds of therapy. I got the word from Rafe Warner. Guess the union has a mole in the administrative offices. The word went out that there was going to be a crackdown on overdue reports, so I made sure that everything I did was up to date."

That sounded like the Rafe Warner whom Sunny knew. He rescued kittens; no doubt he'd warn people who stood to catch grief from the administrator, even if they weren't in the union. It even made tactical sense—worker solidarity against Dr. Reese and so forth.

Elsa glanced at her wristwatch, and Sunny took the hint. "Thanks for talking to me. I know those memories can't have been pleasant."

"It's okay now," Elsa said. "Mr. Scatterwell can't do anything else to me."

They got off the bench they'd been sitting on and went back into the building, which was cooler. But after the heat and humidity, Sunny felt as if her hair had frizzed to about three times its normal size. That was annoying enough, but the tape holding the gauze pad over Shadow's scratches was beginning to come loose. She used her left hand to hold it in place as she made her way to Ollie's room, where she found Ollie had a new roommate, a pale-faced older man with crew-cut white hair. He lay very still in his bed, his breathing shallow and his eyes closed. But they opened as soon as Sunny came inside.

"Sunny Coolidge," Ollie said with excessive courtesy, "meet Charlie Vernon. He's having some breathing as well as walking issues."

"You're not going to talk too loudly, are you?" Vernon had an odd voice, hoarse yet breathy. "If I can just lie and take it easy, I'll be all right. I need to sleep."

Sunny and her boss exchanged glances. She knew Ollie wanted to talk, but that didn't seem likely with Vernon there. She leaned over Ollie's bed. "What do you say you get back in your wheelchair, and I take you for a spin?"

"Good idea," he replied, reaching for the call buzzer. Camille appeared to help Ollie into his chair while Vernon pleaded that she do it with less noise.

The girl rolled her eyes. "I'm trying to be as quiet as possible," she told him.

"I just want to rest," Vernon whined. "It was a tiring trip from the hospital."

As soon as she had Ollie settled, Camille left and Sunny rolled along right after her. *Hope these wheels are quiet enough for Charlie-boy.*

Out in the corridor, Sunny asked Ollie, "Any particular direction you want to go?"

"Just get me as far from that moaner as possible," Ollie directed. "They moved him in while my back was turned. Came in from therapy to find him lying there. The first thing he asked me was if I played the TV too loud. Honest to God, Sunny, I have to wonder if they stuck him in with me as a punishment—or maybe to drive me crazy."

"I'm sure they're just trying to fill the beds, not advancing some master plan by Dr. Reese." She soothed him with a laugh, but Ollie was in a fussy mood.

He turned his pique on her. "Did you *have* to go questioning Elsa?"

"In a word, yes," Sunny told him. "And I think she was glad to have someone to talk to, in a way. If you ask me, sounds like good old Gardner was a letch with a lot to answer for."

But Ollie wouldn't let it go. "That's what I mean," he said. "She's been through enough. I think she deserved a break."

"You can't go exempting people from an investigation just because you like them or feel sorry for them, Ollie. Especially when we still have so little to go on. We have to concentrate on the people parts of the case—motive and opportunity—because we don't have a clue when it comes to means."

"I'll give you means." Ollie nodded toward a rattling sound coming around the bend from the nurses' station. A moment later, a nurse appeared, pushing a cart that looked like a miniature pharmacy on wheels.

"That's everybody's meds," he told Sunny in a stage whisper. "Probably enough stuff there to kill a dozen people."

The nurse gave Ollie a pleasant smile. "Hang on, Mr. Barnstable. I have some things here for you."

"They've got these horse-pill calcium tablets," Ollie grumbled to Sunny. "Wouldn't be surprised if ten percent of the death rate around here is from people choking on the damn things."

Each patient seemed to have an inches-thick binder containing page-sized blister packs of pills, rows of plastic bubbles containing single doses backed with cardboard. The nurse consulted a list, popped the appropriate pills out of their bubbles, and presented them to Ollie.

"Blood pressure pill and your calcium tablets," she announced.

Ollie grudgingly took a small blue pill and two amazingly large ones, along with the plastic cup that the nurse filled with water. He managed to choke down the big pills but told the nurse, "You should be giving people their calcium in ice cream sodas."

The young woman laughed. "There's a thought. But I don't think it works that way."

Now that Ollie had taken his medicine like a man, he was free to go wherever he wanted. But when Sunny turned to go down the hallway ending in the therapy room, her

boss nixed the idea. "Not down there," he said. "I'm beginning to think about that place like the line from the old
movie." He did a passable Bela Lugosi impersonation,
intoning, "'His is the house of pain.'"

Sunny noticed, though, that Ollie waved to Elsa Hogue
when she briefly stepped into that hallway, and Elsa waved
back.

Swinging farther around the nurses' station, Sunny
instead rolled Ollie down the hall to the solarium at the
end of the residential ward on this floor. The various rooms
were quiet, and Sunny caught glimpses of carefully made
beds or a knot of older women watching something on TV.
One of the residents sat in a wheelchair, reading a book
by the light from her window. She looked familiar, and
Sunny realized she was the lady who beat time to Luke
Daconto's music.

She also noted the paintings on the wall, some apparently done by talented amateurs.

Maybe there's a painting therapy guy, too, Sunny
thought. *And maybe a needlepoint therapist,* as they
passed some framed samples of that craft. Just as she was
wondering if she'd end up in a place like this someday, the
murmuring calm was shattered by a strident voice crying,
"I've had enough of this crap!"

"Yep, sounds just like me, say, fifty years from now,"
Sunny murmured.

Ollie glanced up at her. "What?"

"Doesn't matter," she told him. "Just a passing thought."

Sunny wheeled Ollie away and back toward the nurses'
station.

"Have you made it to the front parlor?" she asked him.

"I got a glimpse of it while they were wheeling me in on a stretcher," Ollie told her. "That's about it."

"I haven't really examined it myself," Sunny admitted, her steps taking them down the long hall that led to the front entrance. The sound of muffled bells came through the paneled wall stretching to their right. "I guess the auditorium or activity room or whatever they call it must be on the other side," Sunny said. "Sounds as if Luke is rehearsing his bell ringers today."

"Thank goodness you're not trying to drag me into that!" Ollie gave a relieved sigh.

At last they reached the parlor, where some of the residents sat with guests, enjoying a visit. Sunny noticed that there was plenty of space around the spindly chairs and overstuffed couches to accommodate walkers and wheelchairs.

It was certainly decorated in eclectic (or more likely, donated) style. They passed a fine-looking grandfather clock in a dark walnut case, *tock*ing along in stately grandeur—and running about fifteen minutes behind. Several aquariums dotted the side walls, with rainbows of tropical fish swimming around. The far wall had an enormous, medieval-style fireplace with a make-believe fire dwarfed in the space. Ribbons of red, yellow, and orange cloth danced in a forced stream of air from a fan, their fluttering giving the impression of flames. On the mantel stood several very nice-looking figurines, and above them on the wall hung a slightly mangy hunting trophy.

Sunny peered up at it, trying to identify the species. Something African probably. Antelope? Hartebeest? Okapi?

The taxidermy specimen stared down with an accusatory look in its glass eyes.

"Let's go," Ollie muttered. "That creepy thing is giving me the same look as the stupid deer that put me here."

Sunny started moving again, taking the turn in the corner slowly to avoid an unoccupied armchair—or so she thought.

But a head popped over the side, masked in ginger and black fur.

Sunny stopped. "Hello, Portia."

The cat took advantage of the pause to transfer herself from the chair to Ollie's lap. He sat frozen in the wheelchair, his hands gripping the armrests. "Ah, jeeze."

"Take it easy," Sunny advised. "Portia is a friendly cat. You remember how she sat with Gardner."

"Yeah," Ollie muttered, "right before he went off to the big battle of the bands in the sky."

Actually, Portia showed herself to be a pretty smart cat, resting her weight on Ollie's unhurt leg. Maybe she smelled the surgical wounds on the broken one.

Ollie sat very still, looking down dubiously at the cat in his lap. Portia tipped her head back, staring soulfully at him with her emerald eyes.

Trust a cat to climb all over the person who's not very sure with them, Sunny thought.

"She wants you to pet her," she told Ollie. "That's her and her brother's job here, to visit with the residents and let themselves be stroked."

"Don't say 'stroke' to an old person," Ollie joked. "What do I do?"

"Bring a hand up, don't stick your fingers out, let her sniff the back. When she's comfortable with you, she'll probably make the first move."

Ollie extended his hand hesitantly. Portia sniffed it, examined it, and then stretched her head forward.

"Just pat her gently."

Ollie followed her instructions, barely touching Portia's head. "The fur's so soft," he said in almost a whisper.

Portia evidently thought his petting was nice, but she wanted something a bit more vigorous. She thrust her head against Ollie's palm, and he quickly pulled his hand away.

"She liked what you were doing," Sunny explained, reaching around the side of the wheelchair. "But she wants some of this." She began to scratch Portia between the ears.

Ollie, though, stared at her hand, not at her technique. "What happened there? Did your cat do that?"

A bit belatedly, Sunny realized that her gauze pad must have fallen off somewhere along the way while she was wheeling Ollie around.

"It was an accident," she told him.

He sat looking warily down at the cat. "And this is an accident waiting to happen. Can you get her off me?"

Portia wasn't eager to leave Ollie's well-padded lap. It took Sunny's best cat-handling techniques to lure her away, and even they might not have worked if Portia hadn't been eager to get a good sniff of her.

Good luck with that, Sunny silently told the cat. *Shadow stayed away from me after I took my shower.*

In the end, Portia wound up back in her armchair, looking rather disgruntled.

Ollie wasn't too happy, either. He sat stiffly in his wheelchair, a faint look of pain on his face. Discussion time was over. All he wanted was to get back to his room and stretch out on his bed.

Sunny steered him back to the rehab ward. Just before they reached Room 114, they encountered Camille.

"Do you think you can help get Mr. Barnstable into bed—quietly, so we won't upset Mr. Vernon?" Sunny asked.

Camille took on the challenge, setting Ollie safely back in bed. Sunny whispered her good-byes and left with the aide.

"He'll be able to catch a nap until suppertime," Camille said. "Then maybe he won't be so tired."

"Um . . ." Sunny showed the girl her scratched hand. "Do you think I could get a bandage to cover these?"

"Those aren't from one of our cats, are they?" Camille asked, shocked.

"No, no, I got it at home," Sunny assured her. "I had a gauze pad on, but I lost it."

"Let me go and talk to the nurses," Camille said.

Sunny watched from a distance as the aide walked up to the nurses' station and started talking to one of the nurses on duty.

"Hey," a voice said in Sunny's ear. She turned to find Luke Daconto standing beside her, grinning. "I was just going over to see how Mr. Barnstable is doing."

"By now, he's probably asleep," Sunny told him. "He had a difficult day today, since Portia the cat forced her attentions on him."

"Oh, yeah," Luke said. "It's hard to escape when you're in a wheelchair."

Sunny nodded. "Especially when the cat is in the chair with you."

He laughed. "Maybe it's mean to say, but I'd have loved to see that."

"Yeah, when he was trying to pet her . . ." Sunny tried to duplicate his awkward attempt. Luke caught her hand. "What happened here? Looks as though you had a run-in with a feline fiend yourself."

"My own cat got a little too frisky, I'm afraid." Sunny pulled her hand back. "Frankly, I blame Portia. My guy was zoning out on her scent."

"As you say, that can make male cats a little frisky. We used to have a lot of them running around the house when I was growing up." Suddenly Luke knelt to open his guitar case. "Yeah, I thought I had a little bottle in here."

"Little bottle" was a perfect description. He held up one of those miniature booze bottles usually found in minibars or on airplanes. With this one, however, the label was long gone, as was the booze. Now the bottle held a thick, yellowish, viscous . . . something.

"Mom's all-purpose lotion," Luke explained. "I keep a bottle of this stuff and an emery board around to deal with torn calluses."

He held out his hand. The fingertips he used on the fretboard of his guitar were all heavily calloused. "Screws up my chords and hurts like crazy, when one of these suckers tears free. So I use Mom's lotion. She taught me how to make it over our stove. For a long time, she had a thing for guitarists, so she was very popular." Luke laughed. "Mom used to call herself the 'hippy-dippy chippie.' We lived in a commune in California. She was the local healer, making all sorts of potions and lotions. When she passed away, she left me all her secret recipes."

Sunny looked dubiously at the contents of the bottle. "What's the secret recipe for that?"

"Ham fat and herbs," Luke promptly replied, and then scratched his head. "Or was that her secret recipe for scrambled eggs?" Sunny laughed, and Luke smiled at her.

"Just put a little on your finger and rub it on the end of one of those scratches," he said. "It kills any germs and takes the pain away."

Sunny took the bottle, unscrewed the top, and let a tiny driblet of the yellowish stuff fall on her left forefinger. Then she gingerly dabbed it on one of Shadow's scratches.

"Wow!" she said. Almost immediately, the ache was gone, and her skin felt cool and comfortable.

"Amazing, isn't it?" Luke said.

"Can I use a little more?" Sunny asked.

Luke waved. "Keep the bottle. I've got plenty more at home. Put a bandage over those scratches for now. But when you get home, when you go to bed, just cover them with the lotion. Let them breathe."

Sunny took a little more of the yellow stuff, put it over the other scratches, and flexed her hand. The pain was gone. "I don't know how to thank you."

"I can make a suggestion," Luke replied.

She looked at him suspiciously.

"I have a gig tomorrow evening," he said. "And I'd love it if you could come." *Did he mean, like on a date?* Sunny didn't know how to answer.

"And if you could bring other people, that would be wonderful," Luke went on, not even seeming to notice her hesitation. "It wouldn't hurt if the manager thinks I can draw a crowd."

"Well, sure," Sunny said. "Where is it?"

"A bar called O'Dowd's," Luke said.

"O'Dowd's?" she echoed. "Why would you want to play in the worst dive bar in Elmet County?"

"Where were you when I did the deal?" Luke teased. "One bar pretty much looks like another when they're cleaning up the morning after. I stopped by, they agreed to give me a shot, and that was that."

"I'll do what I can, but it's not going to be easy to get people to go down there."

"All I can ask is that you try." Luke snapped his case together and picked it up.

"I have one more thing to ask you," Sunny said, "something that came out of the stuff you talked about with Will yesterday."

"What?" Luke's brown eyes got a little wary.

"You said somebody gave you the heads-up that Reese was going after people for reports. Where did the warning come from?"

Luke looked a little relieved. "Rafe Warner. He's a pretty decent guy."

And a pretty busy one, Sunny added silently. She thanked Luke again for the lotion, and made sure the bottle was tightly capped before putting it in her pocket. He said good-bye and headed off to the front door.

Sunny glanced to the nurses' station, where Camille was beckoning her over, holding up a gauze pad and a roll of tape.

If only a few drops of magic lotion could take care of everything, Sunny wistfully thought as she went to get bandaged.

*

Mike Coolidge almost dropped his remote when Sunny came home, joined him on the couch, and told him about Luke's upcoming gig.

"O'Dowd's?" Sunny's father said in disbelief. "What was the kid thinking?"

"I think he was just happy to find a place where he could play."

Mike frowned. "The crowd down there will eat him alive."

"Maybe not, if some friendly faces turn up," Sunny said hopefully. "Would you mind coming? Maybe you could ask Mrs. Martinson, too."

"Helena? In O'Dowd's?"

Sunny tried to imagine the fastidious Mrs. Martinson in a rowdy joint like O'Dowd's, but the picture just wouldn't come. "All right," she said, shrugging in defeat, "that probably won't work. But you'll show up for Luke, won't you?"

Now it was Mike's turn to shrug. "I wouldn't mind hearing him do something besides 'You Are My Sunshine.' Just remember, I'm not as good at barroom brawls as I used to be."

"Thanks, Dad." Sunny got up and went to the kitchen, where she found Shadow back in his usual spot on top of the refrigerator. She went up on tiptoe and he leaned down 'til they were nose to nose. She heard him sniff and his eyes widened, but he stayed where he was.

Sunny zipped up the stairs for a quick shower. *That should remove any temptation,* she thought. But just to be sure, she unloaded her pockets and sent her T-shirt and pants down the chute to the laundry. Then, in a fresh shirt and shorts, she went downstairs to see what Mike had gotten off the shopping list.

After checking the fridge, she stuck her head around the entryway to the living room. "I see you got some tomatoes and cold cuts. We still have romaine. How does salad and a sandwich sound?"

Mike thought that sounded pretty good, so Sunny went to the kitchen and got to work. While she was slicing the tomatoes, she looked down at her scratched hand. Luke's lotion had washed off in the shower, and she was getting prickles of pain again. When she finished her preparations, she went back upstairs, applied a little more of the viscous yellow stuff, and taped a new gauze pad over it. She descended the staircase and stepped into the living room again. "Dinner's ready."

Mike got the glasses and poured seltzer for both of them—raspberry flavored this time. Meanwhile, Sunny set out a meal for Shadow.

As they ate, Sunny and her dad made small talk about the events of the day. "I've been hiding in the air-conditioning all day," Mike complained. "Even when I went out this morning to the mall, it was sticky."

"Sticky or stinky?" Sunny said. "Didn't you say it was supposed to break this afternoon? I left the umbrella in the Wrangler—"

Even as she spoke, a thunderclap detonated over the house like a small bomb. The whole place shook, and Shadow abandoned his supper and dashed over to Sunny's feet. But he wasn't cowering. His head and tail were both up, one scanning the area for trouble to be dealt with, the other lashing around in agitation.

"It's okay." Sunny leaned down and petted his bristling fur. "Nothing to get upset about. It's only thunder."

"Yeah," Mike said. "I'm told that it's lightning you have to watch out for."

The sound and light show lasted only about twenty minutes, but the heavy rain that followed stayed on. Sunny and her dad finished their meals and the dishes. While he went back to the living room to see if the storm had done anything to their cable service, Sunny stayed in the kitchen by the phone, trying to think of anyone else she could call to go to Luke's show tomorrow evening.

This is when you realize how much your life has shrunk, she realized. Most of her friends from the old days had, like her, left Kittery Harbor and gone off into the wide world. The ones who remained were all married and didn't have that much in common with her anymore. Finally she punched in the number for her old high school classmate, current vet Jane Rigsdale, who thought a guitarist in O'Dowd's sounded like a hoot. "The problem is, Tobe's got tickets for an outdoor concert in Portsmouth tomorrow night—that is, if the Piscataqua doesn't break its banks and sweep everything away."

Desperate to boost the friendly audience count, Sunny went into the living room. "I tried asking Jane to O'Dowd's, but she has a date for tomorrow. Do you think any of your friends might want to come?"

"I don't think Zach Judson's been in that dump since he was your age," Mike said. "And Ken Howell swore years ago never to mention O'Dowd's in the *Courier*. Every time he'd mention a fight or a drug bust there, it only advertised the place to other lowlives. So he stays away. If he actually saw something there, he'd feel he'd have to write about it."

He gave her a sly smile. "I did talk to one person while you were off phumphing around in the kitchen, and he agreed to come."

"Really? Who?" Sunny asked.

"Will Price." Mike raised his hands to cut her off. "Before you start in, he didn't mention that *you'd* called him. Besides, he'd be a good man to have at our table."

Sunny gave him an unwilling nod. Quite a number of the creepy types in O'Dowd's knew that Will was a cop. If he showed up out of uniform, they'd probably behave themselves, thinking he was there undercover. "I was, um, waiting," she said, realizing how lame that sounded.

"You mean you weren't going to call him because you didn't want Will to know you were going to see another fellow—even if you were only watching him make music." Mike sighed, looking more dadlike than he usually did. "Maybe you don't talk much about it, but I know it bothers you that Will hasn't been a bit more serious."

"I haven't asked for anything more." Sunny winced at the defensive tone that crept into her voice. "I'm just glad there's someone around to go out with every once in a while."

Mike nodded. "Look at it this way. He agreed to go out with you when you're going to watch this new guy in town play guitar. That's got to mean something."

"Right," Sunny said. "Because all us girls just *love* a guitarist."

She decided it was time to find a new conversation topic. "Have you heard anything about Alfred Scatterwell?"

"I asked among my friends," Mike replied. "Seems he's not very political . . . not much of anything really. All he seems to do is sit in his house, counting his money and waiting to inherit the rest. Helena suggested you stop over tomorrow morning. She might have something more for you."

"Okay, thanks." Sunny sat and watched the news with her dad, at least until the weather report.

"Looks like that storm cleared the air." Mike tuned off the air conditioner and opened the window. They heard the sound of a breeze, but no rain.

"Good," Sunny said. She watched a little more TV with her dad, then excused herself to go upstairs and call Will.

"So," he said when he answered, "I understand we're going to watch Luke Daconto perform. That seems awfully chummy, considering he's a possible suspect."

"You never know, he might decide to confess onstage as an encore," Sunny responded, thinking, *Thanks a lot, Dad.*

"Speaking of which, how was your day of interviews? Did you learn anything from Elsa Hogue?"

"Well, she doesn't like Alfred Scatterwell," Sunny said.

"You don't have to like someone to take their money."

"But would you trust them if you thought they had a cruel streak?" Sunny asked. "That's how Elsa described him. Either cruel or very self-absorbed."

Will made a noncommittal noise over the phone. "Anything else?"

"She got a warning about Reese and his demands for paperwork, just like Luke. And, in fact, it came from the same person. Even though the therapists are independent contractors, the union warned them—specifically, Rafe Warner."

"What do you think?" Will asked. "Workers of the world, unite?"

Sunny hesitated for a moment. "There's something I didn't check with Luke. According to Elsa, she went to the nurses' station to bum some caffeine and found Luke there doing the same thing."

"That puts them both pretty close to the ever-popular Room 114." Will's voice got quiet. "But only Elsa Hogue admitted it."

"How about you? Did those lists that Rafe gave you lead to anything?"

"Only to getting my friends pretty ticked off at me," Will admitted. "It was a lot of stuff for them to be checking out. They could have gotten caught."

He sighed. "No one seems to have a criminal record, and they haven't been buying any new cars or boats."

"Huh?" Sunny said, then, "Oh. Spending their ill-gotten gains."

"Right. However, my friend in Boston did find a car service that had a Maine run. The driver was supposed to pick up a passenger on a flight from Hartsdale Airport down in Atlanta, arriving around half-past twelve. But the flight was delayed by almost an hour and a half."

"Factor in another hour and change for the trip up to Bridgewater, given the traffic . . . that would tie in with Gavrik's arrival."

"That's the good news," Will said. "Unfortunately, it also gives the doctor an alibi, assuming Ollie's right about the killer being in the room with Scatterwell. Gavrik would have been on the plane."

"I still wouldn't mind asking her what she was doing out of town," Sunny said. "Or even better, you can ask. Something's going on there."

They agreed to tackle Gavrik the next day—and to have another chat with Rafe about the good doctor.

"Then after Daconto is flushed with success from his O'Dowd's debut, we can ask him about his bad memory on the night that Scatterwell died." Will laughed.

"You don't have to sound so happy about it," Sunny snapped.

"Sorry, I didn't mean it to sound that way," Will apologized. "All I want is for something to let us get a fingernail into this case."

They chatted a moment more, then Sunny said goodbye, hung up the phone, and went back downstairs.

"I think I'm going to hit the hay," she told her dad.

She climbed the stairs, glancing back to find Shadow at her heels. "No AC tonight," she told him. "I really hope we're back to normal." Sunny opened the window, closed the blinds, and changed into shortie pajamas. As she was taking off her watch, she saw the gauze pad.

"Let's give it a try," she muttered, going through the stuff from her pockets. There was the miniature bottle. She undid the top and poured a small dollop onto the scratches.

"Well, it feels better." She peered at the scratches, holding her hand under the bedside light. Was it her imagination, or did they not look so pink? She could only hope so.

But she wasn't the only one who wanted to inspect the

wounds. Shadow successfully dodged the left hand trying to keep him away, bringing his nose to her right. He made a sad noise at the sight of the scratches, sniffed at them three times, then pulled back and sneezed with a vigorous shake.

"Whatever it's made with, the stuff is potent." Sunny laughed and hopped into bed. Shadow followed, snuggling under the sheet and a thin blanket.

Soon enough, they were both asleep.

11

The next morning, Sunny sat at the kitchen table, enjoying a cup of coffee, while Mike prepared to head off to the old school and his daily three-mile trek. She'd awakened to find a clear sky outside her window and a cool breeze drifting in. Except for the smell of damp earth, no trace remained of last night's storm—and even better, the heat and humidity of the last two days were gone as well. The weatherman on the radio said as much.

I guess he looked out his window, too, Sunny couldn't help thinking.

"Sure you don't want to come along?" Mike asked.

"I've got calls to make this morning, and then some visits," she told him.

Mike grinned. "And a date tonight."

"Right," Sunny said sarcastically. "Provided we get

through the day." She waved good-bye to her dad as Shadow came into the room, looked around, and finally settled at her feet. When she finished and got up, he moved to a patch of light from the kitchen window while Sunny went upstairs to shower.

As she washed herself, she couldn't help stealing glances at the back of her right hand. It was incredible: instead of pink scratches, a set of silvery lines barely showed up against her skin.

"For a hippy-dippy chippie, Luke's mother sure knew her stuff," Sunny said.

She came out of the bathroom wrapped in a terry cloth robe and went to her room to pick out the outfit of the day. This wasn't easy. She wanted to look nice for her visit with Mrs. Martinson, but tough enough to deal with the temperamental Dr. Gavrik. In the end, Sunny went with flats, a pair of charcoal gray slacks, and an off-white top.

"When I get home, I'll change into something more suitable for O'Dowd's," she muttered. "Something that can stand up to splinters and won't show beer spills."

She'd just finished wrestling with her hair and putting on some makeup when the phone rang. It was Will Price, calling to tell her he'd secured them a lunch appointment with Dr. Gavrik for twelve thirty. "Should I pick you up around noon?"

"Sure, but I'll be over at Mrs. Martinson's house, so pick me up there," Sunny told him. "See you then."

She hung up and went downstairs.

Shadow perked up and ambled over when he saw Sunny leaving some supplies for him. She gently massaged his fur, then washed her hands and was on her way.

It was a pleasure to be outdoors today, now that the soggy, enervating weather had moved on. As she walked the few blocks, Sunny saw a number of people coming out to take care of deferred garden business, like mowing grass. Mike put his own gardening efforts into cultivating the rosebushes Sunny's mom had planted years ago, but tended to neglect the lawn. As she arrived at the Martinson house, Sunny saw that Mrs. M.'s butterfly bushes were in bloom, bringing blue blossoms and a sweet scent to the air.

She rang the doorbell and heard excited barking inside.

When Helena Martinson answered the door, she had one hand on Toby's collar. "Come on inside, dear," Mike's lady friend said. "Is the kitchen all right?"

"It's fine." Sunny stepped carefully as Toby romped around her feet. "No lack of energy in the little guy, is there?"

Helena got Sunny established at a little table right beside the kitchen window and set out two mugs of coffee and, of course, two pieces of her famous coffee cake.

Toby went to his water bowl and began noisily drinking.

"We just got back from emptying him, and here he is, loading up again." The older woman gave Sunny a wry smile. "There are a lot of things about owning a dog that they don't tell you."

"You're not regretting your adoption, are you?" Sunny asked.

"Of course not. You're good company, aren't you, Toby?"

Toby came over to rest his muzzle on Helena's knee—and leave a wet spot on her tan trousers.

Sunny raised a forkful of cake to her mouth and followed it with a sip of coffee. "Delicious, as usual." She looked at Helena expectantly. "So, tell me—what did you find out about Alfred Scatterwell?"

"As you know, I wasn't very fond of Gardner because of what he tried to do to me—in this very kitchen, as a matter of fact." Helena's eyes seemed to skitter around her spotless kitchen. Sunny had never seen her so reluctant to share gossip; she tried to encourage her with a little humor.

"I know Gardner was a bit of a dog," Sunny said. "Dad started to remember that, when the surprise and the initial reunion feeling began to wear off. First he remembered the good times. After all, it was thanks to that band he had with Gardner that Dad met my mother." She laughed. "Of course, the band broke up after Gardner tried to get between my dad and mom, but that only hit Dad later. Speaking of hitting, did I mention that Dad punched Gardner in the nose?"

"Yes," Helena replied, but it seemed as though she wasn't really following what Sunny was saying. Her expression was distant, as if she were resolving something in her mind.

"So what's the problem? Did Alfred turn out to be a dog, too? Like uncle, like nephew?"

"No." Mrs. Martinson looked closely at Sunny. "What did you think of Gardner? How did he treat you?"

"At first, I thought he was funny and charming—a real life of the party. But the longer I stayed around him, the more I saw of his less nice side."

Helena nodded. "But how did he treat you?"

"He was very buddy-buddy," Sunny replied. "Complimentary. He wanted me to push his wheelchair—said it was the only way to get pretty girls around him."

"Only Gardner would try to turn a disability into a

come-on," Mrs. M. said sourly. She looked carefully at Sunny. "But there was nothing else?"

"Helena, come on," Sunny burst out. "The best he could do was pull the nice old man act. I've got to be—what? Half his age?" She stopped for a second, thinking, *And I didn't have to depend on him for a job, like Elsa Hogue. Maybe I was lucky.*

"That hasn't stopped him in the past." Helena looked deeply into her coffee cup. "Most anyone who encounters Gardner hears something about his travels, and I expect you can guess why he had to leave Piney Brook sometimes. But he came back about ten years ago when Alfred was planning to get married. The only problem is, during the engagement party, Alfred stumbled over his fiancée and his uncle— literally." She pursed her lips. "Let's just say that Gardner got a lot farther with that girl than he ever did with me."

"Yikes!" Sunny stared. "What happened?"

"Gardner got out of town, and Alfred got his ring back," Helena responded. "I'm told that they didn't speak for years."

"And yet, when Gardner got sick, Alfred was over at Bridgewater Hall all the time." Sunny spoke slowly. "I thought he was just keeping tabs on his uncle. But maybe he was watching him more like a vulture. No wonder Gardner kept giving him crap about being the all-purpose heir."

"As the only close relative, Alfred was certainly in an interesting position."

"Yeah, really interesting." Sunny scowled. "Alfred had to toe the line pretty carefully if he wanted to be close enough to enjoy watching his uncle going downhill, but not annoy the old man enough to get disinherited."

Claire Donally

That could explain why Alfred turned a blind eye to Gardner's harassment of Elsa, Sunny thought. *He had bigger fish to fry.*

"Will always says the two strongest motives for murder and mayhem are love and money," she said almost to herself. "Alfred has both—disappointed love and the Scatterwell inheritance."

Sunny bit her lip as counterarguments zinged around her brain. *But if Alfred had been waiting on his revenge for almost a decade, why would he suddenly push it? I only knew Gardner for a little while, but it certainly didn't look as though he was improving. Why would Alfred suddenly lose patience? Why couldn't he just wait a little longer?*

Aloud, she said, "Thanks for digging up this dirt, Helena. Knowing Gardner as you did, it must have been distasteful."

"It was interesting," Mrs. M. replied, "if somewhat seedy." She might have been about to say more, but a crash came from the living room. "Toby!" she called, then shot an embarrassed smile at Sunny. "Looks like the start of another adventure in dog owning."

Sunny followed her host into the living room, where Toby lay whining under the coffee table, peering out at the pieces of a broken vase on the floor. Sunny decided it would probably be best for her to wait for Will outside, so she made a quick good-bye and left Helena to deal with the latest disaster.

When Will arrived, Sunny whistled at his outfit. He was all in black—Henley shirt, jeans, and a jean jacket.

"You look as though you should be riding a motorcycle," she told him.

"Good," he replied, "then I should fit in over at O'Dowd's

later." Raising his sunglasses, he took in her outfit. "Which is more than I can say for you, missy."

She made a face. "I'm going to change later. We can't both go to Dr. Gavrik looking like we intend to beat the truth out of her."

"So while I menace the good doctor, I suppose you can appeal to her softer side."

"That'll be like appealing to the softer side of a rock," Sunny muttered as she climbed aboard.

As they started off to the north, Will asked, "So what did you learn about our new best friend Alfred? What are his vices? Women? Money? Sheep?"

"Well, it looks as though he had an experience that put him off women." Sunny passed along the story that Mrs. Martinson told her.

"His uncle and his fiancée? Ouch. That makes for one tangled motive. Or two, if you count the money." He frowned. "This is the problem with going solely on motive. You can pile it up until, on paper, you've got a prime suspect."

"I detect a 'but' in the underbrush," Sunny said.

Will nodded. "*But* your case doesn't hold together when you apply real-world considerations."

"Like why would he wait ten years and then suddenly rush his uncle off the mortal coil?"

"Or if he had those ten years to plan a murder, he wouldn't at least give himself an ironclad alibi."

"For that matter, why would a guy as—well, 'controlling' is as good a word that comes to my mind—put himself in somebody else's power by hiring them to kill Gardner?"

"I can see you've been thinking about this for a bit," Will said.

"Guilty," she admitted. "And there are always answers you can come up with. He's arrogant, he's conceited, he figures that whoever actually committed the murder for him is in too deep to talk about it . . ."

"You left out a favorite from TV detective shows," Will put in. "Maybe he's just crazy." He sighed. "You can explain and explain until you build a Frankenstein's monster of a theory like the one that Ollie Barnstable came up with against Stan Orton. But you're supposed to apply Occam's Razor."

Sunny grinned. "Also known as KISS—'Keep it simple, stupid!' Start from the simplest causes, and keep to the least complex results."

"Can we do that?" Will asked. "We have a nephew who stands to inherit and who hates his uncle for bad behavior. We also have an occupational therapist who hates the old geezer because he's making her life a living hell. So they join forces . . ."

"Except that doesn't jibe with Elsa's take on Alfred," Sunny objected. "She didn't make a big deal out of it, but I'd say she really resented the fact that he didn't try to help her. Somehow, I can't see him coming to her and saying, 'I'm sorry I didn't rat out my uncle for abusing you, but here's a better way. Let's kill him.'"

"Based on opportunity, Elsa Hogue *was* working late at the facility and could have been the one giving something to Gardner—again assuming Ollie didn't dream it," Will offered. "Lord knows, she had motive."

"She called Gardner a vile sort of person," Sunny agreed. "And yet . . . here comes the real world again.

Gardner had to know how she felt about him. Why would he accept anything from her in the middle of the night?"

"Maybe the great lover thought she'd finally come around."

"With the accent on *final*?" Sunny shook her head. "I thought you didn't like what-ifs and maybes."

"I'm trying to float *some* theory of the crime." Will drove in silence for a moment. "All right, based on opportunity, we do have one other outsider near Room 114 that night."

"Luke Daconto." For Sunny, this was a nonstarter. "You've got opportunity all right, but in terms of motive, there's nothing. He was actually friendly with Gardner, and Gardner was a fan of his."

"I could throw Alfred into the mix, offering money for Daconto to do the deed," Will said quickly. "The guy must be having money problems. He's playing at O'Dowd's, for crying out loud."

Sunny told Will about Luke's commune upbringing. "He still makes his mom's skin cream," she finished. "With a hippy-dippy background like that, do you think he'd really be interested in Alfred's money?"

"They say that whatever one generation wants, the next generation wants nothing to do with," Will said. "The hippies rebelled against the suburban American dream. Maybe Daconto is rebelling against his mom and really wants lots of money. Maybe he only makes her lotion or whatever because he's hoping he can sell the formula for a million dollars."

"Brilliant theory, Ollie," she told him.

Will subsided again as he drove along the country roads around Levett. "There's one theory I'm really not happy to bring up. But now that we're out of the folks who'd not normally be around the ward, we've got to look at the regular staff—and that jump in the death statistics at Bridgewater Hall. What if Gardner Scatterwell was just the latest in a series?"

Sunny stared. "You mean a serial killer?"

"An angel of death—that's what the newspeople like to call killers who turn up in health care."

"I think Frank Nesbit is going to love that theory," Sunny told him. "An angel of death, operating right under his nose?"

"It might be a little . . . politically opportune," Will admitted after a brief pause. "But I'm beginning to think it's either that, or Gardner Scatterwell simply died of a stroke."

"How do you figure to prove this?" Sunny wanted to know.

"We'll have to ask Dr. Reese for patient records—and staff attendance for months, maybe years. Then we'll have to see if the same names crop up around the patients who died."

"That's going to be a lot of paperwork," Sunny had to point out. "And we're coming up on our deadline."

"Yeah," Will replied. "Too bad we've got a date tonight." The route they were traveling became a bit more complicated, and conversation halted as Will went into a series of turns, taking them through more built-up areas, then on a more countrified road again, and after about a quarter of a mile, he turned into what looked like a break in a wall of bushes, and they wound up in a parking lot.

"I didn't think that places like this existed anymore,"

Sunny said, taking in the building sprawling in front of them. It had probably started out as a lodge or log cabin but had grown, throwing out extensions. In his youth, Sunny's dad would have called it a roadhouse. But there was no honky-tonk atmosphere inside. The lighting was subdued, the lunch crowd quiet, and the smell of food delicious.

"A couple of deputies from Levett took me here a few times," Will whispered as they walked up to the hostess. "But I never felt comfortable here. Nesbit turned up too often."

They mentioned Dr. Gavrik's name and were quickly led to a booth in a quiet corner where the doctor was already sitting, her back to the wall, tight-lipped as ever, those piercing dark eyes glancing to her watch and then giving them a "time is money" look.

She had a cup of coffee in front of her. "The fried food is very good—to the taste, if not for the health."

Sunny was surprised. That statement was the most human thing she'd heard from the doctor since they'd met her. Will ordered a burger and cola, Sunny a grilled chicken sandwich with lemonade, and the doctor told the waitress, "The usual."

Will looked at her for a long moment after the waitress left, and then casually asked, "What was so important in Atlanta, Doctor?"

Gavrik's gaze went from piercing to glaring for a moment, "Nothing was interesting there. A storm delayed me." She took a sip of her coffee, her hand moving smoothly. "You think you have found something, but you know nothing. However, I will tell you, to keep you from prying into my personal life. I transferred at Hartsfield Airport, from a flight from Greensboro."

"Okay," Will said. "What was so important in Greensboro?"

"A job interview," Gavrik replied. "Something perhaps I should have done long ago. There is a large Serbian population in that area, so perhaps my language—my accent—will be useful instead of a hindrance."

"You want to leave Bridgewater Hall?" Sunny asked, thinking, *Another defector!*

"You ask why I should leave such a wonderful place?" For the briefest of moments, the woman smiled, and she was striking. Then her lips clamped tightly together again. "I came to this country with excellent medical training, but little English. Working at Bridgewater Hall—that was the best I could get. I was at the top of my class in medical school, and I end up catering to a collection of wealthy invalids? It is enough to make the saints laugh."

"Then why did you come to the U.S.?" Will asked.

"My country . . . is no more. In the town where I grew up, my relatives were trying to kill the neighbors, and they were trying to do the same for us. I worked in a glorified butcher shop, patching holes in people so they could go out and fight again. I dreamed of working in a place where explosions would not bring the walls down on me. And so I came to America, the land of shining hospitals and the finest technology . . . and I worked on people who have shortness of breath or pains in the chest." She grimaced. "Or who need enemas."

Their food arrived. Dr. Gavrik's "usual" was apparently a piece of meat in a pale sauce on noodles, but she didn't touch it. "Do you know how it is to be looked down on, the foreign doctor who does the work no one else wants to do, who does it *cheap*? And all the while, you also see money wasted. Keeping animals for old fools to pet, or paying a person to sing with them . . . these are not necessary things. Yet the new administrator tells me how all departments must suffer if the facility is to go on. To me, that seems . . . ungenerous. So I think it is time to go."

"It seems a long trip," Sunny said.

"They told me six hours to return," the doctor said. "I took the late flight in case my meeting ran long. It did."

"You must have been pretty tired," Will said.

Her black eyes snapped, boring into him. "Not really. The delays allowed me to sleep for a while, and I slept on the ride from Boston. Do not suggest that I made some sort of mistake because of fatigue. I followed all the protocols with Mr. Scatterwell. You can confirm that through the nurses who worked with me."

She braced both hands flat on the table, leaning toward them. "Gardner Scatterwell died of a massive stroke. We did our best for him, but sometimes patients die."

"How about the other patients who've died in the facility?" Will wanted to know. "The ones that have thrown your statistics out of whack?"

"I do not have time for this nonsense." One second, the doctor was sitting across from them. The next, she was rapidly moving in the direction of the exit.

"Well," Will said, watching the disappearing doctor. "I have time for this burger."

"Are you sure?" Sunny said dubiously. "She looks ready to raise hell."

Will only shrugged. "Either we'll get what we want, or we won't. There's only one thing that annoys me."

"What?" Sunny asked.

"The doctor stuck us with the bill for her meal."

There was no use wasting their food, too, so Will and Sunny did their best to enjoy their meals. Lunch didn't sit so happily when they arrived at Bridgewater Hall, however. Dr. Reese only confirmed Sunny's apprehensions.

"I just had a meeting with Dr. Gavrik," the administrator said. "She told me that, apparently having failed to find any convincing evidence about Mr. Scatterwell's death, you want to try a desperate fishing expedition through our mortality records." Reese leaned back in his chair, crossing his arms. "I can't allow that. Our initial agreement stipulated that we would offer as much assistance as possible, but we would not jeopardize patient confidentiality. We are legally obligated to keep patient records private, and this request goes beyond that."

"Does that include patient names?" Will inquired.

"Federal regulations prohibit it," Reese said. "But even if it were solely within my discretion, I still wouldn't give you those records."

"Fine," Will said. "I'll explain that to Mr. Barnstable. And then you'll probably get to explain it to him again."

They went straight from the administration offices down to Room 114. Ollie's roommate was out, which was just as well. Ollie wasn't happy to hear about Dr. Reese's attitude. But he was even more upset when he heard why Will wanted the records.

"You think one of the doctors or nurses is euthanizing patients?" Ollie looked as if more than his leg was paining him.

"It's just a theory," Will admitted. "We've taken a pretty good look at the suspects who shouldn't have been in the ward on the night Scatterwell died. They have alibis, but they're not airtight. But what about the people who were supposed to be there—the staff? We can't 'follow the money' to see if someone received some unusual amount without searching through all their bank records—that's a police investigation. And we don't have the leverage to circumvent patient privacy laws to look into medical records and see if there might be something behind those high mortality rates we heard about. Again, it would have to be an official police request."

"And we all know that Sheriff Nesbit isn't about to do that," Sunny said.

"So, unless something amazing happens, you're telling me your investigation is dead in the water."

Ollie's shoulders seemed to shrink.

"Listen, Barnstable, we were supposed to see if there were any circumstances that suggested anything other than a stroke." Will spread his hands. "Natural causes still seem to be the strongest possibility."

After saying good-bye to a subdued Ollie, Sunny and Will headed for the door in silence. Rafe Warner was working the front desk, but must have caught their mood, because he didn't chat either, merely nodding as they signed out.

Conversation continued to languish in Will's truck all the way home. As they turned onto Wild Goose Drive, he asked, "Should I come and pick you up later?"

Sunny gave him a listless shrug. "If you don't mind taking Dad, too."

"Heck of a date," Will muttered. "Will he be riding shotgun or sitting between us?"

Mike surprised Sunny with a roasted chicken, roasted

potatoes, and two kinds of hot vegetables waiting on the table. "Picked it up all ready-made at Judson's Market," he admitted. "Kinda pricey, but I was in the mood to splurge. Besides," he added, patting his stomach, "we're going to need some fortification before we deal with O'Dowd's beer."

Sunny got some cat food for Shadow, and then all three of them started on dinner.

When they'd finished, Sunny went upstairs to dig out her old pair of Doc Martens and her least disgusting housecleaning jeans. A navy blue T-shirt with a couple of paint splatters and a gray hoodie completed the ensemble. *Hardly the way I'd usually dress for a date*, she thought wryly.

She came down to discover that Mike had changed into some old clothes, too. Shadow circled around them, looking a little skittish. Mike began to laugh. "The last time we looked like this was during spring cleaning. He's probably expecting us to start taking the house apart again!"

Dropping to her knees, Sunny coaxed Shadow over and gently stroked him. "No excitement here," she told him. "We're going away for a while." At last, his tail stopped twitching. Will arrived in his pickup, and Sunny and her dad went outside. Mike told Sunny, "You go up first, honey."

She grinned, climbed aboard, and settled next to Will. Then Mike hauled himself aboard, slammed the door shut, and off they went.

O'Dowd's sat in the middle of a little patch of urban blight at the edge of downtown. Some people called it the source of the blight. It was a long, low, wooden building that had begun life as something other than a bar, but not even Mike remembered what it had originally been. The only hint as to its present business was a beer sign in one of the tiny windows. Mike used to joke that people didn't find O'Dowd's, they just sank to its level. As underage college kids, Sunny and her friends had snuck in there for an illicit beer. But Sunny had still been shocked to see how far the bar's never-high standards had fallen when she and Will visited the place to talk with a suspect.

Warmer weather hadn't improved the ambiance. Will drove into a weed-trimmed parking lot. Sunny saw a few pickups, some vans, a couple of cars that could only be called beaters, and of course, motorcycles. Rolling his truck to a stop, Will got out and opened the door for Mike and Sunny. They reached the plywood slab that served as the bar's front door and heaved at it—last night's rain had swollen the wood in place. With a good yank, Will got it open, and they went in.

A yellowish-gray cloud hung in the air. The state of Maine might have banned barroom smoking, but O'Dowd's didn't follow no stinkin' ordinances. Patrons in here continued to blithely light up. The jukebox with its overamped bass still thumped away, while folks at the bar and at the tables did their best to scream over the noise.

Scanning the room, Sunny spotted a few Bridgewater Hall staff members—they must have all owed Luke favors or something, she figured. They sat in little islands, distinct among the regulars. Sunny spotted Elsa Hogue and Jack the physical therapist sitting at one table, Elsa looking very uncomfortable.

"Let's see if we can join them," Sunny yelled to her dad and Will.

"Do you want something to drink?" Will bellowed.

"Beer—in a bottle," Sunny screeched.

"Me, too," Mike bawled out.

Sunny led the way over to the therapists while Will headed for the bar. Elsa and Jack were happy for company. Mike tried to carry on a conversation while Sunny watched Will's progress at the bar. It was like watching a silent movie—if silent movies were scored by Steppenwolf.

As Will got closer and closer to the bar, Jasmine the barmaid showed more and more interest. Jasmine had been the local sex symbol during Sunny's college days. Now she had too much skin pushed into too little clothing, a bad dye job, and a missing tooth. Still, she did a good come-hither routine until Will was close enough for her to recognize him as a cop. Then her face shut down to a sullen mask as she sold him three bottles of beer.

He returned to the table with a wad of napkins, using them to twist the tops off and wipe the mouths of the bottles. Sunny shouted her thanks, accepted one of the bottles, and took a sip. It had been a while, but apparently some things never change. Cold beer after a warm day remained a good combination.

She saw Luke Daconto come around from the back of the bar carrying a microphone stand and a small amplifier, which he set up on the raised dais that housed the jukebox. Then he vanished, only to return again with his guitar case. Most of the bar denizens didn't even pay attention as he tuned up. Luke looked at Jasmine and nodded. She came from behind the bar, reaching around the back of the jukebox to pull the plug. There were some raucous moans and groans while she vainly signaled for silence. Sunny could barely hear her shouting, "Live music tonight!"

After her third fruitless attempt, Jasmine shrugged, causing a ponderous jiggle to run through her extra flesh, and returned behind the bar. Luke finished arranging the mic, slung his guitar strap over one shoulder, and stood with his hands on his hips, just staring at the seething barroom. It took a few minutes, but people began to glance over in his direction . . . and shut up.

Finally, there were just a couple of drunken boobs laughing at one another's jokes. Luke dropped the microphone down to guitar level and struck a jangling discord that boomed out through the amplifier.

"Sorry," he said, readjusting the mic back in line with his lips. "My guitar farted."

And with that, he launched into a jagged version of "Don't Think Twice, It's All Right."

Will leaned toward Sunny. "Got to give him one thing," he whispered with beer-laced breath. "He's got stones."

12

It wasn't four a.m. when the phone rang this time—it just felt that way to Sunny. After a couple of beers she wasn't accustomed to anymore and a somewhat late night, even an eight a.m. call had her nerves jangling.

"H-h'lo?" Her voice was hoarse and raspy from yelling over the noise at O'Dowd's. Luke had won the crowd over, even doing an encore. But congratulating him on his success had been a little difficult when the jukebox came on again. Sunny coughed, trying to clear away a film of cigarette smoke and beer in her throat—or was that just in her head? "Who is this?"

"Ms. Coolidge? It's Rafe Warner."

That got her eyes open. "Is there a problem? Is Mr. Barnstable okay?"

"Sure," Rafe replied. "I was just talking with him. He gave me your number."

Sunny slowly raised herself to a sitting position. "And why was that?"

"I'm getting off my shift now," Rafe said, "and I've got something to give you." His voice sank to a whisper. "Files."

"What kind—" Sunny got out, but Rafe cut her off.

"I can't discuss this on the phone," he said. "I can be at your house in half an hour. Mr. Barnstable gave me the address."

Thanks, Ollie, Sunny thought.

"Half an hour," Rafe repeated. "I'll see you then." Obviously it wasn't up for discussion, because he cut the connection.

Sunny stared owlishly at the receiver in her hand, hung it up, and then grabbed the handset again. She punched in Will Price's number. When he picked up, he sounded awake and much more human than Sunny felt.

"Files?" he said when Sunny told her story. "Intriguing. Be there in fifteen."

That gave Sunny enough time to run a shower and get the fug of O'Dowd's out of her hair. She sat drinking a large mug of coffee when Will rang the bell. He was in jeans and a T-shirt, and so was she.

"I see we're both dressed to spend the day sorting through files," he said with a smile.

"The question is, what are they, and how many?"

"I'm betting this is the stuff we asked Reese for." Will leaned against the front of the refrigerator.

"The stuff he told us it was illegal to give out?"

Will didn't answer. He stared at the coffeemaker, noticeably inhaling the brewing smell the way Shadow savored a rare scent. Sunny sat up a little straighter. Speaking of Shadow, where was he? He hadn't been in her room, nor was he around when she came downstairs . . . She finally woke up enough to catch Will's hints. "Oh. Sorry. Would you like some coffee?" Sunny poured him a cup and sat at the table.

Will added a little milk and sugar to his cup, took a sip, and sighed. "I told you cops live on this stuff. Do I dare ask who makes the coffee in this house?"

"That pot was my dad's," Sunny told him. "I found it on when I got down here, along with a note telling me he was off for his walk. Stick around, and you'll get to try a pot of mine."

Now that they'd both had their caffeine fixes, the conversation began to flow.

"We know Warner has a mole in Reese's office," Will said. "They must have overheard us with the big guy."

"So Rafe is just going to give us what we want?" Sunny didn't share Will's morning optimism. "Why?"

The doorbell rang. Will grinned. "I guess we'll just have to ask him."

She opened the door to find a jittery Rafe, standing with a sheaf of papers in his hands. He thrust them over to her. "You don't know where these came from, got it?"

When he turned to go, Will caught him by the arm. "We may not know who gave them to us, but I'd like to know what they are. Come in and have some coffee."

Rafe reluctantly accepted a cup. They all sat at the table, the small pile of papers in the middle. Rafe kept looking at them as if he feared they'd explode. "There's a list of the people who passed away in the last year and a half. Well, cases. Their names are blotted out, but I left the dates and the cause of death."

That should give them a long enough time period to average out any normal peaks and valleys in the mortality statistics. Sunny figured that a careful search of the obits from the Portsmouth and Portland papers could probably discover names to line up with the dear departed, but she decided to let Rafe go with a fig leaf of privacy.

Will had more practical considerations. "You mean the official cause of death."

Rafe nodded. "The rest are staff rosters for those days. I figure that's close enough to what you asked for."

"What made you decide to take such a risk getting these to us?" Sunny asked.

"I think you'll look at them and decide you can't use them." Rafe's confidence seemed to come back as he upped his caffeine level. "You've talked about a rise in mortality rates at Bridgewater Hall, and that's true. Right now we're above average. But you're suggesting that the spike is because union people are angry, or aren't doing their jobs, or whatever, because of what Dr. Reese has done since he took over." He took a deep breath. "Reese has definitely made trouble— I ought to know, I've been banging heads with him since he came in—but if you look at the deaths month by month, the spike was higher when Dr. Faulkner was in charge, and we got along better with the administration."

Will frowned. "So you're saying—"

"I'm saying it's not a job action, or people slacking off. As shop steward, I know the folks in the union. They may not all be saints, but they—we—do our best for the patients. I think this information should prove that to you. So you'll either have to go barking up some other tree or just accept that Mr. Scatterwell died of whatever they wrote on his death certificate."

Which is where we'd already reluctantly landed before you brought all this paper to my house, Sunny couldn't help thinking.

"I guess we should say thank you," she said, wishing she sounded more sincere. "It must have been a lot of work for you."

Rafe shrugged. "A little less looking at screens, a little more photocopying. Just promise me one thing. Shred them, burn them, destroy them somehow when you're done. I think once you see that they back up what I told you, you won't have any other use for them."

Rafe thanked Sunny for the coffee and went to stand up. The scrape of his chair seemed to be the cue for a gray-furred form to come through the door.

Shadow's gotten very good at putting in an appearance just as strangers—or Toby—are heading out the door, Sunny thought with a smile.

She wasn't sure if it was cat manners or just cat curiosity. Shadow would come over, give the guest a cursory sniff, accept a little petting if the mood was on him and the person was so inclined, and then move on.

But as Shadow approached Rafe, his standoffishness melted and he became friendly—maybe too friendly. Shadow was all over Rafe's feet and ankles, practically clinging to him.

"Well, hello, fella." Rafe sat back down and went to pet

Shadow, but the cat surprised him—and Sunny—by veering away. It turned into a strange kind of dance. Shadow seemed magnetically drawn to Rafe's bottom half, but repelled by his top.

Then Sunny had a thought. "Were you holding Patrick recently?" she asked.

Rafe looked surprised. "Why, yes. He was feeling a little rocky this morning, so I picked him up to help him feel better."

"Meanwhile," Sunny went on, "Portia was on the floor." She laughed. "I bet Shadow's smelling Portia from your knees down, but Patrick on your upper half. If you sit there and don't pet him, you'll have a new best friend all over your feet."

Rafe did as she suggested, folding his arms and staying still. Shadow twined his way around the security guy's legs, sniffing and purring.

"I've brought Portia's scent home on me a couple of times," Sunny explained. "And Shadow definitely likes it."

"I guess so." Rafe chuckled, looking down at the cat around his ankles, and then yawned. "I'd better be getting home."

But when Rafe rose from the table and started down the hall, Shadow trotted right behind him.

"Uh-oh," Will said. "This could be trouble."

*

Shadow had avoided Sunny since last night when she came home late, smelling of that smoke the humans liked to breathe and the stuff they drank to act silly. He'd found that a bad combination in other homes where he'd lived.

The Old One had gotten up earlier that morning and left something out for Shadow to eat, so he'd left Sunny to sleep by herself. Then the talking-thing had made a noise, and Sunny woke up and stood under the water so the bad smells were gone. But then the human male that spent a lot of time with Sunny had come along. Shadow had learned to give them space when Sunny's He came to visit. He was just about to come into the room and let Sunny know he was around when the noisemaker at the door sounded again—some stranger this time. So Shadow had lain low in the living room while the sound of two-leg talk had drifted down the hallway. After a while, though, he'd decided to go check out the newcomer.

The human didn't seem scared of cats, or angry at seeing one. That was good. In fact, he seemed friendly. Then Shadow smelled the mysterious She on him. He investigated the stranger's feet and legs thoroughly. The scent was so strong, it made his head buzz. Yes, this was definitely the She! Could this be the two-leg the She lived with?

The human bent down and offered a friendly hand—but Shadow hadn't liked that scent at all. It was a He, and Shadow smelled sickness on him. But when the hand went away and the offending He-scent dissipated, Shadow couldn't keep himself away from the traces the She had left.

Then the human rose from his chair again, getting set to leave, and Shadow had an inspiration. This two-leg could lead him to the She!

So, as the human went with Sunny toward the door, Shadow had followed. The scent from the other human's pant legs was a constant distraction. He stepped a little closer, the scent filling his brain . . .

And then hands came from behind and grabbed him up. Snatched from his happy fog, Shadow found himself held helpless as the door opened and the She's human disappeared. Flinging himself around, Shadow managed to tear himself loose, but by then the door had already closed. He flung himself at the heavy wood, scratching and crying, but the two-leg was gone, and the She's scent was already fading.

He heard Sunny's voice. How dare she close the door on him, letting the She's human get away! Shadow was so, so angry. With his back to the door, he hissed at her, one paw up and claws ready—

And then he remembered the scent of Sunny's blood. He couldn't do that again. Conflicting impulses all but paralyzed him. He jammed himself up against the door, the unyielding wood, right at the space where the faintest traces of outside air came in. But it didn't bring the scent he most desired.

Sunny spoke, but she didn't touch him. Maybe that was a good thing. Shadow couldn't trust himself not to draw blood again. He just stayed where he was, letting out his feelings in mournful yowls.

*

"I've seen people going through detox who didn't look or sound as bad as that," Will said as he and Sunny sat back in the kitchen. "Looks as though Shadow has a real case for Rafe's Portia."

"I don't know what to do about it," Sunny said as another disconsolate moan came from the front door. "So I guess we may as well ignore him."

They sat together, reading down the list of names Rafe

had left. Will ran a finger down the page. "I count twenty-three people here. That's like a third of the beds in Bridgewater Hall, isn't it?"

"That shouldn't be so surprising. My dad told me the other day that the average life expectancy for a person in a nursing home is about three years." She held up a hand at the look on Will's face. "Hey, those are the kinds of statistics Dad keeps dredging out of the newspapers."

Will pointed to the lower part of the list. "So, for the past twelve months, there are seventeen cases. But in the six months before that period, I count only six deaths. If that held as the average for the previous year, we're looking at a big jump, almost fifty percent."

"Yes, but remember, you're working with a universe of only seventy-five beds," Sunny pointed out. "A couple of very old or very sick people would cause a big swing in the statistics."

Will divided the files into two piles, and gave one to Sunny. "I think that's all we can get from the deaths. Let's see what the rosters tell us."

By the time she got to the third sheet, she said, "I keep seeing the same names."

"Well, that stands to reason—it's the night shift. Bridgewater Hall isn't like the Sheriff's Department, where people move around every couple of weeks. Soooo . . ." Will drew out the word. "Maybe we should look for names that *don't* turn up all the time."

"Makes sense, I guess," Sunny said. "If the regular staff is a constant, regardless of when the mortality rate was low and when it got higher, we want to look for anomalies."

Will nodded. "Pinch hitters who are hurting the team's

batting average." It was boring work, looking over roster after roster, ignoring the names that were always there and marking the ones that stood out. The problem was that they didn't really stand out. They were just tucked in among the same-old, same-old people.

They switched lists and went back to searching. It wasn't exactly a needle in a haystack effort, but it was tedious.

The exciting world of plodding police work, Sunny thought.

After they had each gone through the entire set of lists twice, Sunny said, "Are you hungry? It just struck me that I never ate breakfast." She put a hand on her stomach. "And Dad's coffee, good as it is, is beginning to feel as if it's burning a hole in my innards."

She left Will to tabulate the results while she went to check the contents of the refrigerator. "Looks like I could do sandwiches, if you don't mind the dreaded roast turkey with lettuce and tomato," she reported, after seeing what Mike had picked up on his latest shopping trip. "I could put a little honey mustard on them."

"Sounds good," Will said, still staring at the papers.

"And to drink there's seltzer, or I could make a new pot of coffee."

"Seltzer, please." A low rumble came from Will's middle. "Maybe coffee on top of old beer wasn't such a good decision." Eventually, Shadow came back into the room, heading for his bowl of dry food. Sunny checked her impulse to go to the cat. *If he wants company, he'll show it,* she reminded herself. *Let's see what kind of mood he's in.*

Shadow was definitely in a bad mood when it came to Will. He elaborately circled around, far out of reach, from the chair where Will sat working. Even so, Shadow kept a wary eye on his new nemesis—at least that was the way it seemed to Sunny, given all the tail lashing that was going on.

Sunny herself he seemed to regard with more sorrow than anger. When she got the glasses from the cabinet over the sink, she discovered Shadow at her feet, gazing up at her. *Sorry,* she silently told the cat. *I'm not sure if this is a love-of-your-life kind of thing, or if it's simple biology. Some days I really wish you could talk and tell me.*

She deposited a plate and glass in front of Will and then did the same for herself. He held up a piece of paper. "As you no doubt noticed, there were a few names that appeared once. Three names appear more than once. I've got one turning up twice, another three times, and a C. Thibaud five times."

He thought for a moment. "You know, five would be exactly the number of extra deaths."

Sunny frowned, staring at the list. She'd only paid attention to the last names, not the first initials. *C. Thibaud,* she thought. *Could that be Camille?*

Aloud, she said, "I guess our next step is to head over to Bridgewater Hall and talk to this Thibaud person," but inside, she really, really hoped that friendly, helpful Camille wouldn't turn out to be their latest suspect.

Sunny closed her eyes, trying to recall the surrealistic scene that night as she rushed down the long, dim corridor to Room 114. The staff had all seemed gathered at the nurses' station . . . Sunny tried to bring that into sharper focus. No, she definitely didn't recall seeing Camille. But it was still possible that the girl had been somewhere else on the floor, tending another patient, or even somewhere mundane, like the ladies' room. *Or hiding out.*

Will's voice interrupted her thoughts. "We never got a chance to talk to Luke, either, what with all his new fans mobbing him."

Sunny managed a laugh. "I hope he didn't take too much of his pay in beer."

The doorbell rang. Over by his food dish, Shadow brought his head up suddenly, but at the sound of barking outside, he slowly brought it down again.

"I'm going to go get that," Sunny said as the bell sounded again, accompanied by more barking. She opened the door a crack, pretty sure she already knew who the visitors were.

Sure enough, she saw Mrs. Martinson wrestling with a leash as Toby tried to stick his nose into the house.

Sunny shot a quick, nervous glance over her shoulder. No Shadow waiting to make a dash for freedom. And no hisses and screams from the kitchen. She relaxed a little and opened the door wider. That got an inquiring canine nose thrust at her and an apologetic smile from Helena.

"Sorry about the delay in answering," Sunny said. "We had a little incident with Shadow trying to get out earlier, and—" She fluttered her hands. "And here I am. What can I do for you?"

"Toby and I were out for our walk, and we heard two very odd stories," Mrs. M. said. "One was from Florence Gaddis. She was driving back from town last night, and she swears that she saw you, Will, and Mike standing in the parking lot of O'Dowd's."

"Well," Sunny admitted, "she's right. We were actually

there last night." She hurried on at the shocked expression on Mrs. Martinson's face. "A friend was playing some music there, the therapist I'd told you about from Bridgewater Hall."

"The young man." Now Helena's expression looked disappointed. Not only had she not been included in an outing with Mike, but she'd missed a chance to meet possible matchmaking material for Sunny.

"We couldn't think of asking you there," Sunny said desperately. "I'm sure you've heard what a cesspool it is."

"I went to O'Dowd's once . . . years ago," Mrs. Martinson said. "If your friend does another show there, let me know."

Sunny knew when she was licked. "Of course," she promised.

Helena nodded and tightened her grip on Toby's leash, not meeting Sunny's eyes.

"You, ah, said there were two odd things?" Sunny finally prompted.

Mrs. M. looked as though she'd been roused from a reverie. "Goodness, where does my mind go sometimes? That's right, another friend mentioned that Alfred Scatterwell is having a memorial for his uncle at the mansion tomorrow evening."

"Oh, really?" Sunny said.

Mrs. Martinson nodded. "It will be the first time the place will be open since Gardner stopped giving parties—which has to be twenty-five years now. With all his absences, traveling and so on, I wonder how the old place has held up."

"You should go and see," Sunny suggested.

But Mrs. Martinson shook her head and looked down.

A simple headshake might have meant that the event was invitation-only and good manners prevented Helena from going. But Sunny knew why Mrs. M. didn't want to meet her eyes. She didn't want Sunny to see the struggle going on inside—between the Kittery Harbor Way, which demanded that everyone's passing be marked; Helena's negative history with Gardner and her desire to have nothing to do with him; and of course, a curiosity as lively as Shadow's own over what had become of what had once been one of the swankiest homes in Piney Brook.

"I know I'm going to see what I can find out about Gardner and Alfred, even if it means crashing, and so is Will," Sunny told her neighbor. "As for Dad, well, if he was visiting Gardner when he was laid up, I'm sure he'll feel obliged to go to the memorial. I don't want to put words in his mouth, but I suspect he'd be glad to have you come along, too."

Helena finally looked up, her eyes shining with gratitude. "Thank you, dear."

"No problem at all," Sunny assured her. "I'll have Dad call you."

Mrs. Martinson got Toby back from the door and waved good-bye.

Sunny waved back. *Isn't that part of the Kittery Harbor Way?* she asked herself. *Helping your neighbors?*

13

Sighing, Sunny closed the door and headed back to the kitchen. "Any excitement here?"

"None whatsoever," Will reported. "No noise, no attempted jailbreaks. The prisoner just drank some water—and sent a few dirty looks my way."

Sunny laughed. "Welcome to my life." She noticed that while she was gone, Will had collected the lunch dishes and washed them. A definite point in his favor. But her heart sank when she saw the pile of paper on the otherwise bare table.

The incriminating files. Or rather, she corrected herself, *the possibly incriminating files. If we're right, they may show a whole series of criminal acts. And of course, the blasted things will be incriminating for us, too, if we get caught with confidential files.*

"Hey, Will, have we got what we needed from these papers now?" she asked.

Will showed her the piece he'd been writing on. "I've got a list of the night shift people plus the three fill-ins, and the dates of the deaths in question. Cause of death is all the same—a stroke. I'd say that's more than we'd have hoped for."

She bit her lip. "Then what do you say we get rid of them?"

"Good idea." Will nodded toward the cat. "I vote we give Shadow the job of shredding them."

Sunny groaned. "I've got a decent paper shredder, but it's in the garage with my New York stuff."

"Will we have to move a lot of boxes to unearth it?" he asked.

"Just the winter clothes," Sunny said. *And maybe a few other things,* she silently added.

*

Shadow followed Sunny and her He out the kitchen door to the little house in the back. Some humans he'd known kept their go-fast machines in these houses. But Sunny and the Old One filled the space with things that were much more interesting—cardboard boxes of all shapes and sizes, just perfect for a cat to climb on—and maybe sometimes use as a scratching post.

When he entered the little house, his eyes went wide. Sunny and her He were rearranging the boxes, piling them up in new configurations. The He made "oof" noises and didn't seem all that happy with the work. But Sunny kept talking, pointing deeper into the space as they cleared a path on the floor.

That wasn't too interesting as far as Shadow was concerned. What he watched was the way the two humans piled boxes higher and higher as they moved farther in.

Maybe Sunny wants the He to make up for grabbing me, Shadow thought, watching a tower of boxes by the door that rose several times his height. He gathered himself, then launched into a vertical leap that just cleared the top. The construction swayed a little as he landed, but that was okay. This was fun!

Shadow played it safer getting back to the floor, jumping down a series of shorter piles, staircase fashion. When Shadow finally dropped to the concrete floor, he looked up to find that Sunny's He had created a real challenge. This was the tallest stack yet, looming not just over Shadow but over Sunny. Shadow backed up—he'd need some momentum for this leap. It would be a record-setter.

Still keeping his eyes on the target, he retreated right out of the little house, until he felt the warmth of the sun on his hindquarters. Then he made a wild charge, moving from a lunge to a lope to a run. The huge pile came closer and closer, he'd have to time this right, or he'd end up crashing into the cardboard tower. Now!

Shadow pushed off with his rear legs, getting the most out of his running start. Up, up, up he went, but the cardboard mountain rose higher. Was he going to fail? He didn't like the idea of taking a tumble back to that hard floor.

But no, there was the flat top of the crowning box. Shadow pounced with his forefeet, his claws sinking into the cardboard, letting him hold on as he scrabbled with his rear legs. It wasn't the most elegant landing, but he'd made it! He was at the top of the world!

Except . . . the pillar of boxes began to sway, a scary, sickening movement. Shadow wasn't sure whether he should hang on or jump.

The decision was taken out of his paws as the pile moved too far over and began to topple. That box he'd struggled so hard to reach slid off and then went out from under him, leaving Shadow scrabbling with all four legs in thin air. He let out a yowl of surprise that was pretty well lost in the crash of boxes landing back in the open space the two-legs had cleared.

Actually, Shadow had to count himself lucky. Some of those boxes were heavy. If one of those had landed on him, that wouldn't have been a good thing. But he managed to bounce from falling box to falling box, getting his claws in another pile of boxes, riding out a vertical descent to the floor, where he crouched as cartons bounced around him, finally coming to rest.

He lay in a sort of cave created when two boxes landed on either side of him and a third dropped to create a roof. The top box landed on its side, and its contents spilled out. Shadow came out to sniff, but it was nothing exciting—just more of those strange paper things that Sunny kept on the shelves in her room. Sometimes she'd take one down and flip papers over, staring at the things for hours. Shadow would come up behind her shoulders to watch, but nothing exciting ever happened. No food fell out from between the papers, and all he ever smelled was dust. He stopped paying any attention to them.

From the sound of things, though, there was plenty of excitement nearby. Sunny raised her voice, calling Shadow's name. And the male human made some loud, angry noises.

The two-legs worked their way back to him, moving boxes out of the way. Sunny gave a great cry when she finally spotted Shadow, scooping him up in her arms, making sure he wasn't hurt, looking concerned.

Shadow relaxed as she cradled him, a faint purr rising from his chest. Yes, she was definitely sorry for the trouble earlier. Shadow was happy until he glanced over to the male human. The look he was getting there made him glad he wasn't living with that one. Glares like that usually meant he'd be out on the street in two shakes of his tail.

The humans went back to clearing space on the floor, but this time they didn't pile the boxes so high. That was fine with Shadow. He'd had enough of jumping for the time being. Instead, he watched Sunny and her He work. Finally Sunny exclaimed something, pulling out a carton.

Shadow couldn't figure out what the big deal was. But Sunny and her male friend took it to the open front of the little house, tearing open the top of the carton and removing a strange, boxy thing. It had a tail, and Sunny took the end and stuck it into the wall. The box started to hum. Shadow got down from his perch and cautiously advanced, almost stalking his way forward. When Sunny touched it and it growled, Shadow jumped back. This wasn't good. Sunny was bigger than the thing, but what happened if it bit her? At least it didn't seem to have legs, so it couldn't chase her . . . or him.

Sunny's male friend came with papers in his hand,

thrust them into the top of the boxy thing—and it ate them! Not only that, but it made loud growling and crunching noises while it did.

Shadow carefully stayed behind Sunny's leg, peering suspiciously at the strange hungry box. This was like a lot of the stuff two-legs kept around. Shadow wasn't sure whether they were alive or not, like the go-fast things humans rode in, or the box with pictures of people inside. This one didn't move around, but it seemed to like chewing up paper. And even stranger, you could look into its belly and see all the chewed-up paper lying in a heap!

That might be a good idea, Shadow thought. *If Sunny could see into my belly, she'd always know when I was hungry and feed me.*

But then, what would happen to his beautiful fur coat? This eat-'em-up thing with its see-through belly lived in a box. Even stupid Biscuit Eaters wouldn't put up with that. They'd want to run around, woofing.

The box-thing stopped growling, and Sunny and her He stepped away from it. Shadow crept forward, extending a wary paw. He gave the boxy thing a tap. It didn't growl; it didn't even move. But that transparent belly-thing seemed to wobble. That gave Shadow an idea. He pushed harder, shoving with both forepaws, and the boxy thing fell over, its clear belly falling away and all those little strips of paper spilling all over the floor.

This was wonderful! Shadow leaped on the largest pile of paper, scattering the strips, rolling on them, having a grand old time until Sunny and her friend came back. Sunny had a big, black, plastic bag, and oh, did she make noise when she saw Shadow in the make-believe snowdrift he'd created.

Shadow expected Sunny's He to make even more noise—human males usually got angry and loud in the houses Shadow had lived in.

But this one just stood quietly, shaking his head.

*

Sunny and Will spent a remarkable amount of time collecting the paper shreds, bagging them . . . and keeping them out of Shadow's reach. "If we ever have to do this again, I vote we burn the evidence instead," Will said, glaring down at the cat. "You are one crazy creature."

Sunny had to go along with that opinion, but it seemed to be the only thing they agreed on for the whole trip to Bridgewater Hall. Sunny tried to lay it out logically. "Okay, maybe we've got a new lead here. But how do we find some proof? More importantly, who even gets to hear it?" she asked. "If we go to Dr. Reese for corroboration, we'll open exactly the can of worms Rafe was afraid of. Reese will know we've been looking at files illegally. Do we talk to Rafe and let him know one of his union people might be a viable suspect? Where will his loyalties lie?"

Will kept his eyes on the road. "I say first we find out who this C. Thibaud is. Then we talk to him or her. Then we make up our minds."

"What kind of questions can we even ask?" Sunny wanted to know. "I can't see us strolling up and saying, "Gee, have you noticed that a lot of people die when you happen to work the late shift?""

Will's lips quirked. "Whenever you talk to a murder

suspect, you have to expect that they're on their guard, even if they're innocent."

"But here we don't even know if there *are* murders," Sunny burst out. "We went to outside doctors, and they told us that Gardner could have died of a stroke. We have a handful of deaths that we think are statistically relevant based on the numbers. Strokes, according to the cause of death in the papers Rafe gave us. Maybe five really sick patients in a row got transferred from a hospital to the nursing home and then died. I don't think it's impossible. That article my dad mentioned to me said that nursing homes get patients who are frailer and sicker these days. That three years is an average life expectancy. Some live longer, and some go quicker. Maybe a lot quicker."

"That's an interesting philosophy for someone who's looking for foul play," Will said.

"I suppose that's what Ollie wants. But call me naïve, I have a hard time believing that someone is stalking the corridors in that place looking to bump people off. I might expect it in a big city like New York, but this is my hometown, for crying out loud. I rode my bike around town. The dangerous neighborhood was the streets around O'Dowd's on a Friday night, because people might get liquored up and drive like idiots."

Sunny glanced over at Will. "I know you're a cop, you see a lot of things I don't. And I know things have changed. Crimes that only used to happen in big cities are turning up in small towns now. But in my heart, I can't imagine that stuff happening in Kittery Harbor . . . or Bridgewater." She grinned. "This isn't like Dr. Gavrik's hometown, where her relatives were ready to kill the neighbors."

"I can understand what you're saying." Will's voice got softer. "I grew up around here, too, remember. But as you say, I've been a cop. I'm trained to look for foul play."

In the end, they decided to ask Rafe about C. Thibaud without explaining the possibilities. Sunny called his number, forgetting until the phone was ringing that he was probably sound asleep after his night shift. But he answered anyway, and didn't sound too upset.

"Sure I know her," he said. "You probably know Camille, too. The last name is pronounced Tee-bow, like the football player."

"Camille the aide?" Sunny asked.

Rafe confirmed it, and she thanked him then clicked her cell phone closed as Will parked his truck at Bridgewater. He gave Sunny a long, thoughtful look. "So you know her."

"I had a suspicion I might," Sunny admitted.

"And you like her, which is why I've been getting this song and dance from you about people possibly being innocent."

"I won't deny that, but I also don't think we have a convincing case to present."

They walked inside in silence until they reached the nurses' station. "Do you want to talk to her?" Will lowered his voice.

"She's little more than a kid," Sunny told him. "I think you'd scare her to death. Why don't you check and see if Ollie is in therapy and I'll look for Camille."

Will gave a nod and strode off. Sunny cruised the hallway and easily spotted the aide in another room. The girl waved to her, and Sunny waved back. A few minutes later, she came out of the room and walked over. "Anything I can do for Mr. Barnstable?"

"I've been thinking about something and don't know who to ask," Sunny replied. She'd been thinking about the approach. "How has my boss been sleeping since Mr. Scatterwell passed away? He's been so upset about it, more than he wants to let on. Do you think there's anyone from the night shift I could ask?"

"I know just about everybody who works the overnights." Camille shrugged. "Whenever someone is sick or can't make it, I fill in."

"Really?" Sunny did her best to look impressed. "Were you here when Mr. Scatterwell had his stroke?"

"Yeah, I was working that night." Camille made a face, but seemed unself-conscious about admitting it. "A patient down the hall did a big load in his bed, and I was in there cleaning him up when the excitement started. So I missed it all. To tell you the truth, what I was doing was pretty gross, but I'm kind of relieved I was busy."

"That had to be tough." Sunny gave her a friendly smile. "Weren't you here the next day, too?"

Camille shrugged. "Look at me—I'm never going to be a model, but my family breeds women who can work and keep working." She leaned forward. "Besides, I need the money. I still owe almost a thousand bucks for my training, so I pick up any extra work I can."

"Still, two shifts in a row, you must be afraid that you'll be tired and make a mistake."

"Oh, no." Camille shook her head, maybe a little too definitely. "I'm always careful. That was something they drilled into us at training." An odd expression flitted across her broad features. "It's different here, though. When we were training, we worked with people—well, let's say people who'd look for free care. But I could get along with them better—they're my kind of people. Here, it's like even when you're wiping their butts, some people will still look right through you." She blinked, blushing. "Wow, we got kind of far away from what you were asking."

"That's me all over," Sunny said easily. "I'm an easy person to talk to." It was a skill she'd cultivated during her years in journalism.

Camille made an effort to adopt a more professional expression. "From what I've seen, by the time Mr. Barnstable has supper and watches a little TV, he's pretty pooped. I think he sleeps right through till morning. If you want someone to check on him at night, though, maybe you should talk to the nurse."

"Thanks, I'll do that," Sunny said, knowing full well that Ollie would kill her if she sent a nurse to check up on him.

Camille pointed at a flashing light. "Uh-oh. Duty calls."

Sunny thanked her and turned to see Will approaching. "Ollie is finished already and resting in his room," he reported.

As they headed for Room 114, Sunny heard a familiar chuckle, so she wasn't surprised to find her father in there with Ollie. She was surprised, though, to find Portia sitting in Mike's lap.

"She followed me here," Mike said, laughing at Sunny's expression while petting Portia's sleek fur. "As soon as I signed in, I had a new best friend. And I have to say, she's a lot more pleasant than your guy."

At the reference to "her guy," Sunny suddenly realized the reason for Mike's sudden popularity. "Before you left today, you put out some food for Shadow, didn't you?"

"Well, he was sort of hanging around me and then looking at his bowl. I figured you might want to sleep in a bit after last night's fun, so I gave him fresh water and dry food."

"And he thanked you for it by hanging around you a little more." Sunny didn't know whether to laugh or impatiently shake her head. "I'm afraid Portia is all over you because of the cologne you don't know you're wearing— eau de Shadow."

Mike thought about that a little, and as he did, Portia thrust her head under his hand for more attention. "Maybe the cologne broke the ice," Mike finally said with dignity, "but I think it's my personality that keeps her around." He scratched the calico cat between the ears. "Right, Portia?"

Sunny didn't even bother to respond to that. Will just laughed. "Where's your roomie?" he asked Ollie.

"His wife and daughter came and took him out to the garden," Ollie replied. "Now he'll be able to tell people on the next bench to be quiet." He shifted in the bed, and Sunny noticed it didn't look so painful for him. "Got anything new?"

"We have a new theory, but it can't leave this room." In a conspiratorial voice, Will explained the fun with numbers they had this morning.

"You say you had staff rosters," Mike said, leaning forward in his chair. "Did any names turn up?"

"Before we answer that, let me ask you something." Sunny aimed her eyes at Ollie. "What do you think of Camille the aide?"

"I like her," he promptly replied. "She's nice and hard-working, and she's the quickest to come if you buzz for help—" His expression soured. "Aw no, you're going to tell me she's the name, right? It's like you're only picking on people I like."

"We just follow the evidence," Will said.

Sunny gave him a look. "But I've got to say in this case, the evidence is thin." With his broken leg, Ollie was pretty much dependent on Camille. Sunny didn't want Will's suspicions to influence the way Ollie treated the girl. She offered her arguments about how fuzzy the statistics they were working from could be.

Ollie slowly nodded, going from patient to hard-nosed businessman. "So you've got a theory and a suspect. Someone who was around on the night shift, a staff member who'd know what was bad for patients and who could probably get her hands on whatever was needed. That's whachacallem—opportunity and means." He gave Will a tough look. "What about motive?"

Will shrugged. "She's beating her brains out for chump change, emptying bedpans for rich people. That would start to get to me. And there's something else." He looked at Ollie. "You think someone was in here that night, giving Gardner a drink. We don't think he'd take one from Alfred or Elsa. But he might have taken it from Camille."

"*Might*," Sunny emphasized. "Here's what I know. She's dedicated and responsible. The reason she's taking all the shifts she can is because she still has to pay off her training."

Ollie pursed his lips in thought. "She didn't like Gardner," he finally said.

Mike shrugged. "She's a nice girl, but plain. Not Gardner's type. I bet he didn't waste much of the old Scatterwell charm on her."

"As a matter of fact, she saw Gardner at his worst, going after Elsa Hogue," Sunny had to admit. "But we're talking cold-blooded murder. Is that enough to make someone go so far?"

"Put it all together . . ." Will let the words hang in the air.

"Put it all together, and do we have enough to persuade Frank Nesbit that he ought to look into this case officially?" Sunny looked around at the others. "He's the one we have to convince, after all. What do you think? Do we have enough to convince him of foul play?"

Mike stopped playing with Portia to offer his two cents. "Admit that he let someone kill patients under his nose at a ritzy rest home? Oh, no."

That got a sour laugh out of Will. "To convince him, we'd have to catch the killer cutting someone's heart out. And even then, he might call it emergency surgery." Will hesitated for a moment, and Sunny could sympathize with him. He'd made a case for some bad things going on here. But he had to face reality. "No," he admitted.

"I could push him, but . . ." Ollie sat still, making the political calculations. "No."

That pretty well killed the conversation. They sat for a moment or two in defeated silence.

"Hey, what's going on, folks?" Luke Daconto came into the room. He was obviously still riding the high of last night's performance, genial and grinning. "With a concert next week, I've been rehearsing my bell ringers pretty hard."

"After all the free beer those folks at O'Dowd's bought for you last night, you were able to listen to bell ringers this morning?" Will stared at him. "You're a tougher man than I am."

"Well, more like the afternoon after," Luke admitted.

"The music was good," Mike said, "but what really impressed me was the way you stared down that crowd to shut them up. That was really something, Luke."

The guitarist shrugged uncomfortably. "It's just something I learned from an old pro when I was on the road, playing in joints a lot worse than the one last night." He grinned at Sunny, a flash of white teeth in his heavy beard. "If you thought that bar was scary, I could show you a few—"

Will rolled his eyes. "That's all we'd need."

Remembering some hair-raising episodes from Sunny's other investigations, everyone laughed—even, after a moment, Sunny herself.

Luke looked a little confused at the big reaction, but pleased. "That's better," he said. "When I first came in here, I thought I was crashing a funeral."

"Oh! Funeral!" Sunny turned to her dad. "I completely forgot. Mrs. Martinson stopped off at the house this morning. She told me that Alfred Scatterwell is having a memorial service for Gardner tonight. She was feeling a little funny about whether she should go, and I kind of promised that you would take her. You'd better give her a call."

"Are you and Will going?" Luke asked.

Sunny nodded, shooting a quick glance at Luke. "Of course. I'll represent you, Ollie."

"Yeah." Ollie started rooting around in the pile of newspapers on his tray table. Sunny noticed he had both the

Press Herald from Portland and the *Herald* from across the border in Portsmouth. "There's an announcement of the memorial in here—not what I'd call an engraved invitation, but it seems to be a public event."

"Do you mind if I use your phone?" Mike asked Ollie. "I want to pass that along to Helena. She's probably worrying herself into a head of white hair over whether it's proper to go."

"On her, it would look good," Sunny cracked. Mike was busy punching in Mrs. M.'s number, but Sunny's comment got a chuckle from everybody else in the room . . . except Luke. He stood very still, as if suddenly he were the one at the funeral.

"Are you okay?" Sunny asked, and then shook her head. "Hey, I'm sorry. I know you'd gotten close with Gardner. You should have heard about this memorial from Alfred, not from me acting scatterbrained."

"If not for you, I wouldn't have heard about it at all," Luke said quietly. "Alfred—well, I guess he didn't approve of his uncle hanging out with me."

"As if you could lead him into bad habits," Mike scoffed. "Believe me, Luke, Gardner tried them all before you were born."

That got a wan laugh out of Luke. "I suppose that's true."

"It's a funny thing, but I understand you were actually nearby the night Gardner died," Will said.

Sunny gave him a "not now" look. *There he is, pure cop, crossing the T's and dotting the I's on the witness statements.*

But Will plowed right on. "Elsa Hogue mentioned bumping into you at the nurses' station."

For a second Luke looked baffled, but then his face cleared. "That's right. I left the office where I was working and came over to see if I could bum anything with caffeine in it. Working on reports makes me sleepy, verrrrry sleeeeeeepy . . ." He slipped into a mad hypnotist voice for a moment, then spoke normally. "I think Elsa was looking for the same thing."

Will looked satisfied with that explanation.

Mike glanced at his watch. "If we want to grab an early supper and get dressed, we should probably get moving."

"Um . . . Mike?" Luke seemed to stumble over his words a little. "Could you give me the when and the where? I'd like to go, too."

"Of course, son," Mike said gently. "It's at eight o'clock, Twelve Brookside Lane." He gave a little laugh. "You know, I haven't been there in almost fifty years, yet I still remember the address. It's funny, what sticks with you."

"Yeah," Luke said. "Funny."

14

Shadow woke up annoyed. He'd been having a dream where he stalked through dark woods, tracking the She by scent. It was nice to open his eyes and find himself in a patch of sun in the living room, but the dream had definitely been more interesting. He'd been awoken by Sunny and the Old One coming through the door, rushing around and talking loudly. There was no hope of going back to his dreams now.

It was still early—Shadow's stomach told him so. But Sunny started preparing food while the Old One went up the stairs. That in itself was odd. The Old One usually spent this time in the room with the picture box. Shadow decided to investigate.

As he climbed the stairs, Shadow heard the sound of running water—much running water. So he wasn't surprised when he found the door to the tiled room closed. But what was the Old One doing in there at this time of day? It made no sense.

Then Shadow noticed that the door to the Old One's room stood wide open. Usually, Sunny's father kept the door closed. He'd made it clear he didn't want Shadow in there.

But if the Old One was busy standing under the water, he'd be there for a while . . .

Shadow trotted into the room. As soon as he was inside, he decided this was a bad idea. He'd been in here just recently, there was nothing to see—definitely nothing he wanted to smell—and there was nothing to play with.

Well, the Old One had thrown his clothes on the bed, and the arm of a shirt dangled down. That was better than nothing. Shadow went over to give it a halfhearted swipe with his paw . . . and froze at the scent that wafted his way as the cloth swung back and forth. How could the Old One smell so much of the She?

Shadow was torn. If this had been Sunny's room, he'd probably climb up on the bed to get more of the fragrance. Besides, it would be mixed with Sunny's scent. He didn't think that mixing She and Old One would be as nice. And the Old One could come in any moment and catch him. That would mean trouble.

So Shadow marched to the door in annoyance, his tail up, its tip twitching. Sunny could be with the She. Even the Old One could be with the She. But Shadow, who really wanted to be with the She, wasn't allowed.

This wasn't fair. This was definitely not good.

*

By the time Sunny had finished chopping up odds and ends into a chef's salad, Mike had come downstairs wearing his dress shirt and a pair of suit pants, toweling his hair.

"You're brave to sit down and eat with your good clothes on," Sunny teased him.

"What am I supposed to do, put a bib on?" Mike demanded, his blue eyes heating up to what Sunny privately called the Laser Glare of Death. "I figured I'd get ready before we sat down. We don't want to be late, and Lord knows how long you'll be up there."

He stuck his face into the refrigerator to get the seltzer, muttering something about interference from the clothing police now. *Guess Dad is feeling stressed about this hoedown, and you were a bit late on the pickup,* the critical voice in the back of Sunny's head commented. At the last memorial service they'd attended, Mike had been all over the place, chatting with various political cronies. She put the glasses on the table, and then took her father by the hand. "What's the matter, Dad?"

"Sorry, honey, I shouldn't have been mouthing off," Mike apologized. "It's just that it's going to be society people, that whole Piney Brook crowd there." Mike's face screwed up as if he'd tasted something bad. "They look at me and see a truck driver. It's kind of funny—Helena was this way and that about going. She didn't want to go there alone. Well, neither did I—with her along, I figure I've got a touch of class."

Sunny smiled and patted his shoulder. "I wouldn't worry about that, Dad. You've got more class than most of the snobs who'll turn up tonight."

*

Sunny took her shower and got dressed as quickly as she could. *Don't give Dad a chance to complain,* she thought as she pulled on the jacket from her lightweight black suit over a pewter-colored blouse. She threatened her curls with a hairbrush and put on a minimum of makeup, added a pair of black flats, and headed downstairs.

Mrs. Martinson had just arrived, and as usual Sunny felt barely adequate when she compared her outfit to the one the older woman was wearing, a classic skirted suit in a deep French gray, the skirt just hitting the right length on a pair of legs that would be the envy of women twenty years younger—or in Sunny's case, thirty-something years younger. A simple white blouse with a brooch at the collar and tiny gold earrings completed the look.

Mike looked proudly at both of them. "Those snooty Piney Brook types may have the big houses, but I'll be walking in with a pair of women looking like a million dollars—apiece!"

Helena smiled. "You clean up pretty well yourself, Mike."

He wore the summer-weight version of his blue funeral suit, an off-white shirt, and his latest Father's Day tie.

Sunny grinned. "You look like you're running for office, Dad."

Mike put a hand to his chest. "Heaven forbid!"

"Well, I think we're ready to go. I take it that Will intends to join us there?"

Sunny nodded.

"Then there's just one thing." Mrs. Martinson reached into her handbag and came out with a set of car keys, which she gave to Sunny. "Would you mind driving the Buick tonight? It will be dark by the time we're coming home, and I'd feel more comfortable."

You might feel downright cozy, sitting in the backseat with Dad, that irrepressible voice in the back of Sunny's head suggested.

"We should have thought of that." Mike looked annoyed with himself. "Your car is the obvious choice."

Sunny nodded. Not only did Helena's sedan have more comfortable seating than Dad's truck or Sunny's SUV, the sedan would fit in better for a Piney Brook funeral.

*

The Brookside district was the most exclusive section of an already exclusive area. As Sunny drove along, she passed estates which kept to themselves behind iron gates or heavy shrubbery, and houses whose architecture screamed, "We've arrived!"

Some of the houses had probably started as summer places. Sunny was particularly taken by one with a cupola. What would it be like to have a round bedroom up there? She didn't much like the place that had turned itself into a McMansion by adding a cream-colored concrete tower to the middle of a classic white-painted spruce building. And the rambling stone buildings, especially the ones that used two-tone fieldstone, seemed a little much to her. Some reminded her of Bridgewater Hall.

When they got to the Scatterwell place, she found a

three-story brick structure built along vaguely Georgian lines, although some Scatterwell ancestor had added a shaded wooden porch to the side of one wing. The brick had mellowed into its surroundings, but Maine winters had not been kind to the porch. Although it gleamed with a coat of white paint, it seemed to be sagging with age.

Mike peered out the window as Sunny parked the car along a curving drive. "Y'know, I never thought about it before," he said, "but this place *looks* like a funeral parlor."

"A rather large, successful one," Helena Martinson added drily.

They got out of the car and walked to the front door, passing a collection of Cadillacs, Lincolns, BMWs, and Mercedes. The door stood open, and a funeral flunkey in a black polyester suit stood in front of a grand staircase padded with Oriental carpeting. "Please go on through to the Grand Parlor," he murmured, gesturing to his right.

The Grand Parlor was indeed pretty grand, an enormous cream-colored room with windows along three sides. *This must be the section that leads out to the porch,* Sunny thought, glancing around. The room had been cleared of furniture, and rows of folding chairs laid out. Up at the front of the room was a lectern and a table with a ceramic urn—something more in keeping with the surroundings than the waxy cardboard box Sunny had seen in Alfred's place. She also noticed the discreet bar at the rear of the room.

Mike had a wry smile when he spotted that. "I think Gardner would approve," he said. "He always called booze a social lubricant."

The other thing Sunny noticed about the room was how warm it was. Although all the windows were open, the more people who joined the growing crowd, the higher the indoor temperature went. And there was something else in the air. Helena gave a discreet sniff. "Fresh paint, which I suppose we should have expected." She pitched her voice quietly. "From what you've said about him, Alfred would value appearances. But there's something else . . ."

Sunny nodded, detecting a faint, acrid smell that seemed to linger in the back of her throat.

"Rot." Mike pronounced the word very quietly. "Let's hope it's only the porch outside. If it's in the house, Alfred will end up sinking his inheritance into repairs."

Sunny in the meantime had been busily scanning faces. "There's Will," she said, "and Luke." They made their way through the crowd. Will looked pretty snappy in a navy suit that made the most of his lean form. Luke didn't clean up quite so well—he seemed about as far out of water as a fish could be, wearing a rather ratty brown corduroy jacket over a pair of black dress pants. He greeted them the way a drowning sailor might welcome a lifeline.

After introducing Mrs. Martinson, Sunny said, "You must be roasting in that jacket, Luke."

He only shrugged uncomfortably. "It's the only one I've got. When you move around a lot, you travel light."

And I bet he wishes he'd traveled with a lighter jacket, Sunny couldn't help thinking.

In spite of his misgivings, Mike quickly spotted a familiar face, too. "Chappie!" He ushered over a tall man with silver hair and a squarish face, handsome in a stodgy sort of way. "Helena, this is Chapman Manning—"

"Leave off the roman numerals at the end," the man boomed, "for heaven's sake."

"Chappie may look respectable, but he's been known to pull some political skullduggery when it has to be done." Mike grinned.

As introductions flew around her, Sunny lost the last names of the two women who accompanied Chappie. They seemed to be called Tavvie and Phoebe. Frankly, Sunny had trouble telling one from the other. Both had graying blond hair cut short, and both wore dark dresses with pearls.

Tavvie nodded toward the urn in the place of honor. "It was rather a surprise, Alfred doing that to his uncle."

"Just a taste of where the old boy was going to," Chappie joked.

"Perhaps it's better than an open casket," Phoebe said. "I'd spent the night half afraid that Gardner would suddenly jump up and shout, 'Surprise!'"

Tavvie's pale eyebrows rose on a face from where wrinkles had apparently been banished. "He could still come leaping in through the window. Gardner always had such a lamentable sense of humor."

"He must have," Phoebe murmured. "I understand he went out with you for a while."

Tavvie's pale blue eyes glinted with malice. "Before he ran around with you—and well before your divorce."

Sunny noticed Helena following the byplay with interest. Luke just looked uncomfortable. Will had a faraway look, as if he appeared to be ignoring it all, but Sunny suspected he was paying more attention than it seemed.

Chappie continued to chat with Mike. "How did you come to know Gardner? He doesn't seem like one of your sort—I mean, I don't think Gardner ever voted in his life."

"Would you believe music?" Mike told the story of the

Cosmic Blade, omitting how the band broke up. "Gardner still had an interest in music, though. That's how he met Luke here. He's a music therapist at Bridgewater Hall."

"Music therapist?" Chappie echoed.

"But he's a real musician," Mike went on enthusiastically. "I saw him play last night. You should have seen how he faced down the crowd at O'Dowd's."

"O'Dowd's? Really?" Sunny could see that Chappie was trying to be polite, but it was also obvious that there was no point where his life and Luke's even intersected.

Tavvie touched Chappie on the arm. "They're about to start. I think we should find some seats."

She was right on the mark. No sooner had the crowd started sitting down than the funereal flunkey led an elderly man in clerical clothing up to the lectern and introduced him.

"They got Bishop Sawyer," Phoebe murmured. "Very impressive." Perhaps, but from the flow of platitudes, Sunny quickly surmised that the churchman had probably never even met Gardner.

Next came Dr. Henry Reese, introduced as Gardner's best friend. He was a bit more personal, telling some funny stories. But Reese mainly dwelt on the boyhood he and Gardner had shared. "Perhaps that's what I think of when it comes to Gardner because to me he never aged. That might sound like a strange admission for a doctor who runs an old-age home, where all too often we bid farewell to an aged resident." He looked over at the urn. "But with Gardner, somehow I never expected that to happen."

The final speaker, representing the family, was Alfred Scatterwell, who came up to the lectern in a sober black suit . . . and with a glass in his hand. Apparently, he'd been fortifying himself at the bar.

"This could be interesting," Chappie murmured.

Sunny silently agreed. *That's the problem with social lubricants—they can get very slippery.*

Alfred looked over the assembled mourners, a sardonic smile on his face. "I suppose a good number of you came this evening to see if the old place had fallen down. Well, you can easily spot that we had to paint in here. Does that make this a whited sepulcher, Bishop?"

He turned to Dr. Reese. "And thank you, Hank, for the wonderful memories you shared. Personally, I wish you'd have talked about the road trip you and Uncle Gardner took after Yale. He always said it made a man of you." Alfred smiled as he spoke, but Dr. Reese stiffened.

Alfred turned back to his audience. "And now it falls to me to say a few words about my uncle. Gardner Scatterwell was well traveled and well liked by all his acquaintances. As for his family, we knew him all too well. You've all heard stories. I, of all people, shouldn't have to go into them. Instead, I'll go back to something that Hank said, about how it seemed that Uncle Gardner never aged. Perhaps that's because we saw him so rarely. He was always going, and now he's gone."

Alfred turned to the urn and raised his glass. "And so, we'll drink your liquor and use your house, and I think you'd probably like that." He shrugged. "And if you don't, it's too late now."

He stepped away from the lectern as the crowd burst into muttering, and then he came back, gesturing toward the bar. "Feel free to accept some Scatterwell hospitality. After all, it's what Uncle would have done."

"Hmmmmm, quite an interesting performance," Chappie said as the crowd began murmuring again.

Mike turned to the back of the room. "I notice it's not stopping some people."

Sunny glanced over her shoulder. The bar now had people lining up to wet their whistles.

"What did you expect, after what Gardner did with Alfred's fiancée?" Phoebe sniffed.

"They found them right upstairs, in the guest bedroom," Tavvie said. "She had to leave town." She gave a low laugh. "And, of course, so did Gardner."

They rose from their seats, and stood in a small group with Mike, Helena, Will, and Luke. "Do you want to go?" Sunny asked.

"It's a terrible thing to admit"—Helena at least had the grace to look embarrassed—"but I'd like to hear some more stories."

So they circulated through the crowd, getting an earful of Scatterwell scandals, all of them starring Gardner.

And then they found themselves facing Alfred.

"What are *you* doing here?" he asked loudly with a slight slur to his voice. The conversations around them grew quiet as people turned.

Mike wasn't about to take that comment lying down. "I knew your uncle before you were born."

"Oh, yes, the townie boy playing in that half-assed band," Alfred said. "Did practicing in Piney Brook get you a better class of groupie?"

He peered at Helena. "Now, back in the day, Uncle might have been interested in you." He rounded on Sunny and Will. "And the gallant investigators. Have you found out the obvious yet? Besides being dead, my uncle is gone." He laughed. "In a puff of smoke."

And you're stinking drunk, Sunny thought. *Not that you'll regret anything when you're sober.*

Alfred then looked Luke up and down with such scorn that the guitarist's face, already flushed from the heat, went a bright red. "And what are *you* doing in my uncle's house?"

But in spite of the heat, the shaggy hair, the mismatched clothes, Luke had a certain dignity as he said, "Gardner was my friend."

But Alfred wouldn't have any of that. He gestured with his drink, sloshing some on the carpet. "My uncle could be pleasant, genial, what you might call friendly. Why wouldn't he be? You were giving him what he wanted for free. But most of the people in this family—in this room— knew how he could get if he wanted something you didn't want to give. And I'll tell you this. He was no friend, no uncle . . . not much of a human being."

For a second, Sunny thought that Luke Daconto was going to grab Alfred Scatterwell and break his storklike, potbellied body over his knee. Instead, Luke turned on his heel and strode off.

Without missing a beat, Mike followed him. He hadn't gone two steps before Helena caught up with him, taking his arm.

Shrugging, Will offered his elbow to Sunny. "Might as well make this unanimous."

By the time they got outside, Luke was gone. The only sign of him was the fading sound of a car engine.

"Maybe it's just as well." Helena Martinson peered into the distance, but the car was long gone now. "What could we say to him after suffering through a performance like that?" She shook her head. "Telling him his friendship was just a figment of his imagination."

"Even if it was true," Sunny said. "Walking around in that crowd, we heard enough stories to Gardner's discredit. By the time Alfred started mouthing off, Luke had to be developing some doubts about his friend's sincerity."

"Alfred was close enough to the truth with me," Mike admitted. "I was the townie kid getting into Piney Brook. It was pretty amazing. I'd never seen a house like this." His face got grim. "But it's not as though I was sponging off Gardner. We were making music, we had some good times together. I found out stuff I didn't like about him, but the guy is dead now. I guess it's true what they say, the good times are buried with people."

"'The evil that men do lives after them / The good is oft interred with their bones,'" Mrs. Martinson quoted. "Shakespeare."

Sunny nodded. "*Julius Caesar.*"

"Much as I hate to admit it, Alfred told the truth about me, too." Helena's lips twitched. "Gardner was interested in me, and showed it in the most disgusting way."

"What was it with that guy!" Mike burst out.

"He was good-looking, had a little charm, and a lot of money." Helena did not make them sound like assets, but Will shrugged.

"With a start like that, I guess he figured he'd take every chance he could—the law of averages says he'd score often enough."

"It seems to have worked with Alfred's fiancée," Sunny had to admit.

"Maybe she was lucky," Helena said. "Looks like Alfred turned out to be a nasty drunk."

That shocked a laugh out of them all.

"Nasty or not, he had us pegged. We've got maybe two days left before the deadline, and our investigation has got nothing." Will turned to Sunny. "We have to map out what we want to do tomorrow."

Sunny noticed a whispered conversation between Helena and Mike. "Sunny," Mrs. Martinson said in her most guileless voice, "would you mind dropping me and your father off at my place for a while? You and Will are welcome, too," she hurried on. "We could all have some coffee cake."

"Thanks," Sunny replied, biting back a grin, "but maybe it's just as well if Dad visits with you alone for a while."

"Yeah," Mike put in. "You'll have the house to yourself, except for the mange-ball."

"Right," Sunny teased back. "And you and Mrs. M. will have some privacy—except for Toby."

That took some of the wind out of his sails.

In the end, Sunny drove the Buick back to Mrs. Martinson's, with Will right behind them. She locked up the car and gave the keys back to Helena, who thanked her for chauffeuring. "No problem," replied Sunny. "I'll see you later, Dad."

"Later," Mike agreed, loosening his tie. "It's already been a heck of a night. I don't know what we can do to top it."

Somehow, Sunny thought, *I don't think it will have much to do with coffee cake.*

Will had the passenger door of the pickup open for her and exchanged "good nights" with Helena and Mike. He'd already ditched his suit jacket and tie.

"I should have brought a change of clothes," Will said, then asked, "Why are you looking at me like that?"

"You're making some interesting assumptions, just because my dad is staying awhile at Helena's."

"I just meant—well, how do *you* feel after spending time in the Scatterwell sauna?"

"Damp," Sunny had to admit, picking at her own clothes. "Maybe we can sit outside on the deck and cool off a bit." She took off her jacket and rolled up the sleeves on her blouse.

When they arrived at her house, she and Will went around the garage to the deck in the backyard. Sunny used the charcoal lighter by the grill to start the citronella candle on the small table back there, offering them a bit of light and some protection from the nighttime bugs.

"So," Will said, settling into one of the webbed chairs, "as a cop, I'd say we've hit a dead end. If we look at the death of Gardner Scatterwell as a one-off murder, we have Alfred—someone with a very strong motive to do him harm, and no alibi—but no proof he was on the premises when Gardner died. We also have two individuals who happened to be working late in the facility, but one—Luke—has no discernible motive, and the other—Elsa—can only be placed near-ish the murder scene. Plus, if we go by the testimony of our eyewitness, Scatterwell accepted something to drink, and I can't see him taking anything from a person he was tormenting."

"But we have another possible theory," Sunny pointed out.

"Yes, thanks to looking at some records we're not legally supposed to be able to see, we can also theorize that Scatterwell's death could possibly be one of a series of medical murders. A significant cluster of deaths seem to coincide with nights when Camille was on duty. However, while she had opportunity, we don't have a strong motive—unless you think it's worthwhile to match obituaries with dates of death and see if she had some sort of beef with the various deceased persons. And other than stroke, we still have no idea of means."

"Not to mention the possibility that Gardner and the other folks did actually die of natural causes," Sunny reminded him.

"Point noted, but we'll put that aside for the moment." Will looked at her expectantly.

"What?" Sunny burst out.

"I, as the cop, have laid out all the logical groundwork. This is the part where you, the amateur, come up with the unexpected plan, and I say, 'It's crazy, but it just might work.'"

Sunny gave him an incredulous look. "Has your TV been stuck on the channel with all the lame seventies mystery shows?"

"Hey, I've seen you pull this off a couple of times."

She sat and thought for a moment. "Maybe we could . . ." Her voice died away and she shook her head. "That's so crazy it *wouldn't* work. Sorry, Will, not this time. I've got nothing."

"Then I think you should use this conversation as the basis for writing up a report in the most persuasive language you can come up with," Will said. "Maybe if you tease him with enough nagging questions, Nesbit might decide this situation warrants a closer look with a bit more legal oomph behind it."

"Can I quote you on that?" Sunny asked.

Will made a face but then grew serious. "I think maybe we ought to meet tomorrow and work on a draft to run past Ollie."

"He won't like having to eat crow in front of Dr. Reese and the sheriff," Sunny told him.

"Well, we can cite the usual constraints of time and the inability to compel the collection of certain evidence," Will said. "Then Ollie can argue with Nesbit, lose, and it won't be our fault."

"Somehow," Sunny told him, "I don't think Ollie will see it that way."

That idea was so depressing, they sat in silence for a minute. Then Will took Sunny's hands. "We still have some time before your father gets back—" He broke off, suddenly pointing upward. "A shooting star!"

Sunny followed his finger, spotting a streak across the sky. "Oh, yeah, the summer meteor showers. It used to be easier to spot them before things got so built up."

Will nodded. "Now they talk about light pollution. When I was a kid, I remember lying on the grass in the backyard with my dad, watching the sky."

"I think we're a little too well dressed to try that," Sunny told him.

But Will moved his chair beside hers so she could rest her head on his shoulder, her eyes on the heavens.

It may not be moonlight, but I guess shooting starlight will do, she thought.

"One in seventy-five million," Will murmured.

"What?" Sunny said.

"The odds of being killed by a meteorite." Will turned to look her in the eyes. "I read it somewhere. "You've got a better chance of being killed by fireworks—or a bee sting."

"I know it goes along with your job, but I really think you should work on your sweet nothings," she told him.

"Maybe this is a case of do, not speak." His lips came toward hers.

But the kiss was interrupted, not by a falling heavenly body but by a yowling furry one that landed on their heads.

*

Shadow heard muffled voices outside the house, but no one came in. Climbing on the couch, he saw a big car at the end of the driveway . . . no people, though. He went down the hall to the rear of the house, and the voices got louder. One of them seemed to be Sunny!

He boosted himself up onto the kitchen table and peered outside. Yes, it was definitely Sunny and her He, sitting on the deck. *Why are they keeping away and leaving me out?* Shadow wondered. It was probably the He, still angry about the boxes and the papers. Shadow stretched forward, one paw against the glass of the kitchen window. If he wanted to get out and join them, he couldn't get through here.

Shadow set off on a determined march to the stairway, climbing up to the second floor, down the hall, and into the Old One's room, worming his way through a door that was almost closed. He knew Sunny's father wasn't in there, and the window was open. Leaping up to the sill, he raised a paw, trying to catch his claws on the corner of the screen without getting them stuck in the screen itself. That's all he needed, to be trapped in here when the Old One came back.

At last the screen moved and Shadow hooked a paw outside, budging the screen a little more until his head and then his shoulders fit through. The roof slanted under his feet, but he could manage that. The problem was finding a way down. Shadow knew the tree wouldn't work. A cat's claws worked fine on the bark going up, but they weren't built for sliding down. That's why he'd seen some friends trapped on branches, calling for help. Maybe he could jump down into one of the chairs or land on the table. It was still a long leap.

As he carefully made his way down to the edge of the roof, it got very quiet down below. Had they gone inside after all? He leaned out to see, his paw slipped, and all of a sudden he was flying through the air.

It could have been worse. He landed on their heads, not as far a fall as it could have been, and quickly bounced over to the table.

But from the noise Sunny and her He made, you'd think he'd dropped on them with his claws out and ready.

*

Sunny screamed, Will yelled, and they both jumped up. It took them a moment to realize that the Unidentified Furry Object was actually Shadow, who now sat on the table, grooming himself. But while he tried to keep up the nonchalant act, Sunny noticed that the cat kept shooting worried glances at her.

"I think this is the first time I've heard of a game called on account of cat. Maybe we *are* stuck in a seventies mystery show," Will groused, trying to recover some sense of humor. "One of the dopey comedy ones."

They left Shadow and walked around to the driveway,

where Will's pickup was parked. "I don't know if I should apologize or what," Sunny said.

"Definitely not your fault," Will replied. "Or mine. When this craziness is over, we'll try for a little more shooting star watching—a private viewing, though, far away from that menace." He leaned down, she raised her lips, and they kissed, but it didn't hold the same promise as the one that got interrupted. After all, they were in front of the house, in public. Not the place for a clinch.

Will climbed into his pickup. "Till tomorrow," he said. Then he drove off. Sunny waved until he was out of sight, then turned to walk to the front door. Shadow stood ready to greet her in the hallway. "Hey, spoilsport," she told him. "Just because you don't get to see your dream girl, you shouldn't go around ruining other people's fun."

She went upstairs to put on something more comfortable, then came back to the living room to make up with Shadow over an exciting game of catch-the-string. By the time the house phone rang, Shadow was tired out and comfortably curled up on her lap. Sunny had to evict him to get up and answer the phone. "Hello?"

"'S Luke," the voice on the other end of the line announced a little mushily. "Luke Daconto."

"Luke?" Sunny said in surprise. "How did you get this number?"

"White pages," Luke replied. "Remembered you lived with your father. Only one M. Coolidge in Kittery Harbor." A crinkling of paper came over the line. "Is there really such a place as Wild Goose Drive?"

Of course, Sunny thought, feeling a little foolish. *Why would Mike have any use for an unlisted number?*

"Are you okay?" she asked. "You sound a little funny."

"Not funny. Drunk," Luke corrected. "I decided to act like Alfred. But now I need to talk to someone, and I hope I can ask a favor."

"To talk?" Sunny said.

"Face-to-face," Luke explained. "See, that's a problem. I can't drive out to While Gootch Drive. I'll probably hit a tree trying."

Sunny sighed, shooing Shadow out of her lap again. "Give me your address," she said. "I'll drive right over."

Scribbling down the address on the notepad beside the phone, she hung up and rose to her feet. "Sorry, Shadow, no more alone time. I've got to go." She looked down at the worn sweatshirt she was wearing. "And I probably should put on some better clothes."

When she came back downstairs, Sunny had on jeans and a less disreputable T-shirt. She left a note for her dad in case he came home before she got back, gave Shadow a quick pet, and headed out to her Wrangler. Luke lived in Levett, in a much more built-up area than Sunny's neighborhood. The buildings and the people were much more crowded there. So were the cars. Sunny circled around several blocks before she found a parking space. She got out of her SUV and walked the rest of the way to her destination, a modest three-story apartment house. As a nod to the old colonial architecture, some of the windows were surrounded by make-believe plastic clapboards. The rest of the walls seemed to be made of rough-cast concrete. She got buzzed in through the front door and mounted the steps to the third floor.

Seems like a neat, clean enough place, she thought,

looking around. *Is this what a music therapist's salary gets?* Luke stood in the doorway to his place, looking a little shaggier and more disheveled than usual. He'd ditched the corduroy jacket and mismatched tie, but he still had the pants—pretty wrinkled now—and the shirt, which looked as if he'd sweated right through it.

"I'm sorry," he said when he saw her. "This was probably a stupid idea."

"Well, I'm here now," Sunny replied. "Let's talk." Luke held the door open for her, and she went into his place. It was a studio, on the small side and sparsely furnished. She saw a couch that looked as if it had been put together from a kit, and a spindly sort of modern chair, arranged on what looked like a piece of remnant carpet. One wall was the kitchen, with a sort of counter arrangement and a couple of stools. Around a corner was the sleeping nook, where Sunny could see the foot of Luke's bed—it seemed to be made— with his jacket hanging precariously off the edge. She saw some very nice sound equipment and a lot of CDs but no television, and some low chests that probably held his clothes. A floor lamp and a spindly table lamp on an end table provided dim light.

When Sunny had seated herself in the chair, Luke made a big, swooping gesture, taking in the whole place. "It ain't Scatterwell Castle, or whatever they call it, but it's home."

He dropped onto the sofa.

"We tried to catch up with you earlier this evening, but you were just a little bit ahead of us when we left." Sunny paused for a moment, trying to figure out what to say. "I guess I wanted to apologize. That's not the way people are supposed to talk—or act—around here."

"Why should I be surprised at Alfred?" Luke asked. "He didn't act much better around his uncle." He took a deep breath. "It was hard to hear all that stuff."

"About your friend?" Sunny said. "I'm sorry. I know that you liked Gardner, and he certainly seemed to like you."

"Yeah. Liked," Luke echoed and then launched into a seemingly unrelated story. "My mom died about a year ago. Something her potions couldn't cure. I managed to get the word and return to the commune before she went. She gave me her book of cures"—he gestured to a battered spiral notebook sitting on the table—"and she finally told me something I'd been asking her about for years."

He sagged back on the couch, looking at Sunny. "You know that saying, 'It takes a village'? I was raised by thirty-seven people on the commune. But I never had a father. My mom had an 'old man' for a while, and especially when she was younger, she had a lot of, well, let's call them overnight guests."

"That must have been . . ." Sunny ran out of words.

"Weird?" Luke suggested. "Hard?" He shook his head. "Actually, it was just life. There was a guy in the commune, Paul, who was a carpenter and woodworker. He was what you'd probably call my role model." Luke laughed. "He believed in doing a good job and not taking any crap . . . and he also loved to sing. He was really into music—got me my first guitar by trading a table he'd made for it. I can't complain about my life. There was just one thing. Whenever I asked Mom, she always changed the subject . . . until she lay dying."

"So who was he?" Sunny asked, afraid she knew the answer. Luke laughed—not exactly a happy sound. "That was the thing; she didn't know. As far as she could narrow it down, he was one of two guys, fresh out of Yale, who were on a road trip. They crashed with Mom, got kind of wasted, and I guess you can fill in the rest."

He moved ponderously on the couch, but his voice got clearer. Maybe his drinks were wearing off. "All I had were first names, and the fact that they came from Maine. So I played detective, managed to get my hands on Yale alumni lists. There are a couple of thousand alums in Maine, but I was looking for people from the class of 1970 and finally managed to find a Hank and a Gardner. One was a doctor who ran Bridgewater Hall. I had a degree in music therapy, had good references . . . and was willing to work cheap. After getting the gig, I just kept my eyes open. It was just a stroke of luck for me that Gardner also happened to be a patient there. I managed to snag a tissue when Dr. Reese had a bloody nose, then I got hold of a couple of glasses that Gardner had drunk from, which was a hell of a lot easier. I sent them off to one of those mail-in DNA places, and here's the answer, postmarked about a month ago." He tapped a finger on a couple of letters lying beside the notebook. "Modern science says there's a ninety-nine percent chance that Gardner was my father."

"So you found him." Sunny couldn't think of anything else to say as she tried to digest all of Luke's revelations.

"And I was even happy. Dr. Reese, well, he came off as a bit of a stiff. It was a relief to find out that Gardner was my dad. He seemed cheerful, even if he was on his back most of the time. He always had a smile and a joke. I was glad I'd found him." Luke fell silent for a moment. "But all I knew was the sick guy at Bridgewater Hall. When I heard all that stuff people were whispering at the memorial, what Alfred said out loud, I had to wonder. Was I a chump to come looking for him?"

"People are rarely all one thing or all the other," Sunny pointed out. "If he was nice to you, enthusiastic, maybe he liked you. Maybe he wanted you to think well of him—to remember the good in him." She hesitated. "Did you tell him?"

Luke shook his shaggy head. "I was sort of edging toward it, working up to it. I almost told him the night he died. See, I did take some time off from pushing papers around and went to see him. He'd been complaining about feeling nervous, but they wouldn't give him anything for it. So I mixed up some of Mom's nerve tonic and smuggled it in for him, gave him a dose—"

"In a glass of brandy," Sunny finished, remembering Ollie's story.

"The stuff tastes awfully strong, and I thought that would cut it a bit. Gardner used to say a good snort was probably as good as a sleeping pill." He stopped, blinking. "How'd you know about that?"

"Ollie woke up and overheard a little while you were visiting with Gardner." Sunny looked over at the wreck of a notebook. "What was in that tonic?"

Luke reached over and turned tattered pages. "Here it is." He passed the book over to Sunny. Luke's mom had unformed, loopy, hard-to-read handwriting that started large on the top lines and progressively shrank as she got closer to the bottom of the page.

"What is this—'toxic'?" Sunny pointed at a word.

Luke tried to focus. "No, 'tonic.'"

They ended up sitting together on the couch, trying to decipher the recipe. It only got harder as the letters got smaller. "What is this here? 'Stop'? Or maybe 'Stup'?"

"Steep, like you do with a teabag. In this case, you do it more than once to draw some bad stuff out of the monkshood."

"That was my next question. I thought it was 'mink stool.'"

"No, definitely monkshood," Luke told her. "'Steep monkshood 2X'—two times."

Sunny peered more closely. "Okay, I can see the rest. But that '2X'—I think that's a seven."

"No, it's a two. Do it twice." He bent over the notebook, "See? There's a bottom on the two . . . or is that the cross-piece on the T in the next line? Oh, man, don't tell me I got it wrong."

Sunny sat very still, her face pale. "Luke," she said gently, "monkshood is pretty dangerous stuff. My mom had some in a corner of her garden. But she rooted it all out when I was very little because she caught me trying to taste a flower. Mom really freaked out. Have you ever made that tonic before?"

Luke shook his head. "I just followed the recipe. I really don't remember exactly what I did now. If I screwed it up—do you think I brought on the attack that Gardner had? It's not the first time I gave him the stuff—he seemed fine the next day. Look, here's the leftover tonic." He went to the kitchen counter and returned with a small bottle of clear fluid. Sunny accepted it into her palm. She didn't want to get any fingerprints messed up.

"I think we'd better have this checked out," Sunny told him.

"Yeah." Luke wasn't just getting more sober with every passing minute. He was getting paler and scareder. "I just wanted to know my father—to do a favor for him. People are going to think I was after his money. That's the last thing I wanted."

"I'll get this to a doctor." She got a pen and wrote down a phone number. "And this is a lawyer I know. I think you'd better call him."

16

Sunny drove through the darkness, the bottle of nerve tonic lying on the seat beside her in a plastic bag. The moment she left Luke's apartment building, she'd gone to call Will, only to realize that her cell phone was in the pocket of her black jacket—which was still on the passenger's seat in Will's pickup. So she drove home at a very sedate speed, not wanting to even jostle the evidence.

You'd think I was driving home with a bottle of nitroglycerine, she thought. *Well, it could blow this whole case sky-high.* Sunny sighed in relief when she at last pulled up in her driveway. Using just her thumb and forefinger, she picked up the bag and walked inside the house—where she found Mike waiting for her in the hallway.

"What's going on with Luke?" He waved the note

Sunny had left. "Is he okay? That was a pretty rough evening he had."

"'Rough' might be an understatement," Sunny reported, giving her dad the highlights of her recent conversation with Luke.

"Wow—he told you he's actually Gardner's son? And that he was in the room giving him something to drink the night Gardner died?" Mike stared at the bag in her hand. "Is that the stuff? What are you going to do with it?"

"I think it's more like, 'What am I going to do, question mark?'" Sunny shook her head. "No, that doesn't sound right. But here's my plan. First, I'm going to call Will so we can decide what to do with this blasted bottle. And get my cell phone back from his truck. Second, I'm going online to learn more about monkshood."

"We used to have some in the backyard, in the shady area by the garage," Mike said. "Big blue flowers. They were very pretty." His expression went from reminiscent to grim. "Your mom got rid of them all when she found you messing with them."

"I know, I remember," Sunny told him. "That's why I got so worried when I heard what was in this tonic. Mom gave me a good scolding—said they were dangerous. Now I've got to find out exactly how dangerous they are."

By the time Will arrived fifteen minutes later, Sunny had finished her research and was ready for his questions. "You think Luke killed Gardner with something made from flowers?" Will asked.

"The active ingredient is something called aconite," she told him. "And yes, it comes from the monkshood. Aconite is used in homeopathic medicine, but it's dangerous stuff. Too much, and it's poisonous. From what I've been reading, the symptoms are numbness in the face, weakness in the limbs, and vomiting. In the end, your heart stops, and you die."

"Which pretty much sounds like what happened to Gardner Scatterwell." Will frowned, opening the bag to look at the bottle inside. "What do you think we should do? Have the contents tested, or go straight to Nesbit?"

"The more I think about it, the more I feel that Luke should turn himself in. After all, what happened was an accident."

"Was it? An accident committed by a poor musician who just happens to be a rich guy's son," Will pointed out.

"In that case, Luke got the order of things all wrong," Sunny said. "He didn't reveal himself to Gardner, didn't get the will changed . . ."

"There are plenty of ways to contest a will. Besides, maybe he did reveal himself to Gardner, who wasn't happy about it," Will challenged, going into full cop mode. "Daconto's suddenly got some pretty strong motives."

"Aren't you jumping the gun? We haven't even tested the stuff in the bottle. We don't even know what killed Gardner."

"Thanks to Alfred having him cremated." Will scowled.

"As for the scenario you're suggesting, there's one big problem—again," Sunny argued. "Would Gardner have accepted a drink from Luke if he'd rejected him? The way Ollie described the whispered conversation he overheard, it sounded cordial, not like someone having poison forced down his throat."

"You're cutting this Luke guy a lot of slack because

you like him," Will complained. "Somebody died here, after all."

"I'm not saying we should keep quiet while Luke makes a quick getaway out of town," Sunny shot back. Then she added in a small voice, "I did give him Tobe Phillips's number, though."

"Oh, great," Will burst out. "You think Daconto is guilty, but you hook him up with the best criminal lawyer we know?"

"*If* the stuff is deadly, then Luke made a mistake, which he'll have to pay for," Sunny replied. "That doesn't mean he shouldn't have good legal advice."

Will fumed for a moment, then reluctantly nodded. "We'll need a secure place to keep that bottle until we turn it in. I nominate my gun safe. Have you talked to Tobe yet?"

Sunny shook her head.

"Well, we should do that, too, get everything set up. Any other details you want to mention?"

"Just one," Sunny told him. "My jacket and cell phone are still in your truck."

*

Sunny got up the next morning at the crack of dawn, yawning. She'd spent a lot of time on the phone before she could get to bed, talking with Tobe Phillips about his new client, Luke Daconto. The plan was to bring Luke to the Sheriff's Department that morning.

Sunny woke herself up under the shower, then made toast and coffee. Mike was asleep, and she decided not to wake him. She poured dry food into Shadow's bowl, figuring that would bring him into the open, but the cat hadn't shown. Then she spotted him trying to hide behind the kitchen doorjamb, eyeing her suspiciously.

"Oh, come on in," she told him. "No strangers, no weird smells. Just me, trying to get out of here." She met him as he advanced with cautious steps, ran her fingers though his fur, and then stood up. "Be a good cat," she whispered to him as she hurried down the hallway, trying not to clomp and awaken her father, "and don't drive Dad crazy."

She got outside just as Will pulled up in his pickup. The ride up north went by without conversation. Will had the news channel on the radio, and they listened for any breaking news bulletins about murders at nursing homes.

They arrived at Bridgewater Hall when most of the residents were still asleep. In fact, in Room 114, Ollie's roommate lay flat on his back, snoring loudly. Ollie, however, was awake. He gave them a bleary-eyed glower. "I guess this must be something big," he muttered.

His eyes got progressively wider as Sunny and Will described the events of the previous night. "Luke is a nice kid," Ollie said when they finished. "Okay, maybe he's a bit of a goof-up. Look what happened when he tried to open that bag of chips for me." Unconsciously, his hands made brushing motions on his chest. "But this is the last thing I'd expect to hear about him." He frowned, figuring angles. "So what's the next move?"

"In an hour, Luke and his lawyer will be coming here," Sunny said. "I figure that will give you time to get washed, shaved, and dressed, not to mention arranging a meeting with Dr. Reese."

Will glanced over at the snoring Mr. Vernon. "And maybe they can get Sleeping Beauty out of the way."

By the time Luke and Tobe arrived at Room 114, a somewhat surprised Vernon had been woken, then wheeled off to rather early therapy. After Vernon was gone, Luke entered the room hesitantly, followed by his lawyer.

Ollie offered his hand. "This is a hell of a thing, Luke."

Luke's shoulders sagged. "I don't know how it could happen. I've made remedies out of that book for years."

Sunny remembered the salve he'd given her. The skin on the back of her hand was as good as new, with no trace of scratches or scarring.

At last Dr. Reese arrived, with Dr. Gavrik at his heels. "I hope we can make this quick, Mr. Barnstable. I have a lot of meetings this morning."

"You may have to cancel them," Ollie replied. He turned to Luke Daconto. "Luke, you have the floor." Luke stumbled a little as he began, but he managed to get clearly enough through his explanation of what happened the night Gardner Scatterwell had died.

Explanation, Sunny thought as she listened to the halting story, *or confession?*

For a long moment, silence filled the room when Luke concluded, until Tobe Phillips spoke up. "There's a definite possibility that due to a mistake in preparing the tonic, Mr. Gardner ingested a heavy dose of aconite."

"Aconite is toxic," Reese said slowly. "You're saying that Mr. Daconto precipitated the whole episode?"

Dr. Gavrik was less diplomatic. "This untrained idiot played at making medicine, administered it without approval, and killed my patient!" She stormed over to Luke, who shrank back. "You fool! You stupid, damned fool!"

Then Gavrik turned on Reese. "I have argued and argued about hiring useless people to make the patients feel better instead of devoting our resources to medicine. Now you see what happens—not only are they useless, they can be dangerous—fatal, even."

She obviously had more to say but bit back her words. Her sharp features tightened, almost clenched, from the effort of keeping them in.

Tobe's handsome face looked disapprovingly at Dr. Gavrik and Dr. Reese as he spoke up. "We came here this morning as a courtesy." He gave the word a slight emphasis and then went on. "Mr. Daconto will now go to the sheriff's office, surrender himself, and make a full statement."

"Oh, yes," Gavrik sneered. "He'll tell everyone how he did wrong, and how he's very sorry, and they'll feel sorry, too, and tell him he's a naughty boy—and do almost nothing!"

She spit the last words out, stepping past Tobe to Luke again. "You practiced medicine without a license, without any training, without any sort of knowledge even, you made a stupid mistake, and now a man is dead. You should be tried for murder." Luke flinched, but he still faced the woman.

"I didn't mean him any harm," he said in a tight voice. "He was my father."

"What?" Reese said.

"Gardner was my father." Luke cleared his throat. "When I came here, I was trying to find out who that was, and I did. I've got the proof at home. He met my mother years ago in a commune in California. He was on a road trip." He paused. "Maybe you remember that."

Reese stared at Luke as if he'd never seen him before. "And you're his son?"

Luke nodded. "Yes, sir. He kept telling me that his nerves were eating him up ever since the stroke, and I knew my mom had used this tonic to help people. So I gave him a couple of doses. I tried . . ." He hung his head. "And I made a big mistake. I have to take responsibility for that, whatever the law thinks is fair."

"And just," Tobe hurriedly put in. Before he could start on the mitigating circumstances, Gavrik cut him off with a disgusted sound.

"Words, words," she said, fanning with her hand as if to dissipate the hot air. Gavrik glared at Ollie, who up to this point had been taking everything in as a spectator. "I suppose you're satisfied now, Mr. Troublemaker. From the beginning, I could tell you were going to be a difficult patient, excitable. And your friends"—she expanded her glare to Sunny, Will, and Luke—"would only make things worse."

Ollie wasn't about to take that tirade lying down, even if he was in bed. "At least this was an accident," he snapped back, glaring up at Dr. Gavrik. "Stupid, sad—but done out of love. But we've still uncovered information that a lot of other people, more than usual, have passed away in this joint. And they may have died on purpose. I know one thing for sure. I'm going to have a chat with my friend the sheriff and ask him to look into that. He'll be able to get into your so-called confidential files to dig out the truth. Hell, after what happened with Luke here, Nesbit will probably feel he *has* to investigate, if only to see how tightly wrapped this place is." Ollie did something Sunny wouldn't have thought possible: he shut up the nasty doctor . . . although the glitter in her eyes promised an unpleasant time in store for the next underling she bumped into.

"Radmila, I don't think there's anything more we can accomplish here," Dr. Reese said quietly. It was the first time Sunny had ever heard Dr. Gavrik's first name. "We have other business."

Like trying to get a jump on the damage control when this comes out, Sunny's reporter alter ego chimed in. It wouldn't be easy. The accident happened in the rehab ward, which had been the source of Bridgewater Hall's excellent reputation. But Sunny suspected that most of the fallout would come from the residential side of the operation, and she could understand why. *Would I want Dad to stay in a place where one of the patients got poisoned by mistake?*

And since the residents were actually the facility's bread and butter, and Reese had said the finances were already on the rocky side, the administrator and the directors might have to decide whether the place would survive at all.

Sunny didn't envy Dr. Reese his job that day. Although it was early in the morning, the tall man already looked tired as he shepherded Dr. Gavrik out of the room.

"Don't listen to her," Ollie told a shaken Luke Daconto. "The only reason her mouth got so mean is because you made her look bad."

"She's right, though." Luke ran a trembling hand over his face. "What was I thinking? Mom at least had years of experience making her mixtures and using them. Me, I just followed the recipes—and I screwed this one up big-time."

"It really comes down to two questions," Tobe said. "Were you indifferent as to whether Mr. Scatterwell would live or die when you gave him that tonic?"

Luke stared at him. "No! I wanted him to be okay, to feel better. That's the whole reason I gave him the tonic in the first place."

Tobe nodded. "And at the time you gave that mixture to him, did you know it was risky?"

"No," Luke said after a moment's thought. "I trust all my mom's recipes."

"Then don't let other people tell you how you should feel about what happened," Tobe told him. "You're the only one who knows what went on, why, and how you felt." Luke nodded, looking a bit better. Sunny couldn't help noticing, though, that Tobe's assured expression quickly faded when Luke turned away to talk to Ollie.

"Thanks for being on my side," he said, shaking Ollie's hand again. "I don't know how much more or how much better I can say it, but I'm sorry. I never meant for anything like this to happen. And I know how much you were upset over it, so I really have to apologize to you."

"Don't worry about me," Ollie told him.

Sure, that irreverent voice piped up in Sunny's head. *What have you got to worry about? This kid won your argument for you.*

"You need to straighten things out for yourself," Ollie went on.

"And we'll start that right now," Tobe said, "by going

to the sheriff." He turned to Sunny and Will. "I understand one of you has the evidence?"

Will reached into his breast pocket and pulled out the little bottle, still wrapped in its plastic bag. "It's either been in Sunny's possession or mine since Luke gave it up."

Tobe nodded, acknowledging the chain of evidence, as he slipped the bag into the side pocket of his suit. He put a hand on Luke's shoulder. "Time to go."

"Don't let Nesbit or the DA push you into something stupid," Ollie warned as they headed for the door.

"That's why I'm coming along," Tobe said over his shoulder, "to make sure that doesn't happen."

Sunny waited until they were out of earshot before she asked Will, "What are Luke's chances, really?"

"Not as good as Tobe's trying to make them." Will sounded serious as he spoke. "Maine has a law on the books for unintentional murder. That can make things pretty rough for Luke."

"Yeah." Ollie grinned and then began to laugh. "But you forget who you're dealing with. I think Frank Nesbit would much rather call this a medical mistake than any kind of murder."

Will's lips quirked. "Well, you've got a point there." He stretched, trying to hide a yawn. "I figure I'd better make myself scarce while the sheriff absorbs these new developments. Do you mind an extended visit, Ollie?"

"More to the point, what about you, Ollie?" Sunny said. "You just dropped a big bomb here. It might not make you popular. Do you want to leave Bridgewater Hall and go somewhere else?"

"Why?" Ollie demanded. "It's not as if they hand out poison nerve tonic every night. I'm settled here, used to the way they do things. I like the therapists. As far as I see it, the only problem is that witch Gavrik, and how often do I have to see her?"

"Soon you may not be seeing her at all," Sunny reminded him. "She's applying for that job down in North Carolina."

"Even better." Ollie rested back on his pillow with a satisfied smile.

"So you're not actually going to press Nesbit on the death rate here?" Will asked.

"I was mostly just going for intimidation," Ollie said. Then his eyes sharpened. "That might make a nice campaign issue for you—if and when you decide to run for sheriff," he said thoughtfully. "But remember, I've been backing Nesbit all these years."

"Sure you don't want to switch horses?" This was the first politicking from Will that Sunny had ever seen. At least he kept it light.

"Not in midrace," Ollie told him. "Besides, even Sunny had her doubts about those figures. I read somewhere there are four kinds of lies: lies, white lies, damned lies, and statistics. The numbers may not pan out, and I don't see much percentage in stirring things up."

"You told Dr. Gavrik you were going to go to the sheriff over it," Sunny felt obliged to point out.

"Aaaaah, she got me annoyed." Ollie waved it away and then gave her an impish grin. "It really did shut her up for once, though."

"That it did," Sunny had to agree. "That it did."

*

Keeping low to the ground, Shadow made his way unobtrusively but quickly down the hallway to the entrance to the kitchen. There he peered suspiciously around the doorway. The Old One sat at the table, drinking hot stuff out of a cup. Although it probably wasn't so hot now. Shadow didn't see any steam rising from the cup.

That was good. Things were normal. Too many odd things had happened since last night. Shadow didn't like it when things changed—well, not unless *he* changed them.

Last night, however, had been more disturbed than in longer than he could remember. First, Sunny and the Old One had each gone to stand under water and then had left the house after eating when it wasn't even eating time. That definitely wasn't usual. Then Sunny had come back after dark with her He, and they'd tried to hide in the backyard. Very, very strange, even for two-legs. Shadow still hadn't been able to figure out what they'd been doing out there. And, of course, it hadn't gotten any better when he'd fallen on them. Then Sunny had gone off again, the Old One had come home late, Sunny had come back, and Sunny's He had turned up again. All these comings and goings were enough to make a cat nervous.

Even this morning, Sunny had gotten up very early and left the house, moving in that funny way the two-legs did when they thought they were being quiet. Shadow hadn't been fooled, of course. He'd been awake when she got out of bed and trailed after her through her whole morning routine. Even when Sunny left some food out for him, and

Shadow's stomach had rumbled at the sound of the dry food landing in his dish, he'd stayed where he was, watching the room and Sunny from afar instead of running in for a bite.

Shadow had considered trying to follow Sunny, discover where she went when she'd come home smelling of that She he found so interesting. But he'd given up the idea. Even if he managed to get outside, it was hard to sneak into her go-fast thing.

She'd even fooled him, going off with her He. So that hadn't worked at all.

The Old One, though . . . he paid very little attention to Shadow. And he moved a lot more slowly than Sunny. Shadow was pretty sure he could get around the Old One's legs and out the door before being noticed.

And the Old One drove a machine that was open in the back. An enterprising cat could jump up there and ride along.

So now Shadow watched Sunny's father carefully as he sat in the kitchen. The Old One wore the loose, floppy clothes he put on before going out and coming back smelling worse than usual. Sometimes he really stank when he came home, but he never came home from wherever place he went to smelling of the She.

Shadow could be patient, though. When the Old One came back, stood under the water, and put other clothes on, Shadow would be ready . . .

17

"**I have to** say, Sunny, I'm impressed," Ollie said, shifting himself to sit higher in his bed. "To tell the truth, I was beginning to wonder if what I thought I overheard the night Gardner died was a dream after all. Figured I'd have to eat crow with these doctors. But you really came through. How did you get Luke to confess to you?"

By being nice to him, the hard-nosed reporter in the back of Sunny's head commented. *It's a technique you don't seem to have much of a handle on.*

"I wouldn't say he confessed to me," Sunny said aloud. "He didn't even realize that he'd done anything wrong. He just wanted someone to talk to after attending the memorial for his father. The gossip was flying, and he heard a lot of not-so-pleasant things about Gardner."

"Oh, man," Ollie said. "Like what?"

Claire Donally

"A lot about his womanizing." Will tried to hit the high-lights without shoveling too much dirt. "His word wasn't all that good, and whenever there was trouble, he tended to disappear."

"Hmph." Ollie frowned. "The guy I knew in the next bed seemed nice enough. Always ready to joke, looking on the bright side, cheerful . . ." He paused for a second. "He gave some people a hard time, but they were usually pains in the butt, like that nephew of his."

"He wasn't very decent to Elsa Hogue," Sunny pointed out.

"Yeah," Ollie admitted. "I never did understand that. She's a nice lady. I figured Gardner must have been hurting when he started therapy with her, and he never got over it."

"So you liked the guy to begin with, and then hear everybody saying nasty things about him," Will said. "I can see it has you feeling a little funny even now. Imagine what it must have been like to know the guy was your father and to discover that the people who knew him best had such a low opinion of him."

Sunny shook her head. "I can see why he'd want to talk it over with somebody."

"And he chose you," Ollie said.

She tried to shrug it off with a laugh. "I guess showing up for his gig at O'Dowd's paid off. I have to admit, he just about floored me when he started talking about being Gardner's son. I never saw that coming."

"Obviously, he got his mother's hair and eyes," Will said. "We can't tell about his chin, not with all those whiskers. But when you look at it, there's a similarity around the nose."

"How can you tell?" Sunny objected. "Gardner had his broken."

"But Alfred didn't," Ollie pointed out. "And his nose pretty much matches Luke's." He shook his head. "I just didn't think to compare them before."

"Who would?" Will asked. "Luke was just a stranger from the other end of the country. Who'd expect him to be the lost heir to the Scatterwell fortune?"

"That's not the reason he came all this way," Sunny said. "After growing up in the commune, he said all he wanted was to get to know his real dad."

"Of course, Gardner would still be alive and Luke would probably be a lot happier if he hadn't found him." Ollie frowned. "Ain't that a kick in the head."

"Mr. Barnstable?" a voice came from the doorway. It was one of the Bridgewater Hall volunteers. "Ms. Elsa says it's time for your therapy."

"Then I guess it is," Ollie said mildly, inching his way to the edge of the bed. "Can you get my wheelchair ready?"

He made the transfer smoothly, then looked up at Sunny and Will. "Want to come and see what we do?"

This is a big change from the way Ollie acted at the beginning, Sunny thought.

"Come on," Ollie said with a big show of generosity. "I'll give you the rest of the day off." He paused for a second. "That girl Annie is taking care of everything, isn't she?"

"It's Nancy," Sunny told him. "And she hasn't called in with any disasters lately." She stopped when she saw the look on Ollie's face. "Oh, take it easy, boss. I do check in with her, and she's doing fine." *So far,* Sunny added silently, her fingers crossed.

With Ollie safely in his chair, the volunteer began wheeling him toward the therapy room. Sunny and Will followed.

They arrived to find Elsa waiting in the doorway. In the week since Gardner Scatterwell had left this world, Elsa had continued the transformation Sunny had noted earlier. She'd had her hair done, was wearing makeup and some tasteful jewelry, and today wore a soft sweater over slacks that showed off her figure modestly but quite nicely. Rubbing her arms in the air-conditioning, Sunny wished she had a sweater, too.

"How are you doing today, Ollie?" Elsa asked.

On a first-name basis now, are we? Sunny thought—but said nothing.

"Ready as I'll ever be," Ollie said. "What's the torture de jour?"

"We'll try you with some table games." Elsa had the volunteer bring him to a table that would normally accommodate six. Two people in wheelchairs and one standing with a walker surrounded it, working on various tasks. "You can take a whack at this."

As soon as Ollie was situated and the volunteer had locked the wheels on his chair, Elsa got a metal box, perhaps a foot square, with dowel handles sticking out of the sides and placed it in front of Sunny's boss.

"You've done this before," Elsa said. "Remember?"

Ollie nodded. "Push it all the way forward, bring it all the way back."

"But to make it a little more interesting, we'll add some more weight." From a pile in the middle of the table, Elsa began adding beanbags to the empty box. But from the way they *thump*ed into place, Sunny realized that they had to be filled with lead shot.

"Can you handle that?" Elsa asked.

"Yes," Ollie replied, moving the box—with effort.

"Okay," the therapist said. "Three sets of ten repetitions."

Ollie set to work, pushing to the limit of his reach and then pulling the box to the edge of the table. He got through the first set of repetitions fairly easily but was obviously feeling a bit of strain as he went through the next ten. Elsa meanwhile went around the table checking on the progress of the other patients. One was working on her grip with some sort of putty, while another was picking up what looked like golf tees and putting them in a large pegboard. The man with the walker was engaged in the same exercise as Ollie, but with an even bigger pile of soft weights in his box.

"Y'know," Ollie said, a little breathless from the exertion, "I keep saying you should put some lamb's wool or fleece on the bottom of these things. Then at least we'd be doing something useful—polishing the table."

Will grinned. "Or maybe they could put you to work rolling out pie dough."

Ollie and his tablemate laughed, and Elsa joined in. "Sorry, boys," she told them. "It's all in the friction."

Like most of life, Sunny thought.

The man with the walker finished his stint with the weighted box, and Elsa moved him over to what looked like a modified captain's wheel set in the wall. Instead of the usual radiating handles, this one had a single handle sticking out from the face of the wheel.

"Very good for the range of motion through the shoulders," Elsa said when she noticed Sunny looking with interest.

"And a real pain to do," the man said, taking the handle in his right hand. "We call it the Wheel of Misfortune." Wincing, he set the wheel in a slow revolution. "There's one."

"Nineteen to go," Elsa told him. "And then you can work the other hand." She watched for a few more turns of the wheel and then came back to the table. Ollie's box sat at the edge of the table, and he dangled his arms over either side of his chair, shaking them out.

"Three sets of ten, accomplished," Will reported. "I counted."

"We're going to try something a little more interesting," Elsa said. "Let's see how you do in bed."

"Excuse me?" Ollie said.

He took the words right out of Sunny's mouth.

Elsa only shook her head. "Come on." She looked at Will. "Could you do the honors with the chair?" Then she led them to a low, padded platform that filled one corner of the room. "This is the area where people do exercises lying down. It's also where we practice getting into bed—and out."

She helped Ollie to a seated, then a lying position. "How's that?"

"Wonderful," he replied. "Where are the blankets? They had me up very early this morning."

"Well, we're going to get you up again," Elsa told him. Then she took him through a series of movements that brought him to the edge of the platform. "Now you want your hands beside either hip," she instructed, setting a walker in front of him. "Push up. I know Jack has been working your opposite leg, so if you need it to, that can take some of the weight. Okay, up, nice and easy."

It definitely wasn't easy, but Ollie managed to rise from the platform, stand, and then take hold of the walker.

"Very good work," Elsa praised him, and Ollie's face flushed with pleasure.

Elsa beckoned Will forward with the wheelchair. "Lock the wheels," she instructed. Then, turning to Ollie, she said, "Do you remember the steps for sitting in a chair?"

"Don't flop." Ollie seemed to be quoting.

Elsa nodded. "That can end up jostling things and being more painful for you. Slow and steady, that's the way."

Sunny watched as Ollie backed the walker in careful steps. It had only been a week, but he was light-years ahead of where he'd been the last time she'd seen him attempting to walk. He transferred his hands from the handles of the walker to the armrests on the chair and then let himself down in the seat.

"Good," Elsa pronounced. "Now you can rest for a few minutes. I figure if I let you lie down on our make-believe bed, we might never get you up."

*

Shadow kept a baleful eye on the Old One. Ever since he'd come back home and stood under the water, Shadow had expected Sunny's father to leave the house and go to wherever the elusive She might be found.

But the Old One hadn't done that. He'd gone into the room with the picture box, but he hadn't put the picture box on. He'd picked up a paper thing with pictures and paged through that. His movements had gotten slower and slower, until at last the Old One had gone to sleep. That wasn't uncommon. Sometimes the Old One took naps on the couch, and Shadow often joined in. It was one of the few activities they could share without annoying each other.

Today, however, Shadow didn't want to close his eyes. What if he fell asleep, and the Old One somehow managed to escape? So Shadow lay glaring up at the sleeping two-leg, who snored away, oblivious, while the cat did his best to hide his impatience, except for the occasional flick of his tail.

The phone rang, and the Old One jerked awake. He spoke for a few minutes, then put the phone back down and pulled himself more upright, rubbing his face with his hands. With a groan, he pushed himself off the couch and went to the kitchen, sticking his face in the box that made things cold and coming out with a bottle. The Old One looked at it, shook it, and then drank from the bottle, emptying it. Shadow took advantage of the distraction to get down a bite or two of dry food and a swallow of water.

As Sunny's father went to toss the bottle away, he stared up at the round thing on the wall. Shadow went on the alert. He wasn't sure what the thing was, but he'd seen similar ones in other human homes. For some reason, the two-legs would look at it and then start rushing around. Still, he expected the Old One to take time checking for his keys and walking to the front door. Instead, the older human was out with the door shut before Shadow could even make a dart for his legs. Frantically, Shadow began leaping up the stairs. He had one chance . . .

Shadow raced along the upstairs hall, into the Old One's room. He struggled with the screen, pushing his way out, and began climbing the roof. This was the hard part. He had to get around to the front of the house, where the human kept his vehicle.

It was scary, especially the trip down the roof. Shadow feared his paws were going to slip out from under him. But the sound of the truck's engine starting brought him scrambling to the edge. The ground seemed a long way down, but Shadow gathered himself for a leap.

After all, it wasn't so bad when you landed on Sunny, he told himself. Down, down he went, landing with a jarring impact that took his breath away. He crouched nervously in the big open space in the rear of the truck. Nowhere to hide. Had the Old One seen anything? Heard anything? But the go-fast merely rumbled and rolled away. Shadow settled down in a more comfortable position, letting his tail encircle his paws.

Wherever we're going, we're on our way.

*

Ollie returned to his room and his bed just in time for the arrival of lunch. Since Mr. Vernon seemed to alternate between carving his chicken cutlet and staring at them, conversation suffered. Finally, Will suggested that he and Sunny go down to the coffee shop and grab a bite to eat.

"Before we go, though, I want to call into headquarters and find out what's happening—and what they want to do with me."

He stepped over to the doorway, took out his cell, punched in the number, and had a brief, one-sided conversation, hanging up with a sour look. "Well, at least I'm free for lunch."

They stepped into the hall, and Sunny said, "Okay, I'll bite. What did they say?"

"They said the sheriff is coming over here this afternoon to see me, and Ollie, and probably Dr. Reese," Will replied. "Until then, I'm supposed to stay put."

Behind him, Sunny saw Camille Thibaud stop dead, her face going chalk white.

"Um, Will, can you give me a couple of minutes? I have to use the restroom. In fact, why don't you go ahead and get a table? I'll catch up with you."

She left Will going around the nurses' station while she walked farther up the ward, but the visitor's restroom wasn't her target. Sunny opened out her stride and caught up with Camille. "What's going on?" she asked the girl. "You looked as though you were going to jump out of your skin."

"The sheriff is really and truly coming?" The words came out in a rush, and a bit too loud. Camille bit her lip and tried again. "People have been talking all morning, saying the worst things, that half the nurses and aides are going to be fired, that we're being taken over by the state . . ." She gulped a breath. "That the sheriff is coming over to close us down."

Obviously the Bridgewater grapevine had been working full-blast, and the gossip hadn't shrunk in the telling.

"I don't think any of that is going to happen," Sunny told the girl. "He needs to talk to some people, that's all."

But instead of calming down, the girl's face only got scareder. "It's me," she whispered. "He's coming to talk to me."

"And why is that?" Sunny wanted to know.

"That night when everything happened, when Mr. Scatterwell passed," Camille said, "it was my fault."

Sunny stared. "Mr. Scatterwell was your fault?"

The girl quickly shook her head. "No, I mean the other patient, the one who got sick and messed the bed. He kept asking and begging for chocolate. I knew he wasn't supposed to have any, but I felt sorry for him. So, on my break, I got a bar of chocolate." A spasm of guilt went over Camille's plain features. "I should have known there'd be trouble from the way he gobbled it up. But he looked so happy. But then a while later, it went right through him. He was so badly off. And now I hear people whispering about patients getting something they shouldn't. It's going to be me. I'm going to be in so much trouble."

Sunny did her best to calm Camille without adding any more fodder to the gossip grapevine. "Mr. Barnstable has something he needs to discuss with Sheriff Nesbit, and since he's laid up, the sheriff is coming here." Camille nodded, but Sunny wasn't sure how successful she'd been in soothing the girl's jitters. She headed off to the coffee shop and told Will about her conversation with Camille.

"Poor kid," he said. "She must be really scared about this job." Then he grinned. "But she's got a lot to learn if she thinks a visit from Frank Nesbit is the same as the Last Judgment."

*

It seemed that they had finally stopped moving. Shadow crouched down, breathing deeply through an open mouth, testing the scents around him. He found an odd combination, catching country smells, grass, trees—and was that a squirrel?—but also the stink of smoke from the go-fast things that humans liked to ride around in. He'd encountered that mix of smells before in his wanderings, usually on heavily traveled roads that went through woods. If only he could look . . .

Instinctively, he pushed upward, aiming to hook his forepaws over the wall beside him. Then he'd be able to see where he was.

But he ducked back down at the sound of the door opening, staying frozen until it thumped shut. He listened carefully—yes, the scraping noises the Old One made as he walked were receding. When they got faint enough, Shadow boosted himself up for a look around.

Now everything made sense. He could see country-stuff all around, the source of the green smells he'd inhaled. But they were in the middle of one of those places where the humans left their go-fast things to rest. Even when there was a breeze, bad smells lingered.

Dropping down to the floor again, he pushed with his rear legs as hard as he could, surging upward, clearing the metal side, and then landing on that weird pebble-stuff that humans liked to surround their houses with.

Shadow hid behind the front wheel of the truck, watching the Old One open a door—a very big, heavy door. This wasn't like the screen door at Sunny's house, where he could climb up, hang on, and make it swing open. It would take patience and luck to get in.

Once the door swung closed, Shadow crept up to inspect it, scratching gently at the wood. No, it definitely wasn't going to shift.

So he went onto the grass at the side of the door and hunkered down. His fur blended with the stone in the wall—at least to a casual glance. After a while, another go-fast thing appeared and rolled to a stop. A pair of two-legs got out—male and female. They were younger than the Old One, but older than Sunny. Shadow kept still until they had the big door open, then he darted in between their legs.

He found himself in a large, echoing space with many-many smells. Shadow got a strong whiff of the She he'd come to find—but that was mixed with the sick tomcat smell he'd also found on Sunny. Shadow crouched, forcing an angry hiss back down his throat.

No noise. Don't make people look at you. Besides, if and when he had to deal with that male cat, he didn't want any two-leg poking into the middle of things.

Shadow trotted along, getting more confused the more he sniffed. He kept catching traces of Old Ones—many Old Ones, more than he'd ever imagined could be in one place.

I lived with an Old One who had many-many cats, he thought. *Could the She live here with many-many Old Ones?*

He had no answer. You could never tell what those two-leggity types got up to.

Now he didn't just smell Old Ones, he heard them . . . and saw them, too. They sat in chairs and couches in a large room. Some even sat on chairs that rolled! Many of them were females, making cooing noises and reaching out to him. One even got up from a chair and tottered toward him, trying to pick him up.

When he lived with the Old One and all the cats, some

of them would fawn and let themselves be petted to get
more food. Shadow never sank so low, no matter how hungry he felt. Not that petting was a bad thing. He quite liked
it when Sunny stroked his fur. But these grabbing hands . . .
Shadow ducked and dodged, finding himself beside one
of those chairs with big wheels. A bony, gnarled hand
landed on his back. He almost flew into the air, darting
away and then skidding to a stop under one of the strange
chairs with wheels.

He shuddered a little, trying to get his fur to lie flat
again. And then the chair began to move. Crouching low,
he slunk along with it, peeking skittishly forward, back,
and side to side through the wires of the big wheels. Nervous as he was, he couldn't control his tail. It kept lashing
around as if it had a mind of its own—putting itself in
danger from the rolling wheels and passing feet.

His mobile piece of cover moved into another room,
small and rather crowded. Now there were feet standing
all around him.

That was bad enough. But then Shadow had to swallow
a real yowl of fright, sinking down to cling to the floor
below him. That just meant he felt the vibrations even more
strongly.

Shadow knew he'd gone faster, riding with Sunny and
even the Old One. On the way to this place, crouched in
the back of the Old One's truck, he'd felt the wind from
their motion ruffling his fur. No, moving wasn't the problem. It was the fact that a whole room full of people had
suddenly decided to move upward like a bird.

18

It wasn't right. Rooms were supposed to keep still. That's the way it had been for all of Shadow's life up to this point. If rooms could suddenly start slowly jumping up, what next? Would houses decide to roam around? The whole idea wasn't good. In fact, it was deeply disturbing.

That was why Shadow lay low, trying to dig his claws into the floor of this moving room, desperate to hold on, especially when it gave a little leap upward and then settled back.

He was so focused on holding tight that he almost missed it when the room stopped moving. Then the door opened and everyone began to leave, including the wheeled chair he'd sheltered under. Shadow had to scramble to keep up.

The chair made a right turn and then went straight for a while. That made it easy to travel along beneath the seat, but Shadow had a hard time getting an idea of where they were going. A pair of legs blocked most of his view to the front. Then the chair made another turn, and Shadow was struck by loud noise—and by the overpowering scent of dozens of Old Ones. It was enough to make him stagger, and when he recovered, he found himself back in the open again. His moving hiding place had rolled on without him.

He found himself standing in a large open area, surrounded by all those Old Ones he'd smelled seated on chairs or those weird rolling chairs. They had all been watching a gigantic picture box where the noise came from. But now the older humans nearby noticed him and began to coo and reach toward him, just like in the other room. Shadow had to dash around as all those hands, bony or plump, crooked or odd-smelling, thrust themselves at him.

As he tried to avoid those clutching fingers, he felt trapped in a nightmare, like the dream he'd had where big angry dogs appeared whichever way he turned. Shadow could feel his heart thudding in his chest as he ducked, darted, and squirmed.

If this keeps up, there's going to be blood, he thought.

To make it worse, he suddenly got a whiff of the She he sought. But it was just the memory of her presence, coming from a blanket on one of the Old Ones' laps.

He finally got away from the hands and ran in terror, not even watching where he was going, just making his legs move as fast as they possibly could. Shadow finally stopped, panting, beside a big metal box with wheels.

It almost seems as it everything in this place has wheels on it, he thought. When he went to explore this new thing, he found that it wasn't solid. One side stood open, and shelves rose up above him. No, actually, they were trays that slid along metal supports along the sides. As he peered in the dimness, he could see all sorts of shapes piled on the trays. He also got a strong whiff of many-many different kinds of food, old food, food that had once been hot and now had cooled.

Shadow heard feet coming toward him and scrambled onto the bottommost tray. It wasn't easy, because the tray had a plate, and cups, and other things on it. But he managed, holding still as the feet appeared in front of him and scraping noises came from above—another tray going onto another shelf. Then the whole big box began to move.

Better to ride than run around with all those old two-legs grabbing for you, Shadow decided. He kept still even as the box rolled into another room that started to move. This time it started falling down very slowly. Shadow wasn't sure he liked this any better than flying, but he tried to be philosophical about it. The last time things had turned out all right. Nothing bad had actually happened.

But as soon as the door opened and they were out of that room, Shadow jumped out of the box. He'd had enough of being trapped in places and forced to go one way or another. Even if more ancient hands came after him, he'd face them on his own four feet.

Maybe the smell of all that food rising around him had clogged his nose, because he wasn't even aware of the other cat nearby until his gaze was filled with the sight of a pair of beautiful green eyes surrounded by patches of brown and black fur. They were nose to nose. He inhaled. It was She!

For a brief, wonderful moment, she rubbed her face

along the side of his. Then she romped past him, running down the long hallway. Shadow turned to follow, racing in pursuit.

*

After finishing their meal, Sunny and Will came out of the coffee shop and walked down the side corridor until they were almost to the nurses' station.

Sunny heard her name called, and turned to see her dad coming down the main hallway, waving. "How did everything turn out?" Mike asked as he reached them.

"Luke's in the sheriff's office, telling them everything that happened," Will reported. "They've already sent the bottle of tonic to the state police lab in Augusta."

Sunny filled in the details of their meetings with Ollie and Dr. Reese. "So now we're waiting on Sheriff Nesbit," she concluded. "Will was told to wait here and report to the sheriff when he arrives. I guess Nesbit wants to pow-wow with Dr. Reese and probably with Ollie as well."

Mike nodded. "Probably trying to figure how to manage the news—and keep your name out of it," he told Will.

"What else is new?" Sunny asked. "So we had ourselves some lunch and thought we'd visit with Ollie awhile more."

"That was my plan," Mike said. "You know, Ollie's not all bad when you spend some time with him. Maybe he grows on you."

Sunny resisted making a crack about any of the long list of things that grew on people. "Maybe it helps that he's not paying your salary," she suggested to her dad.

Mike chuckled and allowed as how that might be so.

Ahead of them, they saw Camille the aide stepping into Room 114 carrying a bedpan.

"Might as well wait here for a few minutes," Will said. "My police instincts say it's going to be pretty unpleasant in there for a little while."

They were all so busy glancing down the hall and joking that they didn't see the disturbance approaching behind them down the hallway until a white, black, and ginger streak zipped past their shins, heading in the direction Ollie's room.

"Portia?" Sunny said, doing a double take. Then came a gray streak that was all too familiar. "Shadow!" She broke into run after them, thinking, *What are you doing here, you crazy cat?* To make matters worse, up ahead she spotted Dr. Gavrik stomping down the hall. The doctor disliked the official therapy animals. How would she react to a strange cat on the premises?

Gavrik turned into Room 114, and to Sunny's horror, so did Portia, hotly pursued by Shadow. A second later, all hell broke loose.

*

Shadow dashed after the She as she led him a merry chase, zigzagging down long expanses of corridor, using pieces of furniture and even people as obstacles for him. Sometimes he nearly pounced on her, but she always managed to evade him. Other times, he held himself back, just so he could admire her running form and drink in the fragrance wafting back from her. When he did that, the She would glance back over her shoulder with challenging eyes and slow her own pace so that he'd come closer,

closer . . . and then she'd take off running again, leaving that intoxicating scent in her wake.

He didn't know how long the game went on. The corridors seemed to pass in a golden glow. Then the She charged into one of the rooms. Shadow followed, detecting familiar smells. Was that Sunny he scented?

He almost stopped to investigate, but the thrill of the chase urged him onward. The She was in a small room now. Surely he could catch her in there!

She vanished behind a curtain, and suddenly Shadow heard harsh words, the sound of a thud, and a cry of pain from the She. The golden glow evaporated as Shadow ducked under the curtain. The She lay crumpled on the floor, whimpering. Over her stood a human female with hate radiating from her like a choking, black stink. On the bed lay a familiar two-leg, one who came around the house sometimes. Shadow had named him the One Who Hollers from the way he acted around Sunny.

But the human wasn't hollering now. He just stared as the Dark One pushed away another female in a white coat while drawing back her leg for another kick at the She. *Not with me here,* Shadow thought. With a rumbling battle cry coming from deep in his throat, he leaped to the attack, claws flashing.

The Dark One drew back with a cry as he raked his way along her ankle. Then she turned to aim a kick at him. He jumped out of the way, riposting with an attack on her other foot. The She rose up, angry, and tried to join in. But she moved clumsily, favoring one side.

Snarling, the Dark One ignored them, swinging to attack White Coat, who made a lot of noise. Not a wise choice, turning her back on Shadow. He launched an attack from the rear, this time slashing the human up behind the knee. Reflexively, the Dark One kicked backward, and Shadow caught a glancing blow. He flew back to land in a heap, knocked onto his side. Quickly, he scrambled to his feet and shook himself. Good. She hadn't hurt him.

But the brief distraction allowed the Dark One to close in on him. She limped slightly, but that wouldn't stop her from another kick . . .

Then, with a loud rattle, curtains suddenly swept open.

*

The billowing fabric in Room 114 blocked the view, but Sunny clearly heard Dr. Gavrik shouting, "What are you doing here?" The noises of feline and human anger and pain pretty much filled in the rest of the picture for Sunny's imagination. How often had she heard Dr. Gavrik crabbing about the waste of resources the facility's therapy animals represented? The notoriously nasty doctor wouldn't have much patience for a pair of them playing around underfoot. From the sound of shoe striking flesh, Gavrik had given one of the cats a painful welcome.

Was that Shadow?

Sunny had no idea how her cat had turned up here—had he somehow hitched a ride with Mike?—and now he'd followed his nose and hooked up with Portia, his dream girl. But Shadow wasn't a therapy animal trained to get along with all kinds of people. If Dr. Gavrik attacked, Shadow would strike back. Sunny finished her sprint, rushing into the room, yanking the curtain aside. Dr. Gavrik was fighting, all right, but with Camille, trying to get a hypodermic needle out of her hand. The aide staggered with one leg drawn back, facing Shadow. She looked like a soccer player poised to score a goal—but with a gray furry body instead of a ball.

On the bed, Ollie Barnstable lay blinking his eyes as if trying to decide whether he was awake or still asleep. One arm lay out of the covers, an alcohol swab on his forearm. The cats must have come flying in to interrupt the doctor just as she was sterilizing the site to draw blood.

"Camille!" Sunny called sharply, trying to draw the woman back from kicking Shadow. "What are you—"

"Watch out for the needle!" Dr. Gavrik called, even as Camille flung her off to crash into a visitor's chair.

As if in response, Camille changed her grip from the three-finger hold for an injection to gripping the barrel of the hypodermic in her fist, stabbing at Sunny.

"Hey! A little help here!" Sunny yelled in Will's direction as she quickly back-pedaled.

But that help came from an unlikely source. Portia launched herself in a clumsy attack, her claws catching uselessly in the leg of Camille's surgical blues. But Shadow, more practiced at street fighting, hurtled himself onto the back of the aide's leg. She stumbled, off balance, her stab at Sunny falling short.

Now Will and Mike came into the room. "What's going on here?" Will demanded in his best cop voice.

"That one was trying to inject the patient!" Dr. Gavrik struggled upright. "She could kill him!"

Will tried to grab Camille's wrist, but the girl was strong, tearing free. Portia made plaintive noises, her claws apparently caught in the blue cloth, dragging behind Camille.

Shadow gathered himself for another charge, a low, unpleasant growl coming out of him.

Sunny's voice didn't sound much more civilized as she spoke through gritted teeth. "Give it up, Camille."

Instead, the aide charged for the door, ready to stab Sunny or go right through her.

Shadow went for Camille's leg again, and Sunny went for her face, landing a solid punch on the aide's cheek. It left Sunny's hand numb, but Camille spun around, the needle flying from her hand.

Mike came forward to grab it, but Will waved him off. "We need her fingerprints on it!"

He had a job subduing the furious woman. She fought him all the way while he got her arms behind her, pinning her to Mr. Vernon's empty bed as he put a pair of handcuffs on her wrists.

"Camille." Sunny tried to rub some life back into her numbed hand. "Why?" She wasn't asking about the attack on Ollie, or even on her. Obviously they had caught an angel of death, the cause of the bump in mortality statistics . . . and Gardner's killer.

"Why?" Camille snarled, glaring over her shoulder. "Haven't you seen this place? They charge four hundred bucks a day to hold a bed for somebody. I don't make that much in a week—and that's before taxes. I'd have been better off finding a job with a landscaping company. The work is just as back-breaking, but there I might get appreciated."

She heaved herself upright. "I put myself into debt, training for this job. Thought I'd be helping folks and moving up from minimum wage. Instead, the pay's lousy, and the work is worse. Still, I stuck with it. I could put up with people puking on me or wiping their butts. It was the eyes I couldn't take—having them look right through me. They thought I was invisible? Fine. I'd make *them* disappear. Who'd notice a couple of extra strokes around here? Especially at night, when everyone has twenty people to take care of."

"An air embolism in the artery," Dr. Gavrik said. "It would seem very much like a stroke."

"Yeah, you didn't catch it, did you, *Doctor*?" Camille made a mockery of the title. "It was one thing, getting my own back on the nasty old ladies, but Scatterwell, he was evil." She turned to Ollie. "And he made all the trouble, bringing the cops in. He knew something, was gonna to talk with the sheriff. I had to go for him—had to shut him up."

Hearing a gasp behind her, Sunny turned to see Rafe Warner and Frank Nesbit staring into the room.

"Did you guys hear that?" she demanded. "I'd call that a pretty explicit confession."

19

It was several days later when Ollie Barnstable finally got to enjoy the gardens at Bridgewater Hall. Will Price pushed his wheelchair, and Sunny strolled along beside. A lot had happened. Frank Nesbit had taken Camille Thibaud into custody, where she'd given a detailed, clinical account of her activities in the nursing home. It made for some sensational newspaper reading and TV news viewing.

"She started off just making patients sick," Will explained. "Then she figured she could come in and be the hero. That really didn't get her anywhere, though . . . except to show how easy it would be to kill a patient right under everybody's nose."

"Camille was on the very bottom of the totem pole, earning peanuts, in debt, afraid of losing her job, power-less. I could see why she wanted to strike back." Sunny noticed an uncomfortable expression on Ollie's face. *Yeah, it's not too far from my own situation.* Her reporter's alter ego was grimly amused. *Maybe he's afraid I'll be sneaking up on him with a pillow.* Aloud, she went on, "Stress can do some pretty weird things to people."

Ollie shook his big head. "I still don't understand why she came after me. That was just plain nuts."

"Well, Frank Nesbit would like to think so," Sunny said. "It might help him put five murders in a different pigeonhole. I think Camille made a string of bad choices. She wasn't what you'd call a criminal genius. The murders were more crimes of opportunity. She never really had a plan."

"And she was scared silly," Will added. "She'd been afraid ever since you got the investigation started on the mortality statistics, Ollie. Then Camille overheard me on the phone with headquarters . . . and talking with you about Sheriff Nesbit coming to the facility." He glanced over at Sunny. "When you tried to calm her down, saying that Ollie and Nesbit had something to discuss, Camille jumped to the conclusion that she was the something to discuss, and so she decided to try and deal with Ollie before Nesbit got here. She decided on her usual trick—she'd give you an air embolism to create the symptoms of a stroke."

Will shrugged. "In the other cases, she gave the injections at night, when there were fewer people around—and less help available. But she was rushed and desperate, and you know what happened."

"It is sort of sad," Sunny said. "Camille loaded herself with debt hoping for a career where she could help people. Instead, she ended up working for minimum wage in a nursing home that might go bust right out from under her."

"Yeah, even a legal aid attorney could make a real sob story out of that." Ollie glanced over at Will. "Then there's the whole whadeyecallit—diminished capacity thing. You think Nesbit is really going for that?"

Will gave him a thin smile. "You know your politics. If you're stuck with a killer, better crazy than cold-blooded."

"If anything good came out of the situation, all the attention Camille is getting pretty much pushed Luke Daconto into the background." Sunny turned to Will. "Tell Ollie about the results from the lab."

He nodded. "The lab rats in Augusta said the tonic isn't as toxic as Luke feared. Looks as if he did actually follow his mom's recipe, so he's out from under on the accidental murder charge."

"Of course, Luke told me there may be some other legal problems—practicing medicine without a license, stuff like that," Sunny said. "And, of course, he lost his job."

Will tilted his head, looking at her with raised eyebrows. "Luke told you, huh? What's this? Making up to the new all-purpose Scatterwell heir?"

"He is a friend," Sunny defended herself. "And considering his legal expenses, I think Luke *will* put in a claim against Gardner's estate."

"That should give old Alfred fits." Will grinned.

"But I don't think Luke is going to stay around here," Sunny said. "He may have found his father, but he's pretty disillusioned."

"That's too bad—Luke's a good kid. I'll miss him." Ollie reached up to mop his brow with the cuff of his sweatshirt. "Can we find a little shade? This sun is getting to me."

"Sure." Will steered a course for a bench overshadowed by a spruce tree.

"That's better." Ollie sat back, fanning himself with his hand, looking out over the various plants and flowers. "You don't think they have any monkshood out here, do you?"

Sunny looked around for the deep blue flowers she remembered so well. "I don't see any."

"Good," Ollie said. "Having them around might give some people ideas. Mike told me your mom had to dig up a whole part of her garden because she was afraid for you."

"Better to dig up a corner of the garden than go through a restructure like this place is doing," she replied.

Bridgewater Hall had lost a number of residents after the story of Camille's angel of death act hit the news. In response, Dr. Reese and the board of directors decided to put more emphasis on the rehab services that had gotten the place such a good reputation in the first place. In the future, one floor would be rehab and one floor devoted to residents.

"They'll probably have to hire more physical and occupational therapists," Will said.

Sunny grinned. "Or hire back some of the ones who left."

Ollie looked more serious. "I don't think they'll be hiring a music therapist anytime soon."

"And I wonder if they'll be cutting down the number of therapy animals." Will sat down on the bench. "The critters don't have a union."

"Speaking of therapy animals, what's going on between Shadow and Portia?" Ollie asked like an expectant godfather.

"I'm supposed to bring Shadow over tomorrow for a

'playdate,'" Sunny said. "Depending on how well behaved he is, Rafe Warner will decide on visitation."

Ollie nodded. "You don't think there's a chance of . . . kittens, do you?"

"I wouldn't think so," Sunny replied. "Shadow was neutered back when he was a kitten." She paused for a moment with a shamefaced grin and then went on, "I am having Jane Rigsdale check it out, though, to make sure it took. When he's around Portia, Shadow acts pretty . . . male."

"Huh. That would be something, wouldn't it?" Ollie laughed.

"They told me I'd find you out here," a voice called from the door back into Bridgewater Hall. They turned to see Elsa Hogue stepping into the garden. "I'm giving up the last minutes of my lunch hour tracking you down," she said, pretending to scold Ollie. "I expect to see you in the therapy room in fifteen minutes, ready to work—and work hard."

Ollie smiled, sat up straight, and gave her a snappy salute. "Wouldn't have it any other way."

Sunny looked from him to Elsa. She had blossomed after her persecution ended, and as for Ollie, his eyes were clearer than Sunny ever remembered, and between the pain from his leg and the healthier diet here, he'd lost some weight. It made a difference. *Could it be my imagination, or is there love in the air?*

Elsa walked back to the building, and Sunny noticed Ollie's eyes following her.

Hmmmm.

"How's the office doing, Sunny?" Ollie finally asked.

Normally, that would have been the first thing out of your mouth, Sunny thought. *Maybe you have mellowed.*

She glanced over to where Elsa Hogue had been. *Or maybe you've been distracted.*

"Well, we finally had the computer catastrophe I'd been expecting," Sunny told him. "I spent a good part of yesterday finding the problem and fixing it."

The boss nodded. "And how's Nancy working out as your backup?"

"Pretty well," Sunny said with a grin. "With her to keep an eye on things, I have the chance to come out and see you."

"Just don't get too dependent on her," Ollie warned. "She'll be back to school come September."

"Yeah, but a little help is nice," she replied. "Of course, she'll go just in time for things to pick up again in the fall."

"So, Will," Ollie said, suddenly changing conversational gears, "how has this big case affected the political landscape?"

"I don't think Frank Nesbit can squirm his way out of this one so easily," Will said. "We're talking about a series of murders that took place over years, almost right on the doorstep of his office."

Ollie gave Will his best poker face. "So you think Frank is vulnerable for this primary."

"I sure intend to find out," Will replied. "Sunny's dad and a lot of other people in Kittery Harbor have been pushing me to make a run. That's why they brought me over from Portsmouth. So I'm going to give it a try."

Sunny looked on and said nothing. She and Will had talked over the idea of him running for sheriff. They probably would never have met except that Mike and his cronies had persuaded Will to sign on as a town constable. Sunny's reluctance over the political fight had surprised her. It was as if, having fallen back into the predictability of her old hometown, she'd become afraid of any change.

Which is ridiculous, considering how much my life has changed in the time since I came back. Change is life, and life goes on, even here in Kittery Harbor, she told herself. *If Will wants to go ahead and make his try for sheriff, the least I can do is help him.*

"I've been thinking." Ollie's air of elaborate unconcern didn't fool Will or Sunny. "Maybe the time has come to align my interests more with my neighbors. Think you could use my support?"

"Oh, I could definitely use it," Will replied, his face wary.

Ollie gave him a toothy grin. "This could be the beginning of a beautiful friendship."

Will still regarded him warily. "I think it will depend on how many strings are attached."

Ollie made an airy gesture. "We can talk, we can talk."

Sunny glanced over at Will. *And if Ollie gets to be too much, we can always remind him that we saved his life.*

"Right now, we'd better get rolling," she said. "After all, you promised Elsa you'd be present and ready to go."

"That's right, you wouldn't want to disappoint Elsa." Will took the handles of the wheelchair and began pushing Ollie back to the building.

They dropped him off at the therapy room and said good-bye, then headed for the front door of Bridgewater Hall. Rafe Warner stood behind the security desk, smiling at them. "Mr. Barnstable doing okay?"

"If he were doing any better, they'd have to invent some new kind of therapy for him," Sunny replied.

As she reached for the pen to sign out, Patrick the cat appeared on the countertop. The black-and-white tux cat was looking less gaunt and better groomed. "He's coming along," Sunny said, trying to avoid his aggressive attempts to be petted. "Maybe too well."

She turned to Will. "Would you mind doing a little scratching and patting on this little guy? I don't want to come home to Shadow smelling of his prospective brother-in-law."

Will sighed but ran a hand along Patrick's back. "I know, I know," he muttered. "In-laws can be such a pain." He glanced over at Sunny. "On the other hand, I hear it'll be a clear sky this evening—the only showers are meteorites."

"Maybe we can go and watch," Sunny said, "as long as we pick a place that's cat-free."